Her brother was very dear to her, but he was asking her to marry a man who was repugnant to her in every way.

"It is the only way for both of us, Leona; there is no other. Promise me."

Leona shut her eyes. She knew that this was the signing of her death warrant if she promised. Hugo knew her well enough to know that she would keep her word, whatever the cost to herself.

"I . . . promise . . . you," she answered dully.

Barbara Cartland

DEBT OF HONOR

Books by BARBARA CARTLAND

- DESIRE OF THE HEART
- A HAZARD OF HEARTS
- THE COIN OF LOVE
- LOVE IN HIDING
- THE ENCHANTING EVIL
- THE UNPREDICTABLE BRIDE
- THE SECRET HEART
- A DUEL OF HEARTS
- LOVE IS THE ENEMY
- THE HIDDEN HEART
- LOST ENCHANTMENT
- LOVE HOLDS THE CARDS
- LOST LOVE
- LOVE ME FOREVER
- LOVE IS CONTRABAND
- THE INNOCENT HEIRESS
- LOVE IS DANGEROUS
- THE AUDACIOUS ADVENTURESS
- THE ENCHANTED MOMENT
- SWEET ADVENTURE
- THE ROYAL PLEDGE
- WINGS ON MY HEART
- WE DANCED ALL NIGHT
- THE COMPLACENT WIFE
- A HALO FOR THE DEVIL
- LOVE IS AN EAGLE
- THE LITTLE PRETENDER
- THE GOLDEN GONDOLA
- STARS IN MY HEART
- MESSENGER OF LOVE
- THE SECRET FEAR
- AN INNOCENT IN PARIS
- METTERNICH, THE PASSIONATE DIPLOMAT
- WHERE IS LOVE?
- TOWARDS THE STARS
- DESPERATE DEFIANCE
- RAINBOW TO HEAVEN
- DANCE ON MY HEART
- THIS TIME IT'S LOVE
- ESCAPE FROM PASSION
- AN INNOCENT IN MAYFAIR
- THE WINGS OF LOVE
- THE ENCHANTED WALTZ
- THE HIDDEN EVIL
- ELIZABETHAN LOVER
- THE UNKNOWN HEART
- OPEN WINGS
- AGAIN THIS RAPTURE
- THE RELUCTANT BRIDE
- THE PRETTY HORSE-BREAKERS
- THE KISS OF THE DEVIL
- A KISS OF SILK
- NO HEART IS FREE
- LOVE TO THE RESCUE
- STOLEN HALO
- SWEET PUNISHMENT
- LIGHTS OF LOVE
- BLUE HEATHER
- THE IRRESISTIBLE BUCK
- OUT OF REACH
- THE SCANDALOUS LIFE OF KING CAROL
- THE THIEF OF LOVE
- WOMAN, THE ENIGMA
- ARMOUR AGAINST LOVE
- JOSEPHINE, EMPRESS OF FRANCE
- THE PASSIONATE PILGRIM
- THE BITTER WINDS OF LOVE
- THE DREAM WITHIN
- THE MAGIC OF HONEY
- A HEART IS BROKEN
- THEFT OF A HEART
- ELIZABETH, EMPRESS OF AUSTRIA
- AGAINST THE STREAM
- LOVE AND LINDA
- LOVE IN PITY
- LOVE AT FORTY
- THE ADVENTURER

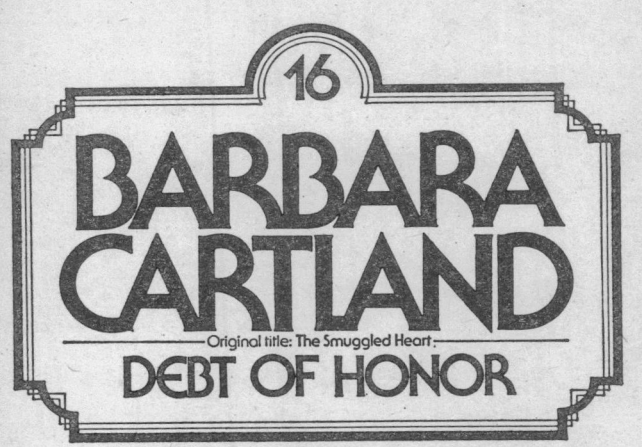

A JOVE/HBJ BOOK

Copyright © 1959 by Barbara Cartland

All rights reserved. No part of this publication may be reproduced or transmitted in any form or by any means, electronic or mechanical, including photocopy, recording, or any information storage and retrieval system, without permission in writing from the publisher.

Ten previous printings
First Jove/HBJ edition published October 1978

Printed in the United States of America

Jove/HBJ books are published by Jove Publications, Inc.
(Harcourt Brace Jovanovich)
757 Third Avenue, New York, N.Y. 10017

1

"LEONA! Leona!"

The man's voice echoed round the hall and up the well of the stairs. It penetrated into a room at the end of a corridor where a girl was arranging some freshly picked rosebuds in a glass bowl.

She dropped them with a little cry and ran towards the door, but before she could reach the top of the stairs the shout came again.

"Leona! Where the devil is the wench?"

"I am here, Hughie!" she called from the top of the wide oak staircase.

He looked up and saw her silhouetted against the dark panelling. Her little pointed face with its halo of fair curls seemed to have an ethereal, almost elfish quality, and her grey dress blended into the shadows so that she might have been a sprite rather than a living person.

" 'Pon my soul, Leona, I've been shouting fit to wake the dead!"

"Oh, Hughie, you are back! How wonderful! I was not expecting you."

"Of course you weren't expecting me," her brother snapped sharply.

Leona knew by the tone of his voice that something was amiss. Knew it, too, by the deep frown which crossed his forehead and the agitated manner in which he was slapping his riding-whip against his high hessian boots.

She reached the hall and ran towards him.

"What is it? What is wrong?"

He stared at her for a moment as if her words surprised him, then answered harshly:

"Everything is wrong, but there is no time now for rattle-prating. Get Bramwell and the maids together. The house has to be got ready."

"Got ready! For what?"

"Stap me! Do as I say, girl," Sir Hugh Ruckley said angrily. And then, as if ashamed of his irritation, he said: "Forgive me, Leona. But I'm in the deuce of a tangle and only you can help me."

"Hughie, what has happened?" she inquired, her hands going instinctively to her breast as she realized by the very intensity of his tone that he was not speaking idly.

"I'll tell you later," he said quickly. "Ring for Bramwell, or shout if the bells are out of order as usual."

"You haven't been losing again? Oh, Hughie, not all that money."

"No, no. I've gained as it happens. And I should have gained a great deal more if it hadn't been for Chard interrupting me. Blast him!"

"Who is Chard?"

"Thunder an' Turf! Don't tell me you have never heard of Chard! What do you think about in this benighted hole? But stop side-tracking me, Leona, and do as I tell you."

Without further comment Leona moved swiftly across the worn rugs towards the door under the staircase which led to the servants' quarters. Her heelless slippers made no sound and it almost seemed as if she floated across the room with a grace that would have seemed lovely to anyone but her frowning brother.

"Bramwell!" she called through the baize-covered doors. "Bramwell! Are you there?"

Her voice was clear and had a musical quality about it which was noticeably missing in her brother's. And yet, as she turned back towards him, there was a resemblance between the two.

The pale, almost ash blonde hair was the same. The same grey eyes like a stormy sea and the same winged eyebrows, which made one think of a bird in flight. But there the resemblance ended. Leona was a piece of thistledown. Hugh was well-built, nearing six foot and wirily athletic after his years of soldiering in France.

"Is he coming?" Hugh asked impatiently.

"Yes, I can hear him," Leona replied.

"He'll take his time as he always does. The doddering old man; he should have been retired ten years ago."

"And where would we get anyone else prepared to work so cheaply and so patiently, especially when the wages are not paid for months on end?"

Leona asked the question without bitterness—in fact there was an almost mischievous smile on her lips and her eyes were twinkling.

"That isn't true," her brother snapped almost angrily. "Since I have been home, he has had all that is owing to him—so has everyone else."

"I know, dear, but they were a long time waiting for it," Leona said soothingly.

"Were you a-calling me, Miss Leona?" an old man asked from the doorway.

Bramwell had worked for Hugh's and Leona's father and for his father before him. He was over seventy, rather deaf and finding it increasingly difficult month by month to get through his work. But Leona loved him. He was part of the Castle and even if they could have afforded it she would no more have thought of dispensing with Bramwell than she would have thought of pulling down the house over their heads.

"Of course Miss Leona was calling you," Hugh said, stepping forward and raising his voice almost to a shout. "Get a move on, Bramwell. There are things to be done—silver to be cleaned, the best table linen to be put out. We've got company tonight. Do you hear me? Company."

"Yes, Master Hughie . . . I mean, Sir Hugh, I hears you. But I don't know how you think I can get everything done without a soul to help me. I suggested having that boy from Seaford, if you remember aright. He was a-willing to come, but you refused him, Sir Hugh, you knows you did."

Hugh looked at his sister. She gave him a little frown.

"We knew nothing about him," she said almost under her breath. "We thought it strange he was so anxious to work here."

"Yes, yes, I recall it," Sir Hugh replied testily. "Well, you must do your best, Bramwell. Get someone in from the garden or the farm. But hurry. There's no time to be lost."

"I don't know how it's going to be done, Master Hugh, that I don't," Bramwell muttered as he turned away, and they could hear him grumbling all the way down the passage which led back to the pantry.

"Hughie, who is coming?" Leona asked.

"Have I not told you already?" her brother said impatiently. "Chard! Lord Chard! And Nicholas Weston, who acts as his secretary, A.D.C. and general factotum."

"But why have you asked him here?"

"Asked him! That's rich." Hugh threw back his head and laughed mirthlessly. "I ask him! Do you think I should be such a sapskull? He asked himself, my girl. And, what is more, it's because he's suspicious. No doubt about it!"

"No, Hughie! No, he cannot be. What did he say? How

do you know?" The questions came quickly and Leona's face turned pale.

Suddenly her brother threw his riding crop across the hall. It struck one of the carved newels on the banisters and then bounced on to the marble floor, its gold handle making a sharp crack before it slithered beneath a carved chest and was lost to sight.

"Hell and damnation! It is the outside of enough that this should happen now!" Hugh exclaimed. "Just when things are going well! Just when I am getting clear."

"What did his Lordship say?" Leona insisted.

Hugh pulled off his travelling coat with its high collar and flung it on a settle. Then he pushed his fair hair back from his forehead with a weary gesture which tried to be sophisticated, but which Leona knew only too well from the trembling of his fingers was a movement born of bewilderment and desperation.

"I was in White's," he said. "I had been winning continuously the whole evening. I was feeling up to scratch, I can tell you, when suddenly I felt someone standing close beside me and a voice said: 'You are in luck I see, Ruckley'. I glanced up, impatient at being interrupted; but then when I saw who it was I naturally got to my feet."

"You recognized him then?"

"Of course I recognized him, simpleton. We were in France together. I was under his command. I saw quite a lot of him before Waterloo and afterwards when we camped near Paris with the occupying armies. Besides, everybody knows Chard."

"What did you say?" Leona prompted.

"I said, 'Good evening, my Lord'—or something like that—and he replied: 'I had no idea you gambled so high, Ruckley. If I remember rightly, you were not so reckless when we were engaged in defeating Bonaparte'."

"What did he mean by that?" Leona inquired.

Again her brother gave that mirthless laugh.

"Chard is no fool," he said. "He knows well enough that my pockets were to let when I was in the Army. Not for me the high tables with the senior ranking officers, but the pettifogging children's games with other impecunious subalterns like myself."

"Do you mean that he was suspicious because you had the money to play with?" Leona inquired.

"That is what it seemed to me," her brother said briefly.

"Then why ask him here?"

"There never was such a girl for asking foolish questions! Bird-brain! He has asked himself. He said in that quiet, disarming way of his: 'I do not know whether you have heard about my new appointment, but I think it will take me into the part of the world where I believe you live'. 'What appointment, my Lord?' I asked. 'I have been instructed to curb the activities of those gentlemen who persist in evading the Customs Officers', he said."

Leona gave a little cry.

"No! No! He couldn't have said that. Not to you."

"He did. And looked me straight in the face as he said it. I'd swear my eyes didn't flicker as I managed to reply lightly enough: 'Congratulations, my Lord. If anyone can bring these fellows to justice, I feel sure it will be you'."

"Then what happened?" Leona inquired.

"He said: 'As it happens, Ruckley, I have to visit the south coast in the Newhaven-Seaford area immediately. I wonder if it would be trespassing too much on your hospitality to ask if I could be your guest?'"

"But there must have been dozens of other people willing to have him," Leona said.

"That is what I thought," her brother answered, "but naturally there was nothing that I could do but say we should be honoured. It flashed through my mind that if I rode through what was left of the night I could have been here early enough to get things ready and to warn everyone. But Chard prevented that.

"'I am most sensible of your kindness', he said. 'Perhaps we could travel down together. It would give me great pleasure to have your company on the journey'. I couldn't say to hell with his company, could I?"

"No, of course you could not. But where is his Lordship?" Leona inquired.

"Only a few miles away," her brother answered. "At the last posting inn he let me off the leash. Perhaps he saw what a fidget I was in, even though I tried to conceal it."

"But, Hughie, if he realized that you were nervous, he may have suspected."

"Perhaps he put it down to the fact that I was impressed with having him as a guest. I warned him that the house was demned uncomfortable, that nothing had been done to it since my father died."

Leona looked around her with a little gesture of helplessness.

"Why should he want to come here?" she asked.

"To watch me, of course," her brother retorted. "I saw

his face as I picked up my winnings—nigh on a thousand guineas. He knew well enough that I could not have made that if I hadn't had the wherewithal to start high."

"But . . . but, what are we going to do?" Leona said helplessly.

"I have got it all planned," her brother replied. "Now listen to me, Leona. Everything depends on you; everything."

"Please Hughie, do not expect too much of me! This frightens me. You know it frightens me. I would rather starve, I would really, than go through all these anxieties and miseries. I swear that I die a thousand deaths every time a cargo is landed."

"Never mind about your dying," her brother said grimly. "You realize what tonight is, don't you?"

"Tonight!" She looked at him and then her eyes widened and her hand went up to her mouth. "The eighteenth! Tuesday, the eighteenth!"

"Exactly!"

"But what are we to do?"

"You've got to do exactly what I tell you, and you've got to do it so cleverly that Chard has not the least suspicion. One false step, one slip up, and I shall be for the gallows or transportation."

"No, Hughie! No! No!"

Leona put her arms round him, but he thrust her aside.

"There is no time for hysterics," he said. "We have got to act. Now, listen to what I have got to say to you. Get the house ready. Give Chard the Chinese room in the East Wing and prepare the Oak room for Nicholas Weston. I will get up the best wine. We must dine well."

"But . . . but, there's nothing to eat."

"Then find something. There's plenty on the farm, isn't there? Chickens, pigeons, a suckling pig. Send down to the village. Order dinner that will make him feel comfortable and not too inclined to turn out on a dark night either."

"They can't come here," Leona cried, but her brother continued as if he had not heard her.

"As soon as dinner is over and you withdraw, you must go to Lew, tell him what has happened."

"I cannot! You know——"

"You'll do as I say," Hugh said roughly. "Fortunately he is not crossing this time. He stayed ashore to reorganize the tub-carriers. He said there were too many accidents last time. You will find him in the caves. Take the lantern with you and walk carefully, the way is rough."

"Hughie, I'm afraid."

"Want to see me hanged?"

"Do not even think of such a terrible——"

"Then you'll do as I say. There's no time to go now. Chard will be here within an hour. There is far too much to be arranged. Besides, Lew may not be there. You're the only person who can carry the message. Slip away after dinner and I will keep Chard as long as I can over the port."

"And then what?"

"Leave everything to Lew. If worst comes to worst, they can sink the cargo in the bay."

"Wouldn't it be better to send them back? Signal or send out a boat."

"What, and lose perhaps four thousand pounds' worth of goods? Do you know how much is at stake? How much this one load is going to bring us? But what's the use of talking? It's action we want. Get the maids. Get Chard's bed made. Get on with it."

"The maids!" Leona ejaculated. "There is only old Mrs. Mildew and Rose—who as you know, is simple. You told me not to engage anyone else, Hughie, for fear they should be spies."

"It's enough to cast anyone into a despondency," her brother cried. "Damme, you'll have to see to it yourself. And for the love of Heaven make yourself look presentable. Haven't you got something better than that rag?"

"I have the gown you bought me last month," Leona said reluctantly. "I will wear that. I know this dress is old, although for the years you were away it was my best—in fact my only one."

"That penury is over," Hugh said. "We are on the way to El Dorado, sister mine. And I intend to get there, Chard or no Chard. But beware of him, he's dangerous."

"Why . . . why does he have to come just at this moment?" Leona cried. "Just when everything was so much better—our bills paid, the servants' wages found! Why must he spoil it?"

"He is not going to spoil it if I have anything to do with it," Hugh answered. "Chard is suspicious, but he cannot know anything definite. Once he sees that he is mistaken, he'll go away and we will never hear of him again."

Hugh's words were reassuring, but his tone was unconvincing and Leona knew by his face that he was afraid inside himself, even as she was. She gave a little sigh and bending forward dropped a light kiss on her brother's cheek.

"I will do my best," she said. "But I hate Lord Chard for coming here, spoiling our happiness and making us afraid and uncertain when all we ask is to be left alone."

"You must play your part well, Leona. Everything depends on you," Hugh repeated.

"I will try; I promise you I will try."

The tears came quickly to her eyes with the intensity of her feelings, and then she turned away from him and ran up the stairs and a few seconds later he heard her voice calling for Mrs. Mildew and her daughter, Rose.

Hugh walked across the hall and into the Salon with its long French windows opening into the garden. The curtains were faded and the chairs sadly in need of being recovered; and there were vases of flowers everywhere and the room gave the impression of being graceful and dignified despite its threadbare appearance.

Hugh looked around him. What would be Lord Chard's impression? he wondered. Would he think it strange that a young man who could afford to risk a thousand guineas at a night's play should not have spent more on his home?

He had wanted to keep every penny piece for his amusement in London: for the women and the dandies he entertained at dinner, and for the green baize tables afterwards which lured him more certainly than any will o' the wisp that the villagers said moved along the river banks at night.

It had been a heady temptation which he could not resist—to gamble and go on gambling, knowing that he had the gold to plunge deep and that when that gold exhausted there would be more to replace it. Why should he worry his head with worn curtains and Leona's moans that the servants and tradespeople had not been paid for years? Why should he care that the farm implements were out of date and the young men had all deserted the Castle grounds for better posts?

Let the fields rot and the house, too, for that matter. So long as the ladies of St. James's flitted with him and there were smiles and invitations on the lips of those who only a year before had passed him by because they thought he was an impecunious subaltern. It had been so easy, too, to attribute the sudden affluence to his father's death.

"Come into a fortune, Ruckley?" someone had asked.

"My father died just before I returned from abroad," he replied. And that was true.

"I heard you'd inherited," was the answer. "Hadn't realized the old man was so warm in the pockets. Never spent much himself, did he?"

"No, a bit of a miser if it comes to that," Hugh had laughed. Even as he said it he imagined that he had seen his father's eyes looking at him reproachfully and felt a shiver down his spine.

Sir George had slaved to keep the estates intact, and when he wasn't struggling against bankruptcy caused by bad harvests and the upkeep of the Castle, he was serving his fellow men. A Magistrate, a County Alderman and finally Lord Lieutenant of Sussex, he had exhausted himself without—as far as his son could see—gaining anything for it.

"Nice obituaries," Hugh said bitterly to Leona when he returned home from the wars. "But we can't borrow money on them, and we certainly can't eat them."

But that was all past. Hugh felt the clink of guineas in his pocket and decided, somewhat belatedly, that he would spend the whole of his last night's winnings on making his home presentable.

A voice behind made him start.

"Master Hughie, what about the wine? You know you forbade me to go down to the cellar, and there's no-one else to bring it up."

"I will bring it up myself, of course," Hugh answered. "You don't want to break your leg on those stone stairs, do you? You keep away from the cellar, Bramwell. And get out the brandy goblets. We'll have brandy as well as port."

After he had spoken, he hesitated. Would Chard think it strange there was such good brandy in the house? Then he shrugged his shoulders. There was no reason why he shouldn't have bought it. He would make some passing reference to the fact that his father always had a good cellar. The thing was to get Chard mellow. Men who had eaten well and drunk well were not so perceptive nor so inquisitive.

He let Bramwell go from the hall and then went towards the oak panelling where it was carved ornately on either side of the fireplace. Hugh glanced over his shoulder. There was no-one about.

His finger sought and found a little spring hidden behind a deeply carved flower. A small door in the panelling flew open. He put in his hand and drew out a bunch of keys.

They were shining as if they had been recently oiled. Then he shut the secret panel again and went towards the cellar.

Upstairs Leona was hurrying Mrs. Mildew.

"The best linen sheets, the ones with the monogram," she was saying. "Thank goodness we put fresh lavender between them last autumn. They smell delicious. And, Rose, lay the fire. If it turns chilly or rains, his Lordship may feel the cold."

"I don't know 'ow I'm going to get everything done, Miss, that I don't," Mrs. Mildew wheezed.

She was fat and found every movement made it hard for her to get her breath.

"And you can be as sure as I'm a-standing 'ere that they'll be wanting Rose to 'elp in the kitchen. Mrs. Barnes will never manage, that she won't."

"Of course she will want Rose," Leona said. "I was hoping you, too, would give her a hand." She saw Mrs. Mildew's face darken and added: "There is no-one who roasts a pigeon like you. I remember my father used to say: 'Give me two of Mrs. Mildew's pigeons and I would not trade them for a haunch of the finest venison'."

Mrs. Mildew mellowed.

"That's true enough, Miss Leona. Very partial the Master was to my pigeons and Mrs. Barnes never could get 'em to 'is liking. 'Tell me your secret, Mrs. Mildew', she's said to me many a time. But there, you can't teach a person 'ow to cook. 'Tis born in them, that's what I say."

"If you could do the pigeons for Lord Chard I should be vastly obliged," Leona said ingratiatingly. "I have sent Jarvis down to the village to see if he can get a leg of lamb and they are plucking some chicken now. It will not be a very stylish dinner, but his Lordship will just have to take us as he finds us."

Mrs. Mildew gave a little snort.

"Take us as 'e finds us, indeed! With you living on half a lettuce leaf all through the war, Miss."

Mrs. Mildew tucked in a linen sheet and pushed the frilled and embroidered pillow-cases over the soft feather pillows.

"That's done," she said. "And now, if you wants them pigeons, Miss Leona, I'd best be a-going to the kitchen."

"Oh, thank you, kind Mrs. Mildew. And if I don't see you again tonight, you will come early in the morning, won't you? And there will be his Lordship's chocolate at eight o'clock unless he prefers ale, and his hot water for washing and shaving. And mind it is very hot."

"I'll be 'ere at six o'clock, I promise you that, Miss," Mrs. Mildew answered. "I've never failed you yet, 'ave I? Not even when Rose was down with chicken-pox and that delirious I 'ad to tie 'er to 'er bed."

"No, you have never failed me, dear Mrs. Mildew," Leona replied.

She glanced at the clock on the mantelpiece and gave a little exclamation of dismay. Lord Chard might be arriving at any moment and she had not yet changed.

She ran down the passage, and it was not only the exertion of running which made her heart beat quicker when she reached her own room. She saw her eyes, big and troubled, looking back at her in the mirror and knew that she was afraid.

She tried to tell herself that these adventures of Hughie's were not of import. She had, indeed, laughed at first when he had told her about them as if they were nothing but the mischievous escapades of a schoolboy. But when she had seen what money was involved and had realized the risks they were running, when she met the men with whom he associated, then she had known it was something very different. Smuggling was no gay-hearted adventure!

And now the whole thing had taken a more sinister turn. Hughie was under suspicion. Lord Chard was coming here to make investigations. What would he find?

Leona saw the sudden terror in her face, the pallor of her cheeks, the dilating of her pupils, the sudden trembling of her mouth. Then she turned away from her reflection as if it was something at which she dare not look.

She hurried to the wardrobe. There were not many gowns hanging there and only one of the least consequence —of soft, white silk—a silk as fine and delicate as if it could be drawn through the proverbial golden ring. It was a gown so beautifully made that it could only have come from France; a gown such as any woman might have dreamed about.

Hugh had given it her and yet she had never worn it. It was one thing to tease him for money to give the people to whom they were in debt, but quite another to take it for herself.

She had accepted the dress from him. She had hung it in her wardrobe, but she had never put it on. She had seen it every time she had taken out one of her old dresses —the ones she had worn for so long and which she had made herself with the help of Mrs. Mildew, of cotton bought by the yard in the market at Alfriston.

They were simple, ordinary dresses that any country girl might have worn. But the silk one was different. It was a gown of a grand lady, one that might have been worn by the elegant society women whom Hugh met in London and whom he described so volubly to his sister.

She had not wanted to be like them. She had been content with her own dreams and her feeling that, whatever she might appear to the outside world, she looked right for the Castle.

She gave a little sigh. Why was she daydreaming when there was so much to do? She supposed it was because she had got used to living with her own thoughts, to being alone, to having no-one in the house.

Her father had been ill before he died. He had not wanted to talk, just to lie in silence. Afterwards, when Hugh was still in France, Leona had been completely alone. And yet she had never felt lonely. There had been the sea, the birds and the animals for company. She had not come much in contact with the world outside and had not wanted to. Now she felt suddenly as if it were encroaching upon her.

She took down the gown from the wardrobe and it seemed to flutter like a captured moth so that she felt as if she held something alive in her hands.

"Why should he come here?" she asked aloud. "Why should he frighten us?"

It seemed to her as if she almost could see him coming down the road, a dark, avenging terrifying man threatening her peace and security, trying to take away the brother she loved.

And she felt as if the gown that she held in her hand was a symbol of him and the world he came from. For one moment she contemplated throwing it back again into the wardrobe, of keeping on the plain grey cotton which she wore every day and which was so much a part of herself. Then she knew it would annoy Hugh and make him more nervous than he was already.

Hastily she began to dress and the softness of the silk against her body gave her no pleasure but only an added feeling of fear. She was only just ready when she heard the sound of wheels outside. She did not even glance at herself in the mirror to see how well the gown fitted. She ran a brush over her fair hair and then, turning towards the door, hurried to the top of the stairs.

But even that last moment of dressing had delayed her long enough to prevent her being in the hall to greet Lord

Chard as he arrived. From the top of the stairs she watched Hugh walk towards the door, heard him say in what appeared to be a voice of genuine enthusiasm:

"Welcome to Ruckley Castle, my Lord. I only wish there had been more time to prepare for your comfort."

"I am quite certain I shall be very comfortable," Lord Chard replied, and his voice was deep and quiet and somehow quite different from what Leona had expected.

She felt her fear and hatred of him heavy in her breast as she reached the bottom of the stairs and came forward towards the outer hall. Her grey eyes were wide in her little face and her lips parted as she waited for her first sight of him—the man who had come here to ferret out their secrets and destroy their happiness.

Then he turned as she approached and she was astonished because he looked so young. She had expected him to be older—at least middle-aged—dark and heavily built, and he was none of these things. Instead, he was young and unexpectedly handsome, with a quiet, grave face and eyes that seemed not suspicious but to look deep into a person's heart. She had a quite ridiculous sense of relief because he was so different, and his hand when he held hers was warm and strong. Then she heard him say:

"Will you forgive me, Miss Ruckley, for putting you to all this inconvenience?" And for the moment she almost forgot how very inconvenient it was.

"Are you really Lord Chard?" she asked.

She had not meant to ask the question. It seemed to slip from her lips. He smiled and his face no longer grave, but attractive and almost beguiling.

"Yes, I am. But you look surprised."

"I . . . I thought you would be . . . different," Leona stammered, and then saw that Hugh was frowning at her and realized that already she had committed a gaff. Why should she have expected him to be anything but what he was? Why, indeed?

"Has your brother been making me out an ogre?" Lord Chard asked as if he guessed what she was thinking.

"No, no, indeed," Leona said quickly. "But he said that you were in France and in a high command, and I had expected someone quite old."

She saw the relief in Hugh's eyes and realized she had said the right thing. At the same time her heart started beating quickly because she had been so stupid and nearly stepped into a trap of her own making.

"I assure you I am very old," Lord Chard said gravely.

17

"I shall be thirty within a year-and-a-half, and that I am sure to a lady of your tender years seems an age of vast antiquity."

Leona laughed.

"No, indeed, my Lord! I think it is surprisingly young for someone of such vast distinction."

She was pleased with herself for doing so well, and then Lord Chard turned to introduce the man who stood behind him.

"My secretary and companion, Mr. Nicholas Weston."

"At your service, Ma'am."

Mr. Weston bowed and Leona took an instant dislike to him. He was small and spikey and rather like a rat, she thought. His pale eyes flickered over her and she was quite certain that he compared her most unfavourably with any other woman he had ever met.

She dropped him a curtsy and led the way to the Salon.

"A glass of wine, my Lord?" Hugh was saying.

"That will be very pleasant," Lord Chard replied.

Hugh hurried away to find Bramwell and to tell him to bring the decanter and the best crystal glasses.

"Nicholas, will you fetch my despatch case? I left it in the coach," Lord Chard said.

Nicholas Weston also disappeared; and feeling suddenly tongue-tied because she was alone with this formidable man, Leona searched feverishly in her mind for something to say. It appeared that Lord Chard was not concerned in making conversation. He just stood beside the mantelpiece and looked down at her.

With a sense of the most foolish dismay Leona realized that her head hardly reached as high as his shoulder.

She glanced up at him. Of what was he thinking as he looked at her? What was there in his eyes that made her breath come quicker, that made her whole body tremble? Then quietly he spoke.

"Why are you afraid?" he asked.

2

Hugh was getting foxed. Leona, watching him from the end of the table, felt herself grow tense and anxious as she heard his voice become louder, his laughter more frequent, and saw the flush deepening in his cheeks.

He had wanted to drink Lord Chard under the table, but the latter remained cool, composed and apparently unaffected by the wine. Hugh, however, was partly intoxicated, and he was joined in this by Mr. Weston, who lost his air of suspicion and repression and became, Leona noticed, quite a different person.

It was as if the liquor released invisible chains and under the mellow influence of the port and the brandy he became free of himself and his own restrictions.

"A-another d-drink, my L-Lord?" Hugh asked, pouring the golden brown brandy into the crystal glass and filling up his own.

Leona had noticed through dinner that Lord Chard, while appearing to drink with the others, did, in fact, imbibe far less than either of them. He never protested when they filled his glass, but it was never empty. He sipped his wine while Hugh and Nicholas Weston had quaffed down the claret and replenished their empty goblets a dozen times.

The conversation had been mostly of the war—anecdotes of friends and acquaintances which made Hugh laugh uproariously and even at times brought a chuckle to Lord Chard's lips. At any other time Leona would have enjoyed herself. She liked hearing Hugh talking of his experiences; she loved to see him happy. But tonight she was anxious, too nervous of what lay ahead, to concentrate on anything save the serving of the food and the fact that the hands of the clock were creeping on minute by minute.

Dinner was actually better than she had expected. Mrs. Barnes had excelled herself and as if by magic had produced a saddle of mutton, two roast chickens and a guinea fowl served with mushroom sauce. There were also the pigeons cooked by Mrs. Mildew, which were so good that even Lord Chard asked for a second helping.

For dessert there was a dish of strawberries from the garden, served with cream from the farm; and Leona felt with relief that at least Hugh need make no apology for the fare they had offered for their guests, especially at such short notice.

She joined little in the conversation, speaking only when someone addressed her direct and thankful when the three men talked amongst themselves and seemed to forget her presence.

She hardly dared look at Lord Chard after the confusion that he had flung her into when he asked her in the Salon why she was afraid. She had known then that her relief when she had first seen him was but an illusion. He was their enemy and all the more dangerous because he appeared charming and because she felt, in some way, that it was going to be difficult to hate him as she had been able to do before his arrival.

She had been thankful that she had been quick-witted enough to hide her dismay at the unexpectedness of his question.

"Afraid, my Lord!" she said with what she hoped was a wide-eyed and innocent expression, even while her heart pounded in her breast. "I am not afraid, but agitated by your Lordship's arrival. It is a great distinction that you have shown us in honouring us with your presence when there are so many other larger and more comfortable houses at your disposal. But I fear we are ill-prepared to entertain such distinguished company."

"I assure you that I am not looking for luxurious accommodation," Lord Chard replied.

"That is, indeed, a relief to my mind" Leona answered with a little effort of dignity which brought a faint smile to his lips.

"Do you run this great house all yourself?" he asked. "You seem very young to have such a burden upon your shoulders."

"There is no-one else," Leona answered. "My mother died ten years ago when I was but a child, and I kept house for my father until his death and now I keep it for Hugh until he marries."

"And you do not find it lonely here?" Lord Chard inquired.

"Why should I?" Leona parried. "It is my home."

"And in a very charming position, if I may say so," he answered. He walked across to the window and looked out to where the sea gleamed emerald and sapphire in the evening light.

The Castle was high above the village and the river, half-way up the cliff-side and at the same time sheltered by the rise in the land and by the trees surrounding the house. It could be bitterly cold when the gales blew, but on summer evenings there was nothing more beautiful than the wide stretch of the Sussex downs and the English Channel, while to the north lay the winding drive and green fields which led down to the village.

"A very charming position!" Lord Chard said again, and his eyes scanned the horizon; and Leona, through the beating of her heart, knew exactly what he was thinking.

"You have not visited Sussex before, my Lord?"

"Yes, indeed, I have been here often," he replied. "My sister lives not far away. You may have heard of her house, Clantonbury, a few miles from Seaford."

"You mean that your sister is the Duchess of Clantonbury?" Leona remarked.

Lord Chard inclined his head.

"I have heard speak of her beauty," Leona said. "Do you visit her often?"

"When she is at home, which is rarely," he replied with a smile. "She prefers St. James's and the gaieties of the London season."

He smiled as he spoke and the twinkle in his eyes told her that he knew full well that he was answering the question that she longed to ask him—as to why he should come to Ruckley when he could go to Clantonbury.

She moved restlessly away from him to pick up her embroidery from the chair and to tidy it away into the inlaid mahogany box which had been her mother's and which she always used.

He watched the young, graceful line of her neck on which her hair grew, soft and golden as a newly born chick. He saw the sensitiveness of her little pointed fingers and the sudden dark sweep of her long eyelashes against her pale cheeks.

"Have you ever been to London, Miss Ruckley?" he asked unexpectedly.

Leona shook her head.

"No," she replied. "And I do not think I wish to go. I am content to stay here where it is quiet and peaceful."

"Are you sure of that?"

The question surprised her. She looked up to face him, her eyes wide.

"Sure of what?" she asked.

"That it is so very quiet and peaceful," he answered.

She drew a quick breath. The warning in his eyes seemed to pierce her as if it were a sword. He knew! He knew! she thought, and then before she could speak, before she could try to frame an answer, Nicholas Weston came into the room and she was able to escape.

Tidying her hair for dinner she had wondered widly what she should do. She had come to no conclusion when she went downstairs to find the gentlemen changed and assembled in the Salon, and the question nagged at the back of her mind all through dinner.

"Another glass of brandy, my Lord? It comes from my father's cellar, but you must admit that it has mellowed well."

Lord Chard held his glass up to the light.

"It reminds me of the cognac I last drank in Calais," he said slowly. "It has the same flavour and, indeed, the same mellowness. I hope you have a good stock of it."

"Enough for all your requirements and more, my Lord," Hugh said boastingly.

Leona rose to her feet. She felt she could bear no more. Could not Hugh see that behind every word Lord Chard uttered there was another meaning? an insinuation that should warn him of the dangers in which they all lay?

"With your Lordship's permission I will withdraw to the Salon," she said gently. "I hope you gentlemen will join me later."

"It will be a pleasure," Lord Chard said.

Nicholas Weston hurried to open the door for her. He was unsteady on his feet and his eyes, when he looked at her, had almost a leer in them.

"We shall not leave beauty unattended for long," he said thickly.

She tried to smile at him and not to show the disgust she felt. She had seen Hugh foxed before, but somehow he had always contrived to look only like a little boy who had been caught stealing the jam. But Nicholas Weston was slimy and unpleasant and she preferred him as he had been when he first arrived.

As the dining-room door shut behind her she picked up the skirts of her gown and ran. She had not long, she knew that. Lord Chard would not be enticed into lazing in the dining-room as Hugh intended him to do. Therefore she must hurry.

She crossed the hall and touched the secret panel in the wall where the keys of the cellar were kept. She drew them out, closed the hiding place behind her, then ran again towards the cellar door. It was heavy, but had been recently oiled. It opened smoothly without a sound.

She went through it, locked the door behind her, and from the light to a small window at ground level saw, standing on an oak bench, what she was seeking.

It was a lantern with a fresh tallow candle in it and a tinder box beside it. It took her a few precious seconds to get the candle lit and then at last, when it cast a warm, rosy light on to the steps going down to the bowels of the earth and on the rough-cast ceiling above them, she set off on the first part of her journey.

The steps led to the cellars of the Castle. There were quite a number of them opening off the arched pillars which supported the house. They looked quite innocent and ordinary with their barrels of wine, iron racks and wine-stools.

Here were the remains of the wines which her father had bought in small quantities and which Hugh now declared were not good enough to drink.

She passed through the first part of the cellar and came to a heavy door opening to the other part. It took all her strength to pull it to one side and when she had done so there was nothing to see but an empty, square cellar and a few casks in the corner of it.

Nevertheless, she closed the door behind her and crossing to the wall on the farther side, felt with searching fingers until, as if by magic, she found the right place and the wall opened to reveal a small aperture just large enough for a man to squeeze through. As she opened it there was the smell of raw, cold air impregnated with salt.

For a moment it made Leona shiver, and then as if she forced herself to do so, she stepped farther down a few more steps and on to the rough floor of a tunnel hollowed out of the very heart of the cliff.

Ruckley Castle was a pot-pourri of every generation. It had originally been built in Norman times, but except for a few walls there was nothing left of the original castle.

Then came the Plantagenets who had a more modest country house, followed by the Tudors with more grandiose ideas. Each owner pulled down some part of his predecessor's efforts and added something different. But it was not until the reign of Queen Anne that this conglomeration of different styles and shapes caused the third baronet to think that it might be put to good use.

Nothing could be a better place for anyone who wished to hide. There were priest holes, several of them, dating from when the Jesuits landed from Spain to threaten Elizabeth I and found a hiding place in the Castle. There were staircases up which Roundheads had chased Royalists and later, with the turn of the tide, Royalists had chased Roundheads.

Sir Charles Ruckley had concealed smugglers and made a pretty penny out of it until he had lost his life in a fight at sea when he and his men were trying to board a French lugger and capture her cargo. According to the local tales is was he who had tunnelled from the Castle to the caves, although legend had it that there had been a passage there for many centuries previously.

But after Sir Charles the Ruckleys became conventional. There was no more smuggling and not much adventuring. They settled down to respectability and anonymity. They were Magistrates and Justices of the Peace, they upheld the King of England—whoever he might be—and farmed their land to the best of their ability.

It was Lew Quayle who found out about the tunnel in some old deeds of the Castle that were lodged in his father's office in Alfriston.

Leona, moving swiftly down the passage, felt her foot stumble against a stone and kept herself from falling only by holding on to the wall at the side of her. She had been moving fast. Now she stopped for breath and put the lantern down on the ground for an instant because her arm was aching from the weight of it.

Lew Quayle! The mere thought of his name had the power to make her draw in her breath sharply. She had an insane desire to run back the way she had come, to tell Hugh she could not do it, could not go any farther.

Only once before had she been down the tunnel. She had hated it then with the feeling of the walls closing in on her. She hated it more this evening because of what lay ahead, because she must speak with Lew Quayle and meet the mockery in his eyes and hear the lust and lechery in his voice.

Lew Quayle! She could not bring herself to say the name aloud. It seemed burned in her mind so that every nerve in her body vibrated to it.

Hastily, as if she was afraid that her courage would fail her, she picked up the lantern. She had got to go on. There was no time to lose. Soon the gentlemen would be coming from the dining-room and she must be there to receive them.

Holding the skirts of her gown with one hand she went onwards, feeling her way a little more carefully now for the tunnel grew narrower, and then widening out, the roof rising until it joined and became a part of a cave. This was only one of many, as Leona knew well, and she hesitated, fearful of the dark shadows, conscious now of the heavy roar of the sea some way below.

It was now that she became aware of another sound, of men's voices and the flickering light of a fire coming through an aperture to the left of her. She followed the light, only giving an involuntary cry as a bat, disturbed by her passage, suddenly swooped down and flew through an opening in the far wall out to sea.

The opening into the next cave was narrow and roughly hewn, so for fear of tearing her gown she must edge herself almost sideways through it. It twisted a little and then suddenly she was in the full glare of the light from a fire. It was not a big fire, but it was enough to illuminate the roughly hewn walls of the cave and the men seated round it.

There must have been at least twenty of them, some of whom she recognized as being local, some of whom she had never seen before. And in the midst of them, bound with ropes, seated with his back against a barrel of wine, was a man with blood pouring from a cut in his cheek and another great gash on his forehead.

She stared at him as if stupefied, and perhaps made an involuntary exclamation, for in an instant every head turned towards her and a rough voice ejaculated:

"Be I a-seeing things or be that a woman there?"

Two or three men jumped to their feet as if in fear and then a voice with a note of mockery in it said:

"There is no reason to be afraid, 'tis only the lovely Miss Leona come to pay us a visit."

The man who spoke came swaggering towards Leona and without meaning to do so she felt herself shrink as he approached her. There was something about him which revolted her to the point when she could feel almost physically sick in his presence.

"This is indeed an unexpected honour!"

There was a sneer in his voice and at the same time a note of interrogation. As he bent to take the lantern from her she shuddered because his fingers touched hers.

"My brother sent me."

She forced the words to her lips and hated the smile which twisted his mouth.

"And I was hoping you had come of your own free will."

He was taunting her as he invariably did and she felt herself stammer, half with anger and half with nervousness as she said:

"He . . . sent me to . . . to warn you."

"To warn us, indeed. Will you not sit down and let me offer you a glass of wine? It is, I assure you, the very best that France can procure."

"There is no time, you must l-listen to me," Leona said hastily.

She looked up at him, and met his dark, bold eyes blazing down at her, taking in every detail of her little frightened face. She had known for a long time that Lew Quayle was attracted by her—known it by his expression and by what he said, known it because at his instigation Hugh was always pressing her to be nice to him.

"You must be kind to Lew. What could we do without him? . . ." "You might be nicer to Lew. He is hurt by the way you cold-shoulder him. . . ." "Can you not be more pleasant to the chap? After all he's filling our money bags for us."

Lew! Lew! Lew! The name haunted her and she would often awake with a scream in the night from a nightmare in which he came nearer and nearer to her and she could not escape.

She hated him now—the smile on his thick lips, the glint in his dark eyes. He was handsome enough, she had to grant him that. She could even understand why the girls in the village, and even those in the county who were better born, ran after him and vied for his favours.

It was rumoured that he was not his reputed father's son but that Arnold Quayle, the solicitor, had adopted him because he had been paid to do so by one of his best clients. There were stories that Lew's real father was a Royal Prince and his mother was from one of the aristocratic families which abounded in the countryside.

There were whispers that old Quayle, who had been good-looking enough in his youth, had seduced the pretty daughter of a nobleman and taken the child when it was born into his home and passed it off as his legitimate son.

It was hard, indeed, to believe that Mrs. Quayle, the dull, homely daughter of a country physician, could have given birth to anything so flamboyant and exotic as Lew. There were stories, too, that she had never been able to conceive a child, and certainly Lew had no brothers and sisters.

Whatever the real truth might have been, Lew had suffered all his life from a sense of frustration. He had hated his respectable middle-class home and his father's dusty, prosaic office with its endless boxes of deeds and documents. Before he was into his teens he tried to seek adventure and excitement in a series of escapades which became the talk of the neighbourhood and got him several serious floggings.

The war with Bonaparte had brought Lew his opportunity. Smugglers were then almost afforded the protection of the Government. They were used for the purpose of obtaining information from the enemy. Spies and counterspies were brought backwards and forwards between France and England, and at the same time the smugglers enriched themselves by almost unbelievable sums.

Lew Quayle, starting in a small way, became more and more ambitious. He had hated poverty all his life and he saw here a chance not only of becoming rich but of obtaining the power he had always craved and which he believed in his heart to be his right by birth.

He organized his gang with the cleverness and the strategy of a general. The special Act of Parliament passed after the war to prevent smuggling merely made him laugh. He could afford to snap his fingers at the Customs men and they, in their turn, were terrified of the very name of Quayle.

Dressed like a dandy, aping the gentry to which he was certain he belonged, Lew Quayle copied the manners and the affectations of the bucks of St. James's. But if anyone crossed or defied him they learned that beneath his elegant exterior he possessed muscles of steel and a ruthlessness and cruelty which stopped at nothing.

"You are looking very lovely tonight," he said now and his voice was thick and seductive, a trick of intonation which had proved irresistible in many unsavoury love affairs.

"I have come here o-only to warn you," Leona repeated.

"And I see you are wearing the gown I chose for you."

His eyes rested on the nakedness of her shoulders and the soft swelling of her breasts where the fashionable, low-cut gown revealed the little valley between them. The whiteness of her skin accentuated by little blue veins.

Instinctively Leona put up her hands, angry now that she had not brought with her a shawl or anything to cover her nakedness.

"You chose for me!" she said angrily, sidetracked for the moment from her main purpose. "Hughie gave it to me."

"Do you really believe that Hugh would have thought of it or remembered his loving little sister?" Lew asked. "I would have given it to you myself but I was afraid you would not have worn it. Nevertheless, you must admit it is a tribute to my good taste."

Leona felt her face grow hot with a flush of shame which dyed her cheeks crimson.

"Had I known that you had bought it for me I would have thrown it out of the window," she said hotly.

He laughed at that, throwing back his head and letting his laughter ring out untrammelled, to echo in the roof of the cave.

"So fiery! So adorable!" he said. "At least you are not indifferent to me."

Too late she realized that he had succeeded in getting under her skin, in arousing her to an expression of her personal feelings. It was something he always did, something which afterwards she regretted bitterly as being vulgar and unrestrained.

If only she could treat Lew with icy detachment. If only she could prove herself really indifferent to him. Then he would have no power over her. She knew that, and yet always he managed to slip through her guard, to force her to a quivering awareness of him when all she wanted was to avoid and forget him.

As if he felt now that he had gone too far he said:

"Tell me your news. I will not tease you further."

She realized then that although their conversation had not been overhead by the men, everyone sitting round the fire was tense. They knew full well that she would not have come amongst them had she not carried news of vast import; and as she looked at the rough yet attentive faces she glanced again at the gagged man with the bleeding cheek and asked quickly:

"Who is he?"

"An informer," Lew said briefly as he followed the direction of her glance.

"An in-informer!" Leona repeated the words beneath her breath and shivered. "Do you m-mean he has given away secrets of . . . of this place?"

Lew shook his head.

"No, he did not know as much as that. He only knew a little and hoped for more. Fortunately we have caught him—fortunately for us, of course!"

"What will you d-do to h-him?"

Leona knew the answer and yet she had to ask the question. There was something horrifying in the blood dripping from the gaping wound in the man's cheek and from the great gash on his forehead. Already with his open mouth and half-shut eyes he looked half dead.

She saw now that his coat had been cut to ribbons and guessed that they had beaten him. His head was bleeding, too, perhaps because they had dragged him by the hair, and his torn trousers revealed that the skin on his knees was bruised and broken.

"You ask what we are going to do!" Lew said raising his voice. "We are going to put out his eyes and cut off his tongue. Even then he might write information to the enemy so we shall cut off his hands—both of them. But after that he might still lead them here so we shall cut off his feet. And then——"

With a little cry Leona put up her hands to her ears.

"Stop!" she said in a quivering voice. "Stop! Do not s-say more. I can-cannot bear it."

"But you must hear," Lew insisted, "and he must hear too. He is a spy, a snake who came among us, worming information from our friends so that he could relay it to those who wish to destroy us."

"Can you not k-kill him outright? It would be kind-kinder," Leona whispered.

"But why should we be kind?" Lew inquired. "He will die. He will die—in time. For now that he has seen our secret places and our unmasked faces how could we let him go out into the world again? But as a warning to others he must die slowly—yes, very slowly. You would not, I am convinced, wish to see it."

Leona's head was drooping.

"I must go b-back at o-once," she stammered. "I only

came to tell you, as Hughie asked me to do, that Lord Chard has come to stay unexpectedly."

"Lord Chard!" Lew repeated the name slowly.

"He is commanded by His Majesty to put down the smuggling on the coast. He is to catch th-those who evade the customs officers and to bring th-them to-to j-justice."

Leona could hardly manage to articulate the words and yet Lew heard them.

"His Lordship is with you tonight, you say?" he asked, and now the mockery had gone and his voice was purposeful, a man whose mind was already reorganizing, planning and replanning.

"We do not know how long he will stay," she replied. "He invited himself and he knows! He knows what is going on, I am sure of it!"

She raised her voice involuntarily at the end of her sentence and two or three men near her jumped to their feet.

"Who knows?" one of them inquired. "Who's been a-gabbing?"

"Keep your heads and be quiet," Lew snapped. "Do you want to start a panic? Miss Leona has come to tell us that there are guests at the Castle tonight. Therefore we shall not bring the cargo ashore, but signal to the cutter to drop it in the bay. We can lift it when the coast is clear."

"Aye, that'll be best," an old man said. "Us don't want t' take no risks."

"Would it not be wiser to send the cutter away?" Leona asked Lew in a low voice.

"Keep his Lordship amused and do not let him look out of the windows," Lew replied. "That should be easy, looking as you do now. He should have no eyes for the sea when you are speaking with him."

Leona's chin went up at the impertinence.

"I have given you my message," she said.

"Tell Hugh I understand and everything will be arranged. And now I will take you back."

"I thank you but I would rather go by myself."

"And if I insist on accompanying you?"

She remembered the narrowness of the tunnel and knew that they would be close together, their bodies touching. Perhaps he would put his hand on hers.

"I shall be quicker alone," she replied. "I dare not delay! They will be coming from the dining-room and I must be there."

She turned as she spoke, and bent to take up the lantern. But Lew moved faster. She was forced to take the lantern from him, and once again his fingers touched hers and tried to linger.

"You will take good care of yourself?"

He was mocking her and she flushed angrily as she pulled the lantern forcibly from his grasp. She heard him chuckle and without another word she ran from him through the aperture into the dark cave and back the way she had come.

Some sure-footed instinct born and bred in her kept her from falling on the sharpness of the stones, but she thought she heard a movement behind her and that sped her on to go even quicker. She passed through the first secret opening and the next and at last reached the main cellar door in which was the key, as she had left it.

She set the lantern down on the oak chest and blew out the candle. She turned the key in the door and pulled it open very quietly. The tapers in the passage seemed almost blinding after the gloom and shadow of the tunnel.

She stepped forward, closing the door behind her. Everything seemed quiet and peaceful, and then a little way down the passage she heard the voices of the gentlemen in the dining-room, the sudden scraping of chairs. She knew then that she was only just in time. They were coming out and she must be in the Salon.

With the swiftness of a hunted animal she sped down the passage, her skirts flying out behind her. As she reached the Salon she heard the dining-room door open, heard Hugh's thick laughter echoed by that of Nicholas Weston.

She ran across the room, slipped the cellar keys into the drawer of the desk and moved towards her usual armchair as if to sit there unconcernedly with a book on her knee.

It was then she remembered her appearance. She stood on tiptoe to see her own reflection in the mirror over the mantelshelf. Her hair was a little untidy but not unduly so. She smoothed it hastily into place. She saw that her face was very pale, her eyes wide and very dark. There was a look of horror in them and she knew now it was because she could not forget what they were going to do to the bound man in the cave below.

There was no time to think. The gentlemen's voices had reached the outside of the Salon. They were coming in. She turned with what she prayed was an easy smile to greet them. She felt as if her lips had to be gouged open.

Lord Chard entered the room first. He advanced towards her, calm, unperturbed, sober and supremely, unaware, she thought, of the tumult raging within her breast which made everything seem chaotic. Lew with his lewd and lustful eyes seeking her fingers; the man who was about to be tortured and killed; the tub-carriers waiting, the cargo that was to be dropped in the bay. They all flashed through her mind as she forced herself to say:

"How nice of you to join me so soon, my Lord."

"I thought myself we had been an unconscionable time," Lord Chard replied. "I was hoping you might have thought so too."

As she spoke his eyes dropped for a moment to the skirts of her gown. Leona instinctively looked too, and as she did so felt, with a throb of horror, as if a sudden chasm of darkness had opened unexpectedly before her.

For on the whiteness of her silk gown, knee high, at just the place Lew must have bent to take the lantern from her, was a long smear of blood—the blood of the man who was about to die.

3

"THERE is blood on your gown," Lord Chard said quietly.

"Blood! Y-yes, it is blood," Leona answered, her voice trembling.

Wildly she tried to think of some excuse, some reason why it should be there. But all she could see was the great, dripping gash on the informer's cheek, his open mouth and half-shut eyes quivering and blurred by pain.

"I . . . I pricked my finger . . ." she began, and then suddenly the effort was too much, the room seemed to swim around her, a darkness descended on her head, she felt herself begin to fall.

She clutched at something or someone, she was not certain what, and then for a few seconds she knew no more. But her loss of consciousness was brief. When she came to herself again she found herself held tightly in strong arms and being carried across the hall and up the stairs.

For a moment she thought it was Hugh, and then she knew that he had never held her in quite this way, with such resolute strength, or with such a sense of security. It took her the space of a few moments while they climbed perhaps a dozen stairs, for her to collect her throughts and realize who it was.

"I am . . . all right, my Lord," she murmured weakly.

"Lie still," he commanded.

She thought that somehow his voice was hard and uncompromising.

"I c-cannot think how I c-could have been so s-silly . . ." she began.

"Do not talk," he replied. "Tell me where your room is."

"To the right . . . at the end of the c-corridor," she managed to reply.

He carried her down the passage, moving as easily as

if she weighed nothing at all. She had the absurd feeling, perhaps due to her weakness, that she was floating along, leaving her unhappiness and difficulties and problems behind. And then she knew it was but a weak fantasy and she must pull herself together and remember who was carrying, and that he was an enemy and dangerous.

The corridor twisted and turned, for they were now in the Tudor part of the house, and the ceilings were low and the floors creaked beneath Lord Chard's feet.

"The room on the left," she said at length.

The door was ajar and he pushed it open. The room beyond was in darkness and he stood still for a moment, still holding her tightly, until his eyes grew accustomed to the dimness and from the light of the tapers outside in the passage he could see the outline of the bed.

Then with a gentleness she had not expected from him he laid her down, easing her on to the pillows and taking his arms away carefully almost as if he felt she was so fragile that any roughness might cause her to break.

She tried to thank him but the words would not come, and without waiting for thanks he lifted the candle from the table beside the bed and going out into the passage lit it from a taper in the sconces and brought the light back into the room.

He set it on a table and stood looking down at her. She was very pale, the pupils of her eyes still dark and dilated with the horror of what she had seen. She felt with an added tenor that his eyes missed nothing— the agitation of her breasts, the trembling of her lips, the dark crimson stain on her white gown and below it the dusty hem where it had swept the floor of the tunnel.

And when his eyes had seemed to see everything he turned and looked down into her face. She left then, as if he searched her very soul. Because she was weak, because her sudden attack of faintness had caught her off her guard, she had no defences left.

Instead she just closed her eyes and let the sudden crimson flood of embarrassment creep up over her pale cheeks, burning and confusing her until the tears sprang into her eyes and trickled very slowly, one by one, from beneath her dark lashes.

"You are ill," Lord Chard said. "I will ring for your maid."

"No-one will c-come," she answered. "They will be in the kitchen. Your Lordship does not un-understand. We were not expecting c-company and there is a lot to d-do."

"Then can I help you? You must have attention."

There was so much sympathy and sincerity in his voice that she opened her eyes in astonishment.

"I . . . I am all right," she answered reassuringly, as if it were he who was ill rather than herself. "It was just a passing faintness. I am b-better now."

As she spoke she would have raised herself on her elbow, but the very effort made her head swim, and with an inarticulate little murmur she lay back again against the pillows.

"Lie still," he said. "I will fetch you some water."

He walked to the washing-stand, poured out a glass of water and brought it to her, raising her head skilfully with his left hand while he held the glass to her lips. She sipped it and the cool, fresh water running down her throat seemed to sweep away clouds of unconsciousness.

"Thank y-you," she murmured. "You might have been a n-nurse."

"I have, indeed, nursed many men in the war," he answered. "I remember how my first sight of men wounded and bleeding shocked and horrified me. I thought I should never grow accustomed to it; but in time I grew hardened to such sights."

Leona closed her eyes again. She knew full well what he was saying. It was as if he was clairvoyant and knew that it was the sight of bloodshed that had shocked and horrified her and guessed that she had been in the proximity of death—and of worse than death.

"I must be careful," she warned herself. She clenched her hands together tightly in an effort to force herself into being on the alert, so as not to be led into any sort of trap.

Lord Chard crossed the room to set down the glass and then he stood looking around him. The light from the candle showed him that Leona had made a little bower of her own with things that she had collected from every part of the house.

The room was small and low with latticed windows which overlooked the garden. On a wide, cushioned window-seat lay several books, as if she had just been reading them. The bed was a Florentine carved gilt, the posts which supported it being held by angels. It had been brought from Italy by the fourth Baronet who had been a great collector of beautiful things. And he was responsible, too, for the exquisite picture over the mantelpiece of cherubs playing with garlands of roses.

There was a *prie-dieu* of carved Spanish walnut. There was a little Queen Anne dressing-table, lovely in the simplicity of its lines, and chairs ornamented with elaborate carving and surmounted by a crown which proclaimed them to be of Charles II workmanship.

Every piece of furniture seemed to have some special meaning and a beauty all of its own. And everywhere there were flowers sending their fragrance into the room, each vase a picture in itself, so gracefully and imaginatively had they been arranged.

"So this is your room," Lord Chard said.

"Yes, I feel that this is my very own place, my real home, the home that I have made for myself," Leona answered, without thinking, without considering her words. It was as if she had told him of her loneliness, of the imaginative world in which she lived almost exclusively when Hugh was away and no-one came to the house except the servants and the tradespeople.

Lord Chard bent and picked up one of the books.

"I see you are reading *Paradise Regained*," he said. "Do you feel that is what you are looking for—Paradise?"

"I do not think that I can imagine it very clearly," Leona replied. "Not the way Milton speaks of it, anyway. To me Paradise lies in the garden with its flowers and its birds, and when the sea is calm, the sun shines through the trees and the wind seems to be a friend speaking of far more exciting things than any person can do. That to me, is Heaven."

Once again she had spoken without thinking, forgetting to whom she was speaking. And now, with a sudden flush rising in her cheeks, she said hastily:

"But I am k-keeping you, my Lord. You will not wish to stay here t-talking to me. I am better, I promise you, and my brother will be waiting for you downstairs."

Lord Chard put the book down and turned towards the door.

"You are certain that you will not swoon again?" he said.

"Quite certain," she replied. "And t-thank you."

"There is no reason for you to thank me," he said. "On the contrary, I feel it is my fault that you are distressed. My coming here must have been a vast inconvenience."

She was certain as he spoke that there was more than the conventional apology in his words. Did he know how great an inconvenience it had been? Did he guess that at this very moment the cutter which had crossed the Channel was being told by signal to drop its cargo in the bay because Lew Quayle and the tub-carriers dare not put out their boats to bring it in?

Leona had nothing to say. She could not contradict his assertion even in politeness, and when she did not speak Lord Chard put his hand on the door.

"Good night, Miss Ruckley! I hope that you will sleep well."

"I trust your Lordship will do the same."

She raised herself to watch him go, to see him pass through the door, to hear him close it behind him. Then she listened to his steps going down the passage until she could hear them no more.

When there was only silence and the beating of her heart, she put her hands up to her face. The whole events of the last few hours swept over her in a wave of horror and fear.

She knew that she had been living on a razor's edge ever since Hugh had arrived unexpectedly to tell her that Lord Chard was on the way. The turmoil over dinner; the tension over what had seemed a long-drawn-out meal; her apprehension of what lay ahead of her; and that blind, terrified dash down the tunnel to warn Lew Quayle.

At the very thought of him her fingers trembled and she drew a deep, uneven breath. How she hated him! The look in his eyes, the familiarity on his twisted lips, the mocking note in his voice. He was evil—everything that was bad, horrible and satanic.

Then, because she shrank from him, because she was trying not to remember the touch of his fingers, she saw again the bound man's face, the blood pouring over his chest. The thought of the blood from his wounds made her remember that she carried it on her and with a suddenly returned energy she sprang from the bed, pulling at the hooks on her gown. She undid it and let it fall to the floor.

When Hugh had given it to her she had thought it beautiful, but she had been too shy to wear it. Now she knew that it had not been Hugh's gift, it became more hateful than anything she had ever owned. Lew Quayle had chosen it—perhaps with the help of one of the women who fawned on him. Lew Quayle had imagined her in it, and because he had a hateful cleverness—which even in her dislike of him she could not deny—he had bought her something which not only became her but fitted her.

She shivered with disgust at the thought that he had

guessed her measurements so competently. She felt sick at the thought that something he had touched and handled had covered her and had in its turn touched her naked skin.

She left the gown lying on the floor, put on her nightgown and crept into bed. But she did not sleep, she lay wakeful, turning and twisting in the darkness, trying, with stumbling prayers to ask Heaven to be merciful to the man who would die before dawn came. She knew it was hopeless to ask that he might die quickly and as painlessly as possible.

Leona had known that the smugglers all along the coast were capable of acts of great brutality. She had heard stories ever since she was a child of the way they had treated Customs men, of how spies had their eyes put out and informers more slowly tortured to death. But it was one thing to hear stories of such actions and quite another thing to see, with her own eyes, what was happening.

All through the long hours of the night she was stabbed with a physical pain of pity for the victim and felt sick with disgust of his captors. And over it all was the terrible sense of frustration and emptiness. She could do nothing, nothing to help except pray, and she felt that even her prayers were inadequate.

She did not hear Hugh and his guests come to bed. Lord Chard and Nicholas Weston were in the West Wing, but Hugh slept only a few doors away from her room. She wondered why he had not come to see her.

She listened and waited, and when at length he did not come she rose from her bed and drew back the curtains. The dawn was just breaking, the garden was still in shadow but the sky was lightening. There was a faint haze everywhere. A promise of heat later in the day. The birds were already awake and the flowers were beginning to unfold as they appeared to wait expectantly for the rising sun. Leona felt the peace and beauty of the garden ease a little the tumult in her heart.

It was then, as she turned from the window with a little sigh, that she saw her gown lying on the floor where she had stepped from it last night, and averting her eyes she began to dress. She slipped into the old grey cotton gown that she had worn for so long; and when she had brushed her hair she picked up the white gown with a little shudder of disgust and went from the room into the passage.

The candles had gutted and she moved sure-footedly and softly, almost like a ghost, her grey gown blending with the shadows in the sleepy quiet of the house. She went as far as Hugh's room and realized that the door was open. She peeped in. The curtains were not pulled and it was possible for her to see at a glance that the room was empty and the bed had not been slept in.

What had happened? she wondered. Surely Hugh had not been foolish enough to go in search of Lew Quayle after Lord Chard had retired.

Fear made her run to the landing and down the stairs; then she sped through the hall and into the Salon. When she opened the door and saw what it contained she was not certain whether her feeling was one of relief or of anger.

Hugh lay on one sofa in the corner, his head fallen back, his feet on a satin cushion. There was a glass of wine smashed on the floor beside him as if it had fallen from his inert hand when he had lapsed into unconsciousness. And on a chair opposite him, with a decanter on a small table between them, was Nicholas Weston. He, too, was asleep, his feet sprawled out, his drunken snoring seeming to echo through the room with every breath he drew.

Leona looked at them for a long moment before she crossed the room, drew back the curtains and threw open one of the French windows. The morning air came freshly in, vying with the fumes of wine and the heaviness of tobacco.

She did not wait to see whether the air awoke the two men but stepped out on to the terrace, and still carrying her gown passed through the rose garden and down into the wild orchard beyond the lawns.

The dew was heavy on the grass, but she did not feel it seeping through her thin slippers on to her stockings. She walked a little blindly, as if deep in her thoughts. Even the loveliness of her beloved garden failed to attract her at this moment.

At the edge of the orchard was a small clearing where a series of bonfires had been built at one time or another. It was here that the autumn leaves were burnt, the weeds from the garden and any other refuse.

There was the charred ash, grey and blowing a little in the dawn breeze; there were half-burned sticks. Picking up one of these, Leona stirred the ash and found, as she had expected, it was still warm and glowing beneath the surface. There had been a bonfire only the day before. She had seen the old gardener making it and had smelt the smoke as it drifted across the lawn when she was picking flowers.

She put down the gown and set about collecting sticks and broken branches. Soon she had quite a pile and putting them on the glowing ashes she soon re-kindled the fire, the flames darting up red and gold.

She turned towards her gown lying where she had left it on the damp grass. She picked it up and with a little gesture which seemed in its very violence symbolic threw it into the flames.

She stood watching it burn——the exquisite silk material which French fingers had fashioned so skilfully, the wide sash which had lifted her little breasts upwards in the Directoire fashion first introduced by Napoleon and which still remained the vogue even five years after his defeat at Waterloo.

And now it was burning. She thought she caught a glimpse of blood stain and turned aside. She would not watch it any longer. It was burned; and if only she could do the same with her memories of what had happened last night, of what she had seen! But she knew that they were seared deep into her soul and never, if she lived to be a hundred, would she be able to forget.

She moved away from the fire, and as she did so she became aware that she was not alone. Someone was standing just at the edge of the orchard where it joined the lawn, someone was watching her and she had no idea how long he had been there.

She went towards him, and because she was no longer weak as she had been the night before, felt her anger rise because he was intruding on her privacy.

"You are early, my Lord," she said as soon as she was within earshot. "I trust that your bed was not uncomfortable."

"I slept well, thank you," he replied. "But I am afraid I am such and old campaigner that I am used to rising at dawn. I find it hard to sleep once the sun is up."

"If you will come back to the house I will ask that breakfast shall be prepared for you immediately," Leona said stiffly.

"There is no hurry," he replied. "I am prepared to wait."

"I would not wish you to be inconvenienced," she answered.

She tried not to look at him, afraid to meet those penetrating eyes, half afraid, too, that she might soften in her anger. She was already only too well aware of the beguiling quality of his smile. When he did not answer her, she glanced towards him involuntarily.

He was looking at her, and she could not help but see how the steel blue gaberdine of his well-fitting coat became him and how his spotless white cravat was tied with a master hand. Why could not Hugh look like this? she wondered, instead of lying dissolute in a drunken slumber, with his mouth open and his hair dishevelled across his forehead.

As if once again he had guessed her thoughts, Lord Chard said:

"I am afraid my secretary lured your brother into making a night of it—or was it the other way round?"

He smiled as he spoke and through his eyes Leona saw what had happened. Two young men had been intent on drinking each other under the table; but their resolution had ended in a draw with neither of them the victor. She could not help but smile in response.

"What a foolish way to spend an evening," she said.

"I agree with you," Lord Chard replied. "There are so many better things to do than to drink. They might have discussed politics, philosophy, world affairs—or been privileged, as I was, to see some very lovely treasures collected by someone who knows and appreciates what is really beautiful."

For a moment Leona did not understand to what he referred, then she gave a little laugh.

"Do you mean the things in my bedchamber?" she asked. "I do not pretend to be knowledgeable about them. I only collected them around me because I liked them."

"I salute your good taste," Lord Chard answered.

"They cannot be valuable," she murmured a little uneasily, as if following a train of her own thoughts. "My father sold most of the things for which he could get a good price—the family pictures, for instance, and much of the silver."

"I do not think money has a great deal to do with beauty or the appreciation of it," Lord Chard replied. "Tell me, what price would you put on this?"

He drew a gold knife from his pocket as he spoke and cut a rose that was just opening from bud to bloom. It was a white rose only faintly touched with pink and the blossom was almost perfect. He held it in his hands looking down at it, and then held it towards her. She gave a little laugh.

"A million pounds!" she answered. "Or, perhaps, the half of my kingdom."

"Perhaps that is exactly what someone will ask of you some day," he said gently.

She looked at him inquiringly and felt her eyes held by his. A little tingle ran though her veins. She did not know why but she felt as if this moment was momentous —the sunshine on their heads, the roses all around them, the silence, broken only by the birds. There was something in his eyes, something in the way he was looking at her which seemed to carry a message . . . if only she could understand it.

"I . . . I . . . do not think I understand," she managed to stammer.

She was not trying to think of what she said, she was only speaking because she must, because the silence between them was something to which she dare not listen.

In answer he held out to her the rose. She took it, conscious as she did so that their fingers touched. Then she moved away from him quickly.

"I m-must see about your b-breakfast, my Lord," she murmured and was gone, her grey gown seeming to melt into the sunshine flashing on one of the open windows.

Lord Chard stood for a moment looking after Leona. Then he turned his back on the house and stared at the garden and beyond it to where the ground sloped down towards the river. He was in a deep reverie which was broken by the sound of steps behind him on the terrace and a rather thick voice which said at his elbow:

"Have you managed to find out anything, my Lord? You are certainly up betimes."

He turned to look at the bleary countenance of Nicholas Weston, his cravat dishevelled, his hair tousled and a full night's growth of beard upon his chin. He did not answer the younger man's question, but merely looked him up and down in a manner which the soldiers whom he had commanded would have recognized as being a reprimand more unpleasant than anything that could have been said to them by any other officer.

Nicholas Weston flushed crimson.

"I am afraid I was a trifle disguised last night, my Lord. Perhaps there was something in the brandy—it certainly seemed strong enough. Maybe it is more potent when no Customs dues have been paid."

"I suggest, Nicholas," Lord Chard said and his voice was icy, "that we leave a discussion on these matters until you are shaved. Miss Ruckley is about and I should not wish her to see a member of my staff in such a condition."

Like a dog that has been whipped Nicholas Weston turned and without a word walked back into the house, while Lord Chard, his hands behind his back, walked slowly up and down the terrace, pacing his steps as if he was on a quarter-deck, a frown between his eyebrows for the first time that morning.

He had not been there long before Leona appeared.

"I am sorry to bother you, my Lord," she said apologetically, "but the cook is wondering what you would like for breakfast. She says she is sure that you would anticipate lamb cutlets and kidneys and perhaps a head of brawn, but the boy who has gone to the village to try and procure these things is not yet back and I am afraid, if you do not wish to wait, there is only eggs and bacon."

"Eggs and bacon is a dish to which I am most partial," Lord Chard said gravely.

Leona's face lightened.

"That is indeed splendid," she said. "Then breakfast will be ready in a very few minutes."

She disappeared again and Lord Chard continued his pacing, but now his frown had vanished and there was a faint smile on his lips.

Inside the house Leona, having given instructions to Mrs. Barnes, was just surveying the dining-room to see that old Bramwell had remembered to put a clean linen cloth on the table, when Hugh appeared, changed from his evening clothes, washed and shaven, but very pale with dark lines under his eyes.

"There you are, Leona," "I have been seeking you everywhere. Where the deuce have you been hiding?"

"I might ask that of you," she retorted with a smile. "I looked into your room early this morning and saw that your bed had not been slept in."

Hugh put his hand to his head and groaned.

"That curst fellow, Weston!" he exclaimed. "I intended to contrive that both he and Chard were well foxed, but Chard slipped away early before I could stop him, and Weston drank me glass for glass until, to tell the truth, I do not recall much more."

Leona gave a little laugh of sheer, unbridled amusement.

"Oh, Hughie, you do look a mess. Is your head aching?"

"Like a fire," he confessed. "My throat is dry and I can tell you I am pretty well up the ropes."

"Breakfast will be ready in a few moments," Leona said.

"Do not speak of breakfast," Hughie groaned. "What happened? Did you tell Lew?"

"I told him," Leona replied, her eyes darkening.

"Then he would have known what to do," Hugh said. "I only hope he had the sense to disperse the pack horses."

"They were in the village," Leona replied. "I do not think it likely that Lord Chard would have seen them."

"We do not know how many damned spies he has following him," Hugh retorted.

"No, of course, there is always that possibility," Leona answered. "But, somehow, I do not feel that his Lordship would do anything underhand. It would not be like him."

"What the devil do you know about him?" Hugh asked angrily. "This is a campaign with Chard just the same as war was a campaign to defeat Boney. He will do it by whatever means lie within his power, and make no mistake about it."

"You may be right," Leona said in a troubled voice.

At the same time she could not imagine Lord Chard instructing people to sneak about the village making investigations in a manner which would belie suspicion until it was too late. She might be wrong, but somehow espionage of that sort seemed contrary to everything she knew about Lord Chard even while she was quite prepared to believe that he, himself, constituted a real danger to them both.

"Where is he now?" Hugh asked, standing up.

"Out on the terrace a-waiting for his breakfast," Leona replied.

"You might have given me the nudge," Hugh complained. "I must go and pay my respects."

As he turned towards the door Leona put out her hand to stop him.

"Listen, Hughie!" she said. "I know that while Lord Chard is here there will be no question of any cargoes being brought ashore; but have you not had enough? Now we know that you are under suspicion would it not be wiser to stop altogether? To tell Mister Quayle that you are no longer interested?"

Hugh looked at her in astonishment.

"You must be bird-witted if you think I can do that," he said. "Do you not understand that I cannot stop now?

Even if I wanted to do so, which I do not, 'twould be impossible."

"But, why?" Leona asked.

"I can tell you exactly why," Hugh answered. "I am in it up to the hilt, and unless we sport the blunt of the next two cargoes at least, I'm a ruined man; really ruined, Leona!"

"But, why? How could you be?" Leona questioned.

"There is no question of 'could' about it," Hugh said almost roughly. "I never was a dab at explaining things, but if you want the truth—I owe Lew Quayle over ten thousand pounds!"

"But, how? Why?" Leona asked.

"No need to put yourself in a pucker," Hugh replied. "He has lent me the money."

"Gambling?" she asked sharply.

"That and other things," Hugh answered abruptly. "Don't look so prim and pie! You don't suppose my share of the cargo was so big at the beginning—do you? After all, I hadn't many rolls of soft to put up at the start."

"But they were using the Castle and our cellars—even the caves really belong to us."

"You try and prove it," Hugh answered. "They used those long before I got back from the war. The tunnel makes things safer, and the hidden cellars have their advantages. But you're not such a green 'un as to imagine they couldn't contrive very well without us. They can run their boats straight from the sea up the river to the village. The inn is nearly as good a hiding place as this and they can always get into the caves up a rope. It is only in an emergency that the tunnel makes a useful get-away."

"Well, Lew Quayle wanted you to be in with him," Leona said desperately.

"Not half as much as I wanted to cut in with him," Hugh answered. "I wasn't even sure he could be persuaded to let me do so. He has always had a grudge against what he calls "the gentry." Everyone knows that. Then he saw you—I think that really clinched the matter."

Leona was suddenly very still.

"What have I got to do with it?" she asked.

"A great deal," Hugh answered with a grin. Then he groaned "For God's sake, Leona, must we have a discussion like this first thing in the morning. With my head busting and Chard as likely as not with his ear to the keyhole."

"I had not realized things were as bad as this," Leona answered.

"I've no wish to throw a damper, but they'll be a damned sight worse if we do not get last night's cargo out of the sea and make plans to land the next. That's due in forty-eight hours. Everything depends on it, Leona. You've got to help me."

"Oh, Hughie! Hughie! I wish you had not got involved in all this," Leona said with a little cry.

She felt the tears start into her eyes, but there was no time to say more. Old Bramwell appeared at the door which led to the kitchen, carrying a huge dish of eggs and bacon. He was followed by Rose with a tray on which there were several silver racks of fresh toast, a large pat of golden Jersey butter and a new comb of honey.

"Good Lord! Is that all you have prepared for breakfast?" Hugh exclaimed with disgust. "Chard will think he is at a charity school. Not that I want any," he added, wincing with pain as he moved his head unexpectedly.

"Eggs and bacon are what Lord Chard asked for," Leona retorted. "And if you take my advice you will have a cup of black coffee. It is better for you than wine or ale which will only make your head worse."

She forced herself to try and speak naturally even while one part of her brain was stunned and agitated by what Hugh had just told her. In debt to Lew Quayle! How could he have been such a fool? How could he have been involved with such a man who, to say the very least of it, was untrustworthy and unreliable?

But apart from all this there was a deeper anxiety, a deeper fear. Worse to Leona than the danger of bankruptcy; worse even than her concern at Hugh's talk of being ruined was the note in his voice when he said: "Then he saw you—I think that really clinched the matter!"

She felt herself shiver. What were Lew Quayle's intentions towards her? What was his real purpose in enmeshing Hugh in his net of crime?

4

"I SHOULD like to ride along the coast this afternoon if that would put you to no inconvenience, Ruckley," Lord Chard said while they were consuming a light luncheon at half past noon.

Hugh looked up quickly from his plate of cold meats and Leona could see the fear in his eyes.

"Not much to see along the Downs," he replied heavily. "Your Lordship would, I am convinced, find more to commend itself in another direction."

"I am also anxious to see the village," Lord Chard said suavely, as if Hugh had not spoken. "I am informed that it can boast an inn which was at one time much used by the gentlemen—of the road."

Leona drew in her breath, she knew that the pause before the last three words was intentional.

"I cannot suspicion where you could pick up such wild rumours," Hugh said, surlily. "The inn is but a ramshackle boozing ken where the yokels imbibe their ale, and could not be of the smallest interest to someone of your Lordship's address."

"On the contrary, I am deeply interested," Lord Chard replied quietly.

Leona saw the frown on Hugh's face and was afraid he might be rude.

"I will order the horses," she said. "You, my Lord, will wish to ride one of your own and Hughie has recently bought a magnificent bay on which I am sure he would value your opinion. You are, I hear, an acknowledged judge of horseflesh."

She had heard nothing of the kind but it was a bow at a venture which fortunately was successful, for Lord Chard said modestly:

"I am flattered that it is my reputation, I am extremely interested in bloodflesh. Do you remember that charger

I had in France, Ruckley? A fine animal if ever there was one. I was really cut to ribbons when he was shot under me in a skirmish with Boney's cavalry."

Hugh immediately began to reminisce of the war and of the monstrous way the French treated their own animals, until Lord Chard's determination to ride along the coast was almost forgotten.

Nicholas Weston said little during the meal. He was looking extremely ill with a green tinge to his countenance and dark lines under his eyes. He pecked at the food and hardly spoke except when he was addressed, but Leona could not help feeling that his ill health served him right for indulging too freely the night before.

As soon as they were finished Leona hurried from the dining-room to send the message to the stables. When she came back Hugh was alone in the hall and taking her by the arm he drew her into the Library and shut the door.

"What maggot has Chard got in his head?" he asked in a low voice. "What does he expect to find? Do you think I ought to send a message to Lew for everyone to keep out of sight?"

"No, no, I am sure it is all right," Leona said soothingly. "There will be no-one about, you can feel assured of that. Mister Quayle knows that his Lordship is here and everyone in the village knows the same thing. They will be on the look-out."

"If only I knew what he was trying to find," Hugh said. "At least I do know, but what will give him a pointer? Boats; pack-ponies; marks on the beach? The Lord knows I'm no hand at this sort of thing, Leona."

"And I am thankful that you are not," she said. "Oh, Hughie, if only you had not got involved so deeply."

"It is too late to wish that now," he said. "But I have no wish to find a rope around my neck or to learn I have been transported. That would be no joke."

"He would not dare do such a thing to you," Leona said fiercely.

"He would do it to anyone if he could prove his suspicions," Hugh answered. "Do not think you are throwing dust in his eyes by being charming. Chard is as hard as steel. He always has been. He is out to get what he wants and if any one man is capable of stopping the smuggling from France to this country it will be Chard."

Hugh spoke with great bitterness, then he walked across the room to stare out of the Library windows.

They looked south and in the distance, over the undulating downland, there was a faint glimpse of the horizon and the sea.

"The cargo should be safe enough," he said reflectively, "as long as they do not try to move it too soon. It was sunk with a drift line in the usual manner. We've done it before but never with so much at stake."

"The tub-carriers will be safe enough going about their usual work," Leona said cheerfully. "And the rest will not have come ashore."

She was trying to reassure Hugh. She hated the troubled, anxious look in his eyes and the way his face seemed to sharpen and look older when he was worried. He always seemed to her so young. It was strange to remember that he was twenty-five and should by this time be thinking of settling down and choosing a wife.

He was so irresponsible, so feckless, that it was difficult to recall that she was very much his junior and that he should be looking after her not she after him. She went towards him now and put her arms round his neck.

"Have no fear! All will be safe," she said with conviction she was far from feeling. "Do not get into such a pucker, my dear one. Just take Lord Chard for a ride and perhaps, if he sees nothing, he will go away tomorrow."

"Blast him!" Hugh said. "Why should we entertain him and that little weasel, Weston? I might have been in London enjoying myself instead of hanging about here startled by my own shadow."

"Be as charming and as easy as you can," Leona advised. "And, Hughie, do not attempt to communicate with Lew Quayle or with anyone else. They can fend for themselves, I am sure of it. After all, they have been warned."

"You made it quite clear to them did you not?" Hugh asked.

Leona nodded. Even now she could not bring herself to speak of what had happened when she had gone down the tunnel to warn Lew Quayle. She had not told Hugh of the man who was about to die. She had not related how Lew had behaved or revealed her own misery and terror. What was the point of worrying him? There was nothing he could do about it.

"You had best go," she said hastily. "Lord Chard will be waiting."

"And what about the village?" he asked sullenly.

"Act quite naturally," she counselled. "Show Lord Chard the outside of the inn—I should not go in if you can avoid it. Visit the Church. There is nothing there which might prove incriminating—not at the moment at any rate."

Just for a second Hugh smiled. There had been occasions when the Church had been used as a dumping ground for the cargo, but it had only been in an emergency. The barrels of wine and the bales of tea and spices, silks and satins and laces, had lain in the aisle for perhaps twenty-four hours, before the pack horses could get them away by devious routes. The Customs men had suspected the inn; they had never thought that the Church might be used as a hiding place.

"No, the Church is safe now," Leona said quietly. "And you might take his Lordship to see Farmer Grundle; he is very proud of his pigs."

Hugh bent swiftly and kissed her cheek.

"I do not know what I should do without you," he said. "I will bore Chard to death with our rural interests and voluble yokels. If that does not drive him back to St. James's nothing will."

He went from the room walking jauntily and Leona knew she had put new heart into him. She followed him a few seconds later and found Lord Chard descending the staircase, wearing an extremely elegant grey riding coat of heavy whipcord, his boots polished so brightly that one could see the banisters reflected on the dark surface as if they were mirrors. He carried a riding whip in his hands and on his head was a high beaver hat in the very latest mode.

"You are not thinking of accompanying us, Miss Ruckley?" he asked as he reached the hall.

Leona had a sudden longing to ride with them, and just for a moment she was tempted to say she would go too, but then she thought it might complicate things for Hugh.

"Alas, I wish I could ride with your Lordship," she answered, "but I have a formidable amount to do at home. I hope indeed that you will enjoy your ride."

"I am sure I shall," Lord Chard said gravely. "Come along, Nicholas," he added, glancing over his shoulder to where Nicholas Weston with a pale set face was descending the stairs at a snail's pace. "A ride will do you good."

"I have an aching head," Nicholas Weston said pettishly. "And I do not anticipate we shall see anything."

Lord Chard shot him a warning glance which in his preoccupation with his aches and pains he did not see.

"What do you expect to see?" Leona asked, innocently. She knew the answer but hoped to embarrass him.

Mr. Weston had reached the hall by now and was forced to face her.

"Nothing in particular, of course," he replied a little sheepishly.

"I am glad of that," Leona said, "for it would be a pity if you were disappointed."

She could not help the dislike she felt for him showing itself in her voice. She had turned towards the front door feeling suddenly angry both with Nicholas Weston and Lord Chard. What right had they to impose themselves on Hugh and herself and use the house as a headquarters from which they could spy on their host and on everyone else in the vicinity?

Lord Chard's voice cut through her thoughts.

"Are you quite sure you will not join us?" he asked. "I would not like to feel that through the inconvenience of our visit we had obliged you to stay behind because we have caused so much extra work in the house."

"No, pray do not blame yourself, my Lord," Leona replied. "I really had not planned to ride this afternoon."

She spoke with a cold reserve in her voice because she was still angry, and he hesitated a moment, standing beside her on the steps, drawing on his riding gloves, as Nicholas and Hugh moved across the gravel to where the groom were holding the champing horses.

"It is a lovely day," Lord Chard said softly.

It was almost as if he was pleading with her, and Leona looked up swiftly. It was somehow difficult to be angry when his eyes were on her face. It was hard, too, to resist the unspoken but nevertheless quite obvious desire that she should accompany them.

She knew he wanted her to go. She knew it even while he just stood and pulled on his gloves, looking down at her, his broad shoulders silhouetted against the blue sky behind him.

"No, I will not come," she said at length in a very small voice. "I think you will do well without me."

"I wish——" Lord Chard began, a sudden urgency in his voice, and then he was interrupted by a shout from Hugh.

"Are you coming, Chard? My horse is fresh and 'tis devilish hard to hold him."

He was wheeling around the drive as he spoke, the bay plunging and bucking.

"Yes, I am coming," Lord Chard said, and the rest of his sentence remained unspoken.

What had he wished? Leona wondered. She had a feeling that what he was about to say was something more important than the mere expression of desire that she should accompany them. Whatever it might have been it was now lost.

She watched him mount. He sprang gracefully into the saddle. His horse was a black stallion and he handled him with consummate skill. Leona had ridden since she was a child and she knew not only a great deal about horseflesh but also when a man was a born horseman.

Hugh was good but Lord Chard was superlative. In the saddle he seemed part of the horse and as she watched the three men ride away, raising their hats to her as they went, her eyes following Lord Chard until he was out of sight. Then with a little sigh she went into the house.

Old Bramwell wanted to speak to her about the arrangements for dinner. Mrs. Barnes was waiting to complain the chickens were tough.

"That dratted poultry man! He's not killing his best for us," she scolded. "He's only a-picking out the birds that are but skin and bone. There's barely a mouthful on 'em. If you ask me, Miss Leona, his mind is on the sea, and that ne'er-do-well brother of his who's been a-coming and a-going this twelve months a' more!"

Leona knew well enough what Mrs. Barnes meant by that. She had not known before that Farley the poultry man had a brother working for Lew Quayle. Was everyone enmeshed in this monstrous spider's web, she wondered despairingly?

"I will speak to Farley," Leona promised. "He must kill the fattened birds. But baste them well and add plenty of wine to the sauce, it makes such a difference."

"And what about th' meat, Miss?" Mrs. Barnes inquired. "Th' butcher says unless he's paid he's not a-leaving th' best cuts."

"But we paid him but a short time ago," Leona protested.

"I know, Miss, but that was a bill that was owed for nigh on three years. He'll not give us much credit again. 'Tis an impudence, if you like, but he swears he can't afford to wait for his money."

"I will speak to Sir Hugh this evening," Leona promised.

"But that'll be too late for dinner, Miss!" Mrs. Barnes said despairingly. "I can't serve to the table what I haven't got in pot, now—can I?"

"I will see what I can do," Leona promised.

She left the kitchen and went upstairs. Hugh had a habit, as she well knew, of throwing any gold or silver that might be in his pocket into the drawer of his dressing-table. He had no idea how much she had grown to rely on the odd change she found in his drawer. It was invariably all he left behind when he rode away to London with perhaps a small fortune in his pocket to risk on the gaming tables, but grudging every penny she begged of him for the running of the Castle.

It had been a continual battle ever since he had returned from France to persuade him to give her anything towards the upkeep of the house. He seemed to feel that money he made through smuggling was his to do with as he liked.

Of course, she reflected, she had no idea that he was so much in debt to Lew Quayle. She had thought that he just had a share in every cargo and it was paid to him in cash, as it was to the other men in greater or lesser degrees. He did not confide in her that he intended to go deeper into the business, and she thought now, with horror, of how much he was involved in buying a new cutter.

Supposing it was sunk before he had a chance to pay for it? There were Naval ships always patrolling the Channel and these had been increased lately so that the smugglers ran a greater risk every time they neared the English coast.

"If only he had asked me," Leona whispered to herself, but realized that she would have been powerless to prevent him. She might feel maternal towards Hugh but he always looked on her as a child.

Leona reached the landing, went along the passage and opened the door of Hugh's bedroom. The sunlight was coming in through the window and before she went to the dressing-table she paused to re-arrange a bowl of flowers that she had set on the tallboy, and to tidy away a coat which had been thrown carelessly on a chair. Bramwell was getting old and could not see to everything. And besides, Hughie had so many clothes.

Leona opened the wardrobe and stood looking at them. Coats of every colour and of every sort of material—whipcord, gaberdine, satin and velvet. They shone in their variety, like a rainbow, contrasting strangely with the shabbiness of her own gown.

But she had no thought of herself as she shut the wardrobe door and went towards the dressing-table. She was only glad that Hugh should have such apparel. Why not? He had been a soldier long enough.

She opened the drawer of the dressing-table. As she had expected, there was the glitter of half dozen golden guineas and quite a pile of silver coins. She picked up three of the guineas. They would pay the butcher and ensure that they had enough to eat for several weeks at least.

Then she closed the drawer again. She felt a little guilty, as she always did when she took any money from Hugh, and yet she knew it was the only way to avoid disagreeableness and grumbles.

"Why are you in need of money?" "Do you think I have it to burn?" "What have you done with what I gave you a week ago?" "I tell you my pockets are to let." "The tradesmen—damn them—will have to wait."

How often she had heard these sentences over and over again. And though invariably he gave her something in the end, it was so exhausting to have to plead and argue and try and prove that she and Mrs. Barnes were as economical as it was possible to be but that they could not live on air.

Never had she taken one penny from Hugh for herself, and when he was away in London she contrived that they lived almost entirely off the estate. There were eggs, rabbits and chickens and they fared well enough although the servants had to wait a long time for their wages.

As Leona came out into the passage from Hugh's bedroom she saw Rose carrying a brush, her mob cap crooked on her head, a smudge of dust on her cheek. She really did look vacant, Leona thought. But she was fond of Rose and no other girl in the village would work as hard as she did for so little.

"Oh, Rose!" she called. "Will you take this money to Mrs. Barnes? Tell her it is for the butcher."

Rose came towards her and dropped an awkward curtsy.

"Lor', Miss! I never 'oped to 'old a golden guinea in me 'and," she said with a giggle.

"It is for Mrs. Barnes," Leona repeated. "Take it straight to her."

Rose closed her hand over the money as if she feared it would try to escape her.

"I'll take it to 'er, Miss, cross me heart," she said, and hurried down the passage, her feet clumping heavily on the old boards.

Leona sighed and turned towards her own room. It would be nice if they could have an experienced maid. She wondered what Lord Chard must think of Rose and her mother, Mrs. Mildew, who was really too old for her work and inclined to stop and gossip. Perhaps he was laughing at the way they lived, despising their uncouth servants with their countrified, unpolished ways.

She had seen a smirk several times on Nicholas Weston's face when old Bramwell had made a mistake in serving the meals or had joined familiarly in the conversation as he had been wont to do ever since Hugh was a child.

"No! Lord Chard is different," she reassured herself. She had a feeling he did not laugh at them. It was only Mr. Weston with his supercilious, dandified manners who thought they were a joke.

She felt herself suddenly grow hot with resentment at the thought and tried to laugh away her own anger. How foolish to feel sorry what someone like Mr. Weston thought! Soon he would be gone and he would never think of them again.

Lord Chard was not to be compared with his ferret-faced secretary. She had a feeling that somehow he would remember them. Then she almost laughed aloud at herself. What a ridiculous idea! The one thing they did not want was for Lord Chard to remember anything about Ruckley Castle, or Hugh, or anyone else.

She had a sudden strange and unaccountable conviction that this was all predestined, that Lord Chard's coming was something which could never have been avoided and could not have been prevented. She had a feeling there was a reason behind it all. And then she shook herself. How ridiculous she was being. She was just imagining things.

To escape from her own thoughts she hurried a little faster down the passage. There was work for her to do in her own room. She thrust Lord Chard from her thoughts. She must remember all the things she had to do—practical, sensible things.

She opened the door of her bedroom, then gave an exclamation that was almost a scream. A man was sitting in the chair by the window. A man who rose when he saw her, blocking out the light it seemed to her.

"What . . . are you . . . doing . . . here?"

Her voice seemed to be strangled in her throat and yet to come harshly from between her lips.

"I was waiting to see you," Lew Quayle replied.

"But here! In my room! How did you get here?"

"I came up the tunnel, of course," he replied. "I had a reason."

"Get out!" Leona said. "Get out of here and go back to where you came. You have no right, no right at all."

She was angry with an anger that was all the more violent because it was born of fear.

"What a little spitfire you are," retorted Lew Quayle, smiling.

"You are not permitted to come into the house, you know that," Leona said.

"Your brother, who I believe is the owner of the castle, has invited me to enter whenever I wish," Lew replied suavely. "Besides, as you well know, he gave me another set of keys. The fact that I do not use them often is due, I assure you, entirely to my consideration for your feelings in this matter."

"Then go now," Leona said. "This is my room and I will not have you in it."

"I came in here," Lew replied, "because I thought it was the safest place for me to speak with you. I knew your guests had gone riding. I waited until I saw them go but I did not think you would wish the servants to see me. They talk too much."

"What do you want?" Leona inquired.

She still stood in the half-open doorway and Lew still faced her from the other side of the room.

"That is a more sensible question," he said, grinning. "Will you not come in and close the door behind you? I assure you that I shall behave with the utmost propriety."

He was mocking her and she hated the smile on his lips. She felt herself shudder as she saw it and yet, as if he compelled her, she closed the door, and came a little farther into the room, standing stiffly, every nerve of her body tense and her face very white and her eyes wary as she watched him.

"That's better," he said approvingly. "I do not know why you should be so afraid of me."

"Why have you come?" Leona asked.

"I'm going to tell you that in a minute," Lew replied, comfortably at his ease in the armchair. "But first I wish to know what is occurring. Where has Hugh gone with Lord Chard?"

"His Lordship wished to ride along the coast," Leona answered. "He also signified his desire to visit the inn and the village."

"The devil he did!" For a moment Lew looked discomposed, then he added quickly: "He will find nothing for there is nothing to find. The place has been searched often enough, if that is what he is after."

"I do not think, somehow, that he expects to find anything," Leona said carefully. "He is just looking over the ground as if he were planning a future campaign."

Even as she said this to Lew she realized it was the truth. That was what Lord Chard was doing. It was as clear to her now as if he had told her so with his own lips.

"May his soul rot in hell!" Lew said with a sudden violence. "I anticipated he would be gone by now and we could have moved the cargo tonight."

"He has not spoken of leaving." Leona replied.

"Then you must try to make him leave. Tell him you are shutting up the house; that the servants are sick. Tell him anything but be rid of him."

"I cannot imagine anything more likely to arouse his suspicions," Leona retorted.

"Yes, you may be right there," Lew conceded. "So you are taking an interest in our fortunes, are you? I believed you to be superbly indifferent."

"I am interested only in Hughie and how much he is involved in all this," Leona retorted. "You know as well as I do that if I had my way he would never see you or an illicit cargo again."

"If that were so how he would hate the poverty in which he would have to live," Lew said softly. "Can you imagine him pinching, saving and becoming threadbare? That is not the life for Hugh—not the Hugh I know."

As he spoke his eyes roved over her, taking in every detail of her old, worn, grey gown. What he left unspoken was so obvious that Leona felt the colour rise in her cheeks.

"You looked very beautiful last night," Lew said suddenly, his voice altering.

Leona drew herself up as he continued:

"I thought of you in that gown long after you had gone from the cave. You looked like a vision of another world when you came from the darkness. Even the men remarked on it."

"I burned that gown this morning," Leona said.

"Burned it!"

The exclamation was sharp. Even Lew, for once, had been taken off his guard.

"Yes, I burned it because you gave it to me," Leona replied. "And because there was b-blood on it. The blood of the man you were mur . . . murdering."

Lew stared at her for a moment, then threw back his head and laughed.

"Was there ever a girl with such spirit?" he asked. "Gad, but I like it in you. You are like a horse that is unbroken. But one day I shall be your master."

There was not so much a threat in his voice as a statement of fact. Leona felt the blood suddenly drain away from her face. She saw the sudden fire leap into his eyes, heard the passion rising in his voice and knew that he was dangerous, knew that one false move and she might not be able to hold his desire for her within bounds. Proudly she faced him.

"Tell me what you have come here for," she said harshly, "and then go."

She knew as he did not answer that a battle raged within him. He debated within himself as to whether to take her in his arms, and yet at the same time he still had some sort of respect for her that he could not entirely overthrow. He hesitated and Leona spoke again.

"If you do not tell me why you have come, I myself shall leave the room. Besides, the others may be returning. I do not know how long they will be away."

She won the battle—the battle which seemed to vibrate between them so fiercely that it almost brought her to her knees. Then, with a sense of relief, she heard Lew reply.

"I have come because I need your help."

"My help! In what way?" she inquired.

"One of my men has been injured."

"How?"

"He was cleaning a gun and it exploded, the bullet passed through his right shoulder. I dare not take him home because it is so obviously a bullet wound that noone will believe for one instant that he did not get it in a fight with the coastguards. It is all the more infuriating because the truth is that we never saw the shadow of one last night."

"I think the truth is that the man was fighting," Leona said slowly.

"You are quick, are you not?" Lew inquired. "That

is what I like about you—'tis hard to pull the wool over your eyes."

"I do not want your compliments." Leona retorted. "How can I help this man?"

"He has been running a fever for the last few hours," Lew replied, "so I have brought him here."

"Here!"

The word was jerked out of her mouth by astonishment.

"Where else can I take him? He will die if I leave him in the cave. Besides, I cannot hang about there and the others have gone home."

"So I am to do your dirty work for you, am I?" Leona inquired.

"Not at all. I am asking you to do a woman's work—to be a ministering angel to someone who is suffering. Is not that the sort of job at which women are supposed to excel?"

"Perhaps," Leona admitted. "But not to men who are really criminals, men who are being hunted by those who uphold the law."

"Well, try to think that Hugh might be in the same position and you would be sorry if no-one would help him," Lew said brutally. He laughed as he saw her wince and added "That has gone home has it not? Well, come and see the fellow and then perhaps that hard little heart of yours will soften towards him."

"Where have you put him?" Leona asked.

"In the room at the far end of this passage. I remember Hugh told me once that you never used those rooms. They certainly do not look as if anyone has slept in them for years."

"Nobody has," Leona said.

"Then there is no reason why your servants should give themselves extra work by going into them," Lew asserted. "The key was in the door and I turned it on him. If you can keep him warm he should be all right in a day or so."

As if he felt she still needed convincing he continued:

"If I take him home in this state his wife will have hysterics and start sending for the physician or the neighbours. Everyone will be blabbing and in next to no time one of those nosey coastguards will be making inquiries as to what sort of illness he has contracted. A gunshot wound is enough to convict any man along the coast these days."

"Then you should see that your followers are more

careful with their firearms," Leona said. "I'm crazed to listen to you but I suppose I had best have a look at the man."

She realized as she spoke that she was committed to looking after him. But what else could she do? There was a lot of reason in what Lew was saying, she was well aware of that. Besides, something instinctively within her would have prevented her from ever refusing to help a man who was in pain, however bad he might be, however criminal his actions.

She walked across the room and went to open the door. As she touched the handle Lew's fingers closed over hers.

"Allow me," he said with a hint of laughter behind the conventional politeness.

She snatched her hand away as if he had stung her. Then he waited for a moment, looking at her and holding the door still closed.

"Do you really hate me so much?" he asked.

"I loathe you," she retorted.

"You attract me as no other woman has ever attracted me before."

"If that is meant to be a compliment it merely disgusts me," Leona replied. "And let us hurry. If I have to nurse this man there are arrangements to be made before the others return."

She was vividly conscious that Lew could prevent her from leaving the room if he wished. She knew the danger which threatened her every second when she was in close proximity to him. But now, though she knew it was madness to linger, she could not help but ask the question which had been trembling at the back of her mind ever since she had first come into the room.

"That man," she said almost in a whisper, "the one who was to d-die. Is he . . . d-dead?"

"He died quicker than he deserved," Lew replied roughly. "Because of the message you brought us we had no time to play with him as we had intended. He was dead within five minutes of your departure."

Leona gave a little sigh of relief. That at least was something.

"Is that a mark in my favour?" Lew inquired. "Do I get a prize for such forbearance?"

"Take me to this wounded man," Leona said sharply. "I have told you there is no time for words."

She heard him chuckle beneath his breath as at last

he opened the door and let her pass through it. She moved down the passage, tense and stiff because he followed her.

The house was very quiet; the passage twisted a little and there were several rooms on the other side to her own which, as Hugh had rightly said, were never used. They were small, damp and faced north. Most of the furniture from them had been moved or else they had become a repository for things from other rooms that were not needed or which Leona had decided were unnecessarily ugly.

As they reached the last room Lew drew from his pocket the key of the door. He fitted it in the lock, turned the handle and Leona entered.

A man was lying on the bed covered with a blanket. He was muttering to himself and she saw at one glance that he was in a high fever. She walked across to him and put her hand on his forehead. It was burning hot and his skin was dry. It was impossible to understand what he was saying but it was obvious from the movement of his lips that he was thirsty.

"Fetch a jug of water from my bedroom," Leona said to Lew, and meekly he obeyed her.

She pulled back the blanket when he had gone and saw that the man had no coat. His shirt had been cut away from his damaged shoulder and the wound was roughly bound up with a handkerchief. She undid it, experiencing a feeling of horror mingled with pity, as she looked at the battered shoulder.

She was staring down at it, trying to see if the bullet had been removed, when Lew came back with the water.

"The bullet has been extracted," he said as if he guessed that was the question she had been about to ask him. "One of my men took it out last night. He was a bit rough about it and I daresay his hands were none too clean."

"Stay here with the man," Leona said.

She went from the room and when she got outside she turned the key in the lock. She guessed her action would surprise Lew but she had no desire to take any risk however unlikely.

She went downstairs and found a china basin in the pantry and half a bottle of brandy which had been opened the night before. There were also bandages and fresh linen in a small drawer in the corridor where she always kept them in case anyone had an accident in the house or in the grounds.

She carried all this upstairs and with it a jug of hot water which she fetched at the last moment from the kitchen, telling Mrs. Barnes that she needed it to clean a mark off her gown.

It was not likely, she thought as she passed along the stone-flagged passages, that anyone would take any notice of her. They were too used to seeing her move about the house while they were at work, knowing that she, too, worked—dusting, tidying, and even scrubbing when there was no-one else to do it.

She re-entered the bedroom and knew by the quick glance that Lew gave her and the movement of his hand towards the pistol he carried in his coat that he was on the defensive, ready in case by some ill chance it had not been she but someone else. Just for a moment she wondered what his life must be, eternally on the alert, always ready for the unexpected, anticipating every move of friend and stranger alike.

She crossed to the bedside and put the things that she carried down on the table.

"Who is the brandy for?" Lew inquired.

"It is to clean the wound," Leona replied briefly. "My father told me that wine, or preferably brandy, has saved many a man's life when a wound has become infected."

The man on the bed was hardly conscious and yet she felt a shudder go through him as the brandy stung against the torn flesh. Then she washed the wound by adding a little brandy to the hot water. Then she bound it up with her clean bandages and set a cool compress of linen wrung out in cold water on his forehead.

"He will be better in a little while," she said. "I will prepare a special tea of herbs to make him sleep."

"If he is well enough tomorrow I'll take him home," Lew said.

"I hope he will be," Leona answered. "It is not going to be easy to keep him here. If Lord Chard finds him what do you expect me to say?"

"Your imagination and your woman's instincts should need no prompting from me," he said, impertinently.

She turned towards the door carrying the bowl of bloodstained water.

"Do you not want me to thank you?" he asked with that note in his voice that she most disliked.

"The best thanks you can give me is to keep away from here," she retorted.

"And if I replied that I was glad of the excuse to see you, what would you say to that?" he asked.

Once again he was standing between her and the door but Leona looked up at him defiantly.

"If you do not open the door for me immediately," she said, "I will fling this bowl of water over you."

"Every word you speak, however cruel, merely entrances me," Lew murmured, and he was smiling as he opened the door so that Leona felt that although he had done what she said, in some obscure way his was the victory.

"Get out of here, and quickly," she said over her shoulder, speaking almost below her breath, and walked along the passage, determined in her own mind not to look back, not to see whether he was following her.

She reached the housemaid's cupboard, emptied away the dirty water and cleaned out the basin. When she had finished she realized almost guiltily that she had been listening all the time, tense and fearful, for the sound of Lew's voice, for the awareness that he was behind her.

He must have gone. She felt herself relax with relief and, at the same time she knew that this was the beginning of a new régime, something she had always feared and which until now had never come to pass.

Never before had Lew Quayle entered the Castle uninvited. Never before, presume as he might, had he dared to visit her unless Hugh had been there. Now he had come without invitation and found his way, by some knowledge or instinct known only to himself, into her bedroom, the one room in the house which she could really call her own.

She had a feeling of horror at what this might lead to. The idea of finding Lew at every turn of the passage, in any room that he might wish to visit—even her own— filled her with terror. Then she tried to tell herself it was only because the man was wounded, only because he needed her help so desperately.

The full consequences of what she had done in accepting this new burden swept over her in a sudden tide of apprehension and despair. A sick man on her hands; Lord Chard returning at any moment; and Hugh deeply in debt to the man she most hated in the whole world.

She felt it was almost too much for one person to face, especially someone so resourceless as herself. She had a feeling that she could not do it, could not go on. And yet what else was there she could do?

It was as she came from the housemaid's cupboard to walk back along the passage, she heard the sound of horse's hoofs outside—the riders were returning. She heard Hugh's voice call out to the grooms and as she reached the top of the stairs, she looked down into the well of the hall and saw someone come in through the door.

It was Lord Chard drawing off his riding gloves, and she saw him stand, preoccupied, below her, flexing his fingers as if they were stiff.

And then suddenly as if the fact that he was being watched communicated itself to him by some sixth sense, he threw back his head and looked up at her. Their eyes met and for the moment she had the strangest feeling that here was someone who could help her, here was someone to rescue her from the terrible dilemma in which she found herself.

She felt as if her worried and troubled heart leapt downwards to tell him of all she was suffering. And because for a moment she forgot who he was or why he was here, and knew only that he seemed so different in every way from Lew Quayle, she was not surprised when with his eyes still holding hers, he said quietly:

"Leona! I was thinking of you!"

5

LORD CHARD came slowly up the stairs and it seemed to Leona as if his eyes never left hers. She wanted to turn and run to her own room and yet she was unable to move. She could only stand as if paralysed until he reached the top of the staircase and came the few steps towards where she stood, one hand resting on the balustrade of the balcony, the other holding the small basin in the crook of her arm.

She felt as if in some extraordinary way time stood still. It might have taken a century or only a few seconds for him to reach her. She had no idea how long it was; nevertheless she felt as if the passage of time was in itself interminable.

He seemed extraordinarily tall and broad-shouldered as he came nearer and nearer, until he stood looking down at her, his eyes on her face, his expression grave and serious, at the same time, inquiring, as if he asked a question of her.

"I have been thinking of you," he said again.

And now, because she felt some answer was expected of her, she faltered:

"I am . . . honoured, my Lord. But . . . why should . . . I occupy your . . . thoughts?"

"I consider your life here is strange," he said unexpectedly. "A young girl—so very young—alone in this great castle without anyone to chaperon or guard you. It is not right."

If Leona had not known that such a thing was impossible she would have thought there was quite a violence of feeling beneath his conventional words.

"I have . . . Hughie," she said.

"And is he often here?" Lord Chard inquired, making it more of a statement than a question. And then he went on: "Your brother enjoys the gaieties of St. James's. I often see him in the gaming hells, at Newmarket and at Almack's—in fact anywhere the *beau monde* chooses to congregate. I do not blame him for seeking the social whirl, but what about you? Would you not also enjoy London?"

"I should hate it above all things," Leona said frankly. "Besides, my Lord, what sort of figure do you think I should cut without the right clothes and without someone of import to sponsor my *début*? No, this is the place for me—the wilds of Sussex."

"How can you be sure of that?" Lord Chard persisted. "You are but a child. You have never known anything but what you call "the wilds of Sussex". London can be very alluring to anyone as lovely as you."

She stared at him in frank amazement. It was not only that she had not expected such a compliment to pass his lips but also because she had never thought of herself as lovely or, indeed, as even passably pretty.

"I . . . I think, my Lord, y-you are r-roasting me!" she managed to ejaculate at length as the blood rose crimson in her cheeks, and then she was angry with herself for appearing to take a fulsome compliment so seriously.

Lord Chard shook his head.

"No, indeed!" he answered. "And I am persuaded that you would enjoy London and would make a considerable stir should you care to do so."

"Now you are, indeed, making fun of me," Leona said.

"I am speaking in all seriousness," Lord Chard replied. "Shall I arrange it for you? Shall I ask my sister—or, better still, my grandmother—if you might stay with her for the rest of the season?"

There was no mistaking now that he was in earnest and Leona felt a sudden warmth in her heart at his kindness.

"I think, your Lordship," she said, "it is indeed kind of you even to think of me. But I assure you that in London I should be a fish out of water. I am very happy here. I love my home and I am never lonely—not even when Hughie is away for months at a time."

"But it is an unnatural life for a girl," Lord Chard persisted."

"Unnatural, perhaps, amongst the people you know, my Lord. But my father and I had very simple tastes. It was only Hughie who wanted to be gay, who desired to go out in the world and cut a dash. We were content with the farm—our sheep, cows and pigs—and looking after the people whom we employed and who have served us faithfully for many years."

"And your brother has not been content with that? Not even when he came home from the war?" Lord Chard said, his voice grave and full of meaning.

Leona realized this was dangerous ground.

"I . . . I must go, my Lord," she said hastily. "I have many things to do. Thank you again for your consideration for me. I would not have you believe me ungrateful, but I am like the wild flowers that you will find growing on the downs. Transplant them, or even bring them into the warmth of the house, and they die."

"We will discuss it further," Lord Chard said, as if he could not believe that her answer was final.

"I shall still say no," she smiled at him. "But thank you again."

She turned to leave him and as she did so her hand brushed inadvertently against his coat. She gave a start.

"You are wet, my Lord. I had not realized it was raining."

"Indeed, it was pouring," he replied. "That was why we returned so early. I am afraid all the things I desire to see will have to wait until the morrow."

Leona glanced towards the high, long windows of the hall, the small latticed panes of which were ornamented in stained glass with the heraldic crest and coat of arms of the Ruckleys. The glass was old and not particularly well cleaned, but through it she could see, somewhat indistinctly, the rain pouring down straight and grey against the background of the green trees in the drive.

"It is, indeed, raining hard!" she exclaimed. "You must be soaked to the skin. Please go and change your garments. I would not wish you to catch cold."

"I have stood far worse than this in France," Lord Chard said with a smile. "In fact I would not have returned if it had not been for your brother and Nicholas. They protested volubly against continuing our ride."

"They were right," Leona said positively. "What is the point of taking such risks with your good health? Please change your coat and breeches, my Lord. Later I will send someone to your room to light a fire so that they can dry."

"That would of course be most sensible," Lord Chard said with a smile. "And I shall see you later?"

"Yes, of course," Leona replied. Her eyes flickered before his and she turned hastily away from him. She hurried down the passage towards her own room, stopping on the way at Hugh's room to rap sharply on the door. She entered without waiting for a reply, to find her brother with his coat in his hand, holding it to the light of the window.

"I declare this damned material is going to mark!" he exclaimed as he saw who stood in the doorway. "That cursed crook Shultz assured me that it would make a perfect riding coat. Perfect indeed! These rain marks are going to make me look like a spotted dog if they do not dry out."

"Let me see," Leona said.

She crossed the room and took the coat from him, inspecting it closely, then put it over the back of the chair.

"It will be all right," she said soothingly. "That sort of material always marks when it is wet. I have noticed it with several of your other coats and Father had one like it once."

"Egad Father!" snorted Hugh. "He spent as little as possible on his garments and bought them from that tailor in Brighton whom I would not employ to make a grave cloth."

"Father was not a dandy like you," Leona smiled.

Looking at him she thought how handsome he was with his straight nose and shining grey eyes. But he would be more handsome still, she added to herself, if he did not look so worried and if there was not a querulous look about the droop of his mouth.

She suddenly remembered that she had to add to his worries, and, first glancing over her shoulder to make quite certain she had shut the door behind her when she came in, she said in a voice a little above a whisper:

"Hughie, I have got something to tell you."

"What is it? Something wrong?"

She heard the anxiety in his voice and instinctively her arms went out towards him and pulling his head down to hers she laid her cheek against his.

"Oh, Hughie!" she said softly. "I hate to worry you. You have got so much to trouble you as it is."

"Stap me, but that's true enough!" ejaculated Hugh. "What's happened now? Do not hide anything from me."

"I shall not," she answered with a little sigh. "But you will not like this. Lew Quayle has brought a wounded man here. He is in the green dressing-room at the end of the passage."

"A wounded man! By thunder! If this is not the outside

of enough! Is Lew queer in the attic? His brains must have blown away in the breeze."

"He did not know what else to do with him," Leona explained. "Apparently there was a shooting accident. The man was cleaning his gun and shot his own shoulder—at least, that is what Lew says. I think actually he must have been fighting with someone else in the cave. Anyway, the wound is festering and he is in a fever."

"A deuce of a dust! But why here? Why didn't Lew take him home?"

"It was quite obviously a gunshot wound," Leona explained, "and Lew thought that if it were seen he would be arrested on suspicion. What ordinary farmhand is likely to be injured by shot or to own a gun which needed cleaning?"

"No smoke about Lew!" Hugh said admiringly. "But it makes me devilish nervous to have a wounded man in the house with Chard nosing about!"

"That is what I said," Leona told him. "But he is unconscious—or rather, delirious. I am just going to brew him some herbs which will take away the fever. Perhaps by the morrow he will be well enough for Lew to take him home."

"I'll serve Lew a trick and tie for this!" Hugh ejaculated, walking backwards and forwards across the room in an agitated manner. "Supposing Chard wants to go round the house, and finds him?"

"He is not likely to do that," Leona said soothingly. "The man is right at the end of this wing. Lord Chard could not be farther away from him. And, besides, I do not believe that his Lordship would walk in and out of the rooms without asking our permission."

"No, I grant you that," replied Hugh. "He does not appear to snoop about. At the same time, he misses nothing. Do not let him pull the wool over your eyes. He is looking for evidence against us and if it exists he will find it."

"I am sure he will," Leona said, feeling her heart drop a little at the thought. "And that is why Lew Quayle must keep out of sight. You must tell him, Hughie, that he is not to come here. I found him this afternoon sitting in my r-room."

Her voice trembled on the words. All the indignation and horror she felt at discovering Lew Quayle had invaded her privacy was coming to the surface in a sudden outburst of indignation.

"I will not have it, Hughie, do you hear?" she stormed.

"I will not have him treating this house as if it were his own, walking in and out at his pleasure and even daring to enter my bedchamber."

"I suppose he knew it was a safe place in which to wait for you." Hugh said mildly. "He had to sit somewhere, did he not?"

"But not in my room; not again," Leona retorted. "I shall lock the door and take the key away with me. But you are to tell him Hughie, do you hear? You are to tell him that he is not to come here."

"All right, old girl! No need to put yourself in a pucker!" Hugh exclaimed, putting his hand affectionately on her shoulder. "I know Lew is a bit of an outsider but he is of such vital import to me—to us—if the truth be told, that I can afford to offend him. But I'll tell him to go easy, I promise you—and to get this damned man out of here as quickly as possible."

"I must go now," Leona said. "I must go and give him the herbs. It will take away the fever and then, if he is properly bandaged, he can go home. There is no reason for Lew to come into the house again. Tell him that you will see the man downstairs and let him out by the garden door. If he is too weak to walk Lew and his friends can have a carriage waiting for him a little way down the drive. Will you arrange that, Hughie? Promise me."

"Of course! Of course!" Hugh said, airily. "I'll attend to it all. I'll tell him, too, to keep his casualties to himself. It's too damned dangerous bringing them here!"

Leona started to say something then changed her mind. She was well aware that Hugh was missing the point. He was not concerned whether Lew came into the house and to her bedroom or not. He was only concerned with the danger to himself.

Oh well, there was no use labouring the point. She knew that Hugh was as weak as water where Lew was concerned. She would just have to look after herself.

She hurried to her bedroom and taking a small bowl of herbs from a shelf in the cupboard, descended to the kitchen. There she brewed them with hot water and a spoonful of wine, and when they were ready she strained them into a teapot and returned upstairs. There was nobody in the passages, she reached her own room in safety and then hurried on along the corridor to the green dressing-room.

The man was still delirious; the fever was mounting and he was tossing from side to side, beads of perspiration standing out on his brown forehead. He was obviously thirsty, however, and when Leona raised his head he drank the herbs down greedily—two big cupfuls—and would have drunk more if Leona, thinking he had had enough, had not set his head back again on the pillow.

He had thrown off the bedclothes with the heat of the fever, but she covered him again and pulled the curtains a little closer to prevent the light falling on his face. After she had given him the herbs she waited in the room for over ten minutes. By that time he had ceased muttering, his breathing was deeper, less fitful, and he had ceased to toss and turn.

She had previously seen how the herbs worked and knew exactly what would happen. In a little while he would fall into a very deep sleep, and while he was in that condition the fever would break. In about six to eight hours he would awake to find himself weak but perfectly clear, the inflammation in his wound subsided, the fever gone.

She fetched a pitcher of water and a glass and set it beside the bed. Then, when the man's breathing was steadily growing more and more rhythmical, she stole from the room, shutting the door quietly behind her.

When she was back in her own bedchamber she found it was nearing the time for dinner, and went to her wardrobe to take out her only other gown. It was a very plain little white batiste which had become rather tight. It was sadly out of fashion and just for a moment, as Leona stared at it, she had a sudden regret for the gown she had burnt that very morning.

Then the memory of the look in Lew Quayle's eyes when he told her that he had chosen it for her and the thought of that long smear of blood on the skirt convinced her that even if it had hung there she would never have put it on.

She took down the batiste gown from its hanger and had just changed when the door was flung open and Hugh came rushing in. He shut the door behind him, listened for a moment as if he half suspected that he had been followed, and then with his eyes alight, turned towards her.

"Leona, they are moving the cargo tonight! Whatever happens we must keep Chard amused and not let him put his nose outside the door."

"Moving it tonight!" Leona repeated. "But surely that is a risk, is it not?"

"To be sure it is a risk!" Hugh ejaculated. "Everything is a damned risk and you know it. But Lew says we can wait no longer. We've got another cargo waiting at Dieppe and the bay must be clear of this one. He says there is no sign of the Customs men or the Dragoons. He's had men out looking for them all day. The place is as peaceful as a graveyard."

Leona shuddered at the simile.

"Are you sure, quite sure, Hughie?"

"Lew is convinced it's all right," he replied. "Unless Chard has set a trap which nobody can suspect, we should be able to raise the stuff tonight, get it on the pack ponies and away before it is dawn."

Leona looked out of the window. It was still pouring with rain.

"His Lordship is not likely to venture out in this," she said doubtfully.

"We've got to make certain that he does not," Hugh answered. "It's your deal, my dear!"

"Why me?" Leona asked.

"You must entertain him, keep him amused. Lew is certain you can do so if you set your mind to it."

"Lew! What has Lew to say in the matter?" Leona asked with a sudden flash or anger. "I am not taking my orders from him whatever you may do."

"Now, Leona, do not get in a fret," her brother begged. "You know what this means to me. And if Chard should happen to put his nose outside and see the men coming up from the beach—well, I'm for the Colonies, and you know it."

"Yes, yes," Leona answered. "But, oh, Hughie, are you certain that this is the time to take such a risk? Supposing he has a naval cutter out at sea? Supposing the Dragoons are waiting on the downs?"

"Lew says he will stake his life there is not a Dragoon or a coastguard within miles of the Castle," Hugh answered. "As for the sea, we have a couple of look-outs in boats keeping watch beyond the bay!"

"It ought to be all right," Leona said doubtfully.

"It has got to be all right," Hugh said with a sudden vehemence. "God, Leona! When I think what is at stake it makes me feel quite sick."

Because Hugh was agitated and upset Leona instantly forgot her own fears. She crossed to him and put her hand on his arm.

"It will be all right," she said. "Lew is not likely to risk his own neck, and you will be here in the house, will you not?"

Hugh nodded.

"There is nowhere else I dare be," he said. "Chard will think it highly suspicious if I disappear after dinner. But God knows how I am going to amuse the chap. He does not drink, he does not seem to want to play cards."

"You and Mr. Weston play together," Leona said. "He is far more dangerous than Lord Chard when it comes to spying out the land. Keep him engaged and I will strive to occupy his Lordship's attention."

Even as she spoke she felt ashamed that she was not more reluctant to do this very thing.

Hugh bent and kissed her cheek.

"You're a good sport, Leona," he said. "And if only we can get this cargo away there will be some rolls of soft in my pockets."

He spoke with a sudden elation and Leona said quickly:

Whatever money you get from it, Hughie, you must promise me one thing. You must give it back to Lew; set it against the debt you owe him. Promise me."

She saw a little of the excitement die out of Hugh's eyes.

"Curse the debts!" he exclaimed irritably. "When I get my hands on some gold I want to enjoy it, I want to spend it."

"Yes, I know," Leona said soothingly, as one would to a child. "But you have got to pay Lew first. You said yourself that with one or two more cargoes you would be clear."

Hugh kissed her cheek again.

"To hell with Lew!" he said. "He'll be fine and dandy so long as you're nice to him. Don't forget what I told you; you've got to be nice to him."

"I cannot——" Leona started to say, but before the words had hardly reached her lips Hugh had interrupted them with an exclamation as he glanced at the clock.

"Thunder and turf! But I'm going to be late for dinner," he said. "And Chard is always punctual to the minute."

He went from the room slamming the door behind him. Leona turned slowly across the room to the mirror. The white batiste gown was much too tight, she thought, looking at herself critically.

" 'Twould be hard to hold a stable boy's interest in this," she whispered to herself a little ruefully. And then she sat down at the dressing-table and tried to arrange her hair in a more fashionable manner. But the small gold curls seemed to insist on haloing her little pointed face and making her troubled eyes seem unnaturally large.

After a while she gave up her efforts to be fashionable as hopeless. In an effort to disguise the inadequacy of her gown she took two pink roses from the bowl on the table and pinned them at her breast. But she was sadly dissatisfied with herself as finally she walked slowly down the stairs to the Salon.

Lord Chard was already there. He had changed into white evening breeches and a blue satin coat which contrived to make him so resplendent that Leona felt more dowdy than ever. His cravat was of snowy whiteness and she noted how the diamond seal on his fob glittered in the light as he turned at her approach.

"I hope you will excuse me for helping myself to a glass of Madeira," he said.

"I must apologize that I was not down earlier to offer you one," Leona replied.

She knew his eyes were on her as she approached but after a quick glance at him she dropped her eyes to the ground, angry with herself and with him because, inevitably, whenever he spoke, it seemed to her that his words, however ordinary and commonplace, threw her into confusion.

There was now a silence between them, a silence that somehow seemed more pregnant with meaning than any words they might speak. And after a moment, because she was afraid, Leona said quickly:

"It is still raining."

"Yes, indeed," Lord Chard replied. "I can hear it."

"I am sorry for anyone who is out in it tonight," Leona said. "Not that there will be many of course!"

"There are always those who have to be abroad, wet or fine," Lord Chard remarked.

"Yes, yes, I suppose so," Leona said, trying to think what sort of people those might be, except smugglers.

"This must be a very lonely place in the winter," he remarked.

"It can be frightening when there is a storm," Leona admitted. "The wind seems to whistle round the house. Sometimes it even shrieks as if there was someone outside crying to come in. I feel frightened when I hear that."

"And yet you will not come to London," Lord Chard said.

"No I could not go away," Leona answered.

"Not even for a short while?" he persisted.

"Not to London," Leona said. "I should be far more frightened of London than of a storm at sea."

"But, why? There are also nice people in London as well as nasty ones. There are also people who do not always wish to be gay and even those who can talk seriously. Many indeed have country estates of their own."

"I know that," Leona answered. "I am not so stupid that I do not realize that country people go to London too. It is "just that I should be out of place there."

"Yes, I think you would," Lord Chard said surprisingly.

She raised her eyes and looked at him because his reply was so unexpected.

"You are different from all those people," he said looking down at her. "I sometimes wonder if you are wholly human and if you are not, in fact, a nymph coming in on the mists from the river or part of the white crested waves as they beat against the cliffs."

"I wish I were," she said almost involuntarily. "Instead I am very human, my Lord, with all the worries, anxieties and troubles of a human being."

"If you went away would you not leave them behind?" be inquired.

She shook her head.

"No, indeed, they would come with me because they are a part of my life."

"Shall I try and persuade you that you are wrong?" he asked.

There was an eagerness in his voice she had never heard there before and once again she found her eyes held by his and felt something strange and exciting awaken within herself. She did not know what it was. She only knew she wanted to hear what he had to say— she felt inexplicably interested and excited.

"Shall I?" he asked very softly.

"If I am late, Miss Ruckley, I must apologize!" a voice said from the doorway and Leona turned with a start to see Nicholas Weston come through the door, his voice grating unpleasantly across the room.

"No, you are not late, Mister Weston," she said after a moment, when she had collected her thoughts and remembered who he was and what he was doing here.

She felt as if she had been rudely awakened from a dream—a dream that had a touch of magic in it; a dream that now she was awake had no substance of fact or reality and yet in some strange way the feeling of it remained.

"I believe, my Lord, I have caught a cold," Nicholas Weston said to Lord Chard. "We should never have stayed out so long in the rain."

"You are getting soft, Nicholas, that is what is wrong with you," Lord Chard remarked.

Hugh appeared a few moments later full of apologies, and as soon as they were assembled Bramwell announced dinner and they all walked towards the dining-room.

Leona had worried as to what the food would be like and tonight her apprehensions were not unfounded. The household could make an effort for once but it was difficult to repeat their triumph of the night before. Leona found herself apologizing that the turbot was not as hot as it should be and the guinea-fowls were a little overdone.

"I am afraid, my Lord," she said, "our household is getting old. They can contrive a palatable meal for one evening but that is all. If Hugh and I were alone here this evening we should be having cold roast mutton while Mrs. Barnes put her feet up."

She laughed as she spoke, thinking it far better to be frank than pretend that the meal was all it should be.

"I understand only too well," Lord Chard said. "And I know that Nicholas and I are a confounded nuisance imposing ourselves upon you in this manner. You must forgive me, Miss Ruckley, but as a rough soldier I had forgotten the difficulties of domestic life in England."

"Oh, I did not mean that exactly," Leona said, flushing as she realized that her words could be interpreted as a wish to be rid of him. "I was only explaining. . . ."

"I understand exactly what you were trying to say," Lord Chard said. "But I know, too, that I am outstaying my welcome. May I propound an idea of my own which I hope you will find acceptable?"

"Y-yes, of course," Leona stammered, feeling ashamed that she should have been so tactless.

"It is, in fact, an invitation," Lord Chard said, "for you and your brother to drive over with me tomorrow to Clantonbury. My sister returns there from London and will, I know, be delighted to see you. I have, too, a great desire to show you the mansion which, in my opinion, is one of Robert Adam's finest efforts."

"By Jove! That is a very nice invitation," Hughie said from the end of the table.

He looked at Leona as he spoke and she knew by the sudden expression in his eyes and the note in his voice that the idea delighted him. She was not so dense that she did not understand why. Lord Chard had suggested going away. They could be rid of him, then it would be easy for the second cargo to arrive.

"I have always wanted to see Clantonbury," Hugh went on. "I hear it is magnificent. Weston was telling me that it cost nearly a quarter-of-a-million pounds. Can that be true?"

"I should imagine the final reckoning was not far short of that figure!" Lord Chard replied. "It was built, of course, by the last Duke, who travelled all over the world looking for treasures with which to furnish the different rooms. He spent a fortune on it but, fortunately, my brother-in-law, the present Duke, inherited considerable wealth from his mother, and my sister is not entirely penniless."

"Well, I personally have only one answer to your invitation," Hugh said, "and that is that we cannot go there too soon as far as I am concerned."

"And what does Miss Ruckley say?" Lord Chard asked, turning directly to Leona.

"Th-thank you, it is very kind of you," Leona replied.

There was nothing else she could say with Hugh's eyes upon her, and yet when she reached the Salon she remembered miserably how she would look in front of the Duchess and perhaps other fashionable women who might be visiting Clantonbury.

How embarrassing to have only two gowns, the grey, worn and faded, and the white batiste which was too tight for her. Both were so out-moded that she was quite certain it would be difficult for them to hide their smiles when she appeared.

She was seeking frantically in her own mind for an excuse not to go when the gentlemen came from the dining-room and joined her. Hugh gave her a warning glance and settled himself with Nicholas Weston at a card table. Lord Chard sat down on the sofa beside Leona, who had hastily picked up her embroidery in order to occupy her hands and have an excuse not to look at him.

"You embroider very beautifully," he said after a few seconds.

"I am fond of it," Leona replied. "I am trying to cover all the chairs in the dining-room. But it will take me a long time."

She looked to be sure that Hugh and Nicholas Weston

were too engaged in their game to overhear what she was saying, then bent forward and said softly:

"My Lord, I have something to ask you."

"What is it?" Lord Chard replied.

He spoke quietly but she had the impression that he was alert and suddenly tense.

"Do not make me come to Clantonbury," she said. "Take Hughie—he will enjoy it. But I would rather stay here."

"But if I tell you that I want you to come," Lord Chard replied, "that the reason for my invitation was that you should see my sister's house—what then?"

"It is very amiable of you," Leona replied. "But I cannot . . . cannot. . . ."

She somehow could not find the words and her voice trailed away ineffectively.

Lord Chard bent forward and put his hand on hers. At his touch she was suddenly very still, the words dying upon her lips. She had not realized that his fingers could seem so strong and yet, at the same time, be warm and almost comforting.

"What is it?" he asked. "What is the truth of why you do not wish to visit my sister?"

'I . . . I have nothing to . . . wear," Leona stammered.

She had not meant to say it so bluntly and yet, because of the pressure of Lord Chard's fingers, the truth seemed to be squeezed from her.

She felt his fingers tighten for a moment and then instinctively she knew that what she said had not been what he expected to hear. She did not know whether he was relieved or not. She only knew that he had expected something else, though what, she had no idea.

"You need not worry about that," he said. "My sister is about your size, though in many other ways you are unlike each other. I promise you she would be only too glad to lend you anything you need—in fact it would be a pleasure to her. She loves clothes and loves dressing up herself—and her friends too. I often say she behaves like a child with a lot of dolls, for she is always exchanging her hats, her necklaces and her shawls for those belonging to someone else."

"With her friends that is a very different thing," Leona said. "Besides, she might not like me."

"You need not worry yourself on that score," Lord

Chard answered. "I can answer for my sister and I say that I know that she will love you."

There was a kind of finality in his tone which kept Leona silent for a moment, and then, when she would have protested further his hand covered hers once again and he said:

"Trust me in this. I promise you that these little matters are not of the least account. Your brother wishes to come to Clantonbury and I want, above all things, that you should be a visitor there and meet my sister. Let the details sort themselves out, for they will, I promise you."

It seemed to her as if he ironed all the difficulties away; they vanished almost as if he mesmerized them with the quietness of his voice.

But, even as she felt soothed, the pressure of his fingers on hers made her heart suddenly start beating in a quite unpredictable manner. She felt the quick thump of it, her fingers trembling beneath his. And then, even as he freed her, her eyelids lifted and she knew that once again he was looking into her eyes, holding her spellbound, weaving some magic web around her from which she could not escape.

"That is settled then," he said softly, and she felt as if there was nothing she could say, no irresistible argument she could raise could have any effect.

"Come and play to me," he said. "I know that you do play the pianoforte because I was looking at your music earlier today and realized there were many tunes amongst it I had not heard since I was a child. They were the tunes my mother used to play to me when I was ill and I want to hear them again."

Obediently, because he seemed to have sapped her very will, Leona rose, laying her embroidery aside, and went to the piano.

She played softly so as not to disturb Hugh and Nicholas Weston, and after a time Lord Chard rose and came and leaned over the piano, watching her fingers so that she played softer still.

On and on she played: the music was propped up in front of her but she ignored it and played other tunes, which she had composed herself. They were what she played when she was alone in the Castle and the candles had gutted and gone out and she was alone in the darkness.

And into her music she had woven all her thoughts of life—of her home, the sea, and of all the things she dreamt of and which she found sometimes a faint echo in the books she read.

At first she played a little self-consciously because Lord Chard was listening; but after a time she knew that he wanted to hear more and so with her fingers she told him all the things that she had never told anyone else and which it seemed to her no-one else would have understood.

It was growing late when at last she stopped, her hands falling to her lap from sheer tiredness.

"Thank you!"

His voice expressed far more than his words and she knew, although he did not say it, that he had understood what she had been telling him.

She rose from the piano at the same time that Hugh rose from the card table.

"Damme! Weston's taken a monkey off me," he exclaimed. "My pockets are to let and I'm for bed before I lose my breeches!"

"And I also!" Nicholas Weston ejaculated. "I have a sore throat. That rain this afternoon went right through my coat. I was soaked."

"Would you like a hot drink?" Leona asked.

They were the first words she had spoken for a long time and she knew that Lord Chard was watching her as she moved across the room towards the grog tray.

"No, thank you," Nicholas Weston answered. "I shall sleep well without it."

"Then I will say good night, gentlemen."

Leona picked up one from the row of silver candlesticks standing by the door which Bramwell had left ready before he retired. Lord Chard lit it for her with a taper and opened the door.

She crossed the hall and went upstairs, the light from her candle casting strange shadows as she moved slowly along the passage towards her bedroom. She was still in the dream into which her music had carried her and it took her a moment to remember that she must look in at the sick man before she went to bed.

She opened the door of his room softly. As she expected, he was sleeping soundly and snoring a little. She held the candle up to his face and saw that the heavy flush of fever had subsided but that he was sweating profusely. She covered him up with another blanket so that he should not catch cold and went quietly from the room. There was nothing she could do. The herbs would work their own course, for they never failed.

Back in her own room she undressed slowly, still strangely happy and almost before her head touched the pillow her happiness and the music had mingled into a long dream.

She was awakened suddenly by a knock. It came again, and yet again, and suddenly she realized that someone was knocking on her door.

With an effort she came back to reality. She was in her bed in the darkness. The knock was repeated. It was only faint as if a finger tapped against the wood, but she remembered suddenly that she had locked the door before she undressed.

"It must be Hugh," she thought. "Something must have gone wrong."

In a sudden panic she got out of bed, reaching for the soft, white shawl that she used to cover her nightgown.

She reached the door.

"Is that you, Hughie?" she asked.

"Open the door."

It was only a hoarse whisper but there was urgency in it, and without thinking she turned the key and the door flew open. The light was still burning in the passage. It was low but light enough to see who stood there.

She gave a sudden gasp as Lew Quayle, carrying something in his arms, pushed past her into the room.

"Why have you locked the door?" he asked. "'Tis dangerous and I was affeared lest someone would hear me knocking."

"What do you want?" she inquired. "You have no right to come here. I told Hughie to tell you I would not have you in the house."

"I got your message," he said, and though she could not see his face she knew he was smiling.

He put something down and then before she realized what he was about he stepped through the door, took a taper from one of the sconces in the passage and brought it into the room. He closed the door behind him and set the taper down on the dressing-table, kindling another candle which stood there so that both illuminated the room.

"What are you doing?" Leona asked. "And what have you brought here?"

She looked down at what he had set upon the floor and saw that there were two large rolls of material.

"I brought you a present," Lew said, following her glance.

"Is that what you have come for?" Leona asked in astonishment.

"You should be grateful," he replied. "You told me you had burned the gown I gave you. Well, I have brought you some stuff to make another. Look at it! Straight from Paris!"

He pulled open the rolls as he spoke and instantly the room seemed filled with the glitter and shimmer of the Orient. There was a great roll of silver lamé, glistening and shining in the candlelight; and the other was of white satin embroidered with sprigs of gold. Both of them, as Leona knew full well, were materials that would fetch their weight in gold when they reached London, from ladies of fashion who wished only to wear materials from France.

She stared at them incredulously and then she said in an ominously quiet voice:

"Do you really credit that I would want to take such a present from you? Do you really believe that I covet anything such as this when you have risked men's lives and Hughie's freedom to smuggle it in?"

"I believe you to be a woman," Lew answered. "And what woman could refuse such as these? I have never seen finer. Just think of their value!"

"I would not care if they were made of diamonds," Leona answered. "I do not want them. You can take them away."

"Do you really mean that?" Lew asked, his eyes narrowing. "I filched them off the last pack-horse as it was leaving. When I saw them I thought of you. I knew what you would look like wearing them so I brought them here. Does that mean nothing to you?"

"It only means once again I have not made myself clear," Leona answered. "I do not want your presents. I do not wish you to come into this house."

Even as she said the words defiantly she remembered how Hugh had pleaded with her to be nice to Lew. Awkwardly she tried to soften the blow.

" 'Tis too dangerous," she said hastily. "You must not take such risks. It is kind of you to think of me but please take these th-things away."

"That is better," Lew said. "You are weakening, as I knew you would. Think of yourself wearing the silver lamé, think of it against the whiteness of your skin, the gold of your hair. Come, let us look at you in the mirror."

He pulled at a length of silver material as he spoke and before she realized what was happening had thrown the long, glittering stream of it over Leona's shoulder. Then he turned her round so that she could see herself in the mirror.

She saw her own reflection—her hair, a little tousled from her sleep, gleaming in the candlelight, her face pale and frightened, her eyes wide open. And then, behind the shimmering silver on her shoulder, which seemed to her like the river in the moonlight, she saw Lew's face— saw the sensuousness of his lips, the fire in his eyes which she knew spelt danger.

"No . . . no!" she cried, trying to turn away.

But it was too late. His arms went round her, holding her captive.

"You look a Queen!" he said. "And that is what I will make you—the Queen of the Coast. A Queen whom all men shall acknowledge because she is invincible."

His lips were very near to her but by some superhuman strength which she had not known she possessed she twisted away from him.

"Let me go!" she cried, and he clutched at her too late, for the silver lamé came away in his hands with the white shawl which it had covered and Leona fled from him in her nightgown.

She wrenched open the door and sped with bare feet along the passage to the safety of Hugh's room. She burst open the door, closed it behind her, feeling with trembling hands for the bolt she knew was there. Then she groped her way in the darkness to the bed. She sat down, her breath coming sobbingly from between her lips, her heart thumping against her breasts as if it would burst out of them in her agitation and terror.

"Hughie!" she called, her voice hoarse and shaking with fear. "L-Lew is in my bedroom again. H-he has brought me p-presents—m-material from F-France. I-I tried to be n-nice to him but I cannot. He frightens me; f-frightens me, Hughie, and you must tell him once and for all to go away. I cannot b-bear it. I cannot go on fighting and escaping from him k-knowing that he will c-come b-back!"

She gave a little sob, piteous and heart-breaking.

"Yes, he will come b-back, Hughie, because he is determined to get me sooner or l-later. Do not let him. . . . Please . . . please . . . Hughie, do not . . . let him!"

Her voice broke as the tears came tumultuously, and then she flung herself forward, grasping at her brother's shoulders, trying to hide her streaming eyes against him.

Then, even as she touched him, even as she felt him move, her tears were checked and a sudden scream was stifled in her throat. For a voice, grave and quiet which she knew so well, said from the darkness of the bed:

"I am afraid I am not Hugh!"

Leona felt as if all the breath left her body—it was to Lord Chard she had addressed her pleas!

6

FOR a moment Leona was thrown into such a panic she could not think coherently. She wanted to escape, to run away, to hide herself. And yet, at the same time, she could not move.

"I must apologize for startling you," Lord Chard said quietly. "The chimney in my bedroom was smoking and your brother insisted that I should sleep in his bedchamber."

Still Leona could not move. She felt as if she was gasping for air, her heart thumping, every pulse and vein in her body throbbing intolerably.

Then suddenly a realization of what she had said swept over her in a crimson flood tide. At least her limbs seemed to obey her and she made a hasty movement to rise to her feet.

It was too late! Lord Chard's hand covered hers where it rested against his chest and she felt as if he imprisoned her.

"I have frightened you! You are upset," he said gently. "Be quiet for a moment. Shall I light a candle?"

'No . . . no . . . do . . . not look at me," Leona cried wildly.

She felt Lord Chard move and sit upright in bed, but he still had hold of her right hand, holding it with gentle yet strong fingers as if he half held her captive, half tried to soothe her agitation.

"I would not have embarrassed you for the world," he said. "But you are in distress and I must help you."

"No, no, it is nothing," she said hastily. "Nothing . . . I . . . I had a . . . bad dream."

"A very bad one it appears," he said drily. "You imagined there was someone in your room."

There was a faint accent on the word "imagined" and Leona shivered. Too late she saw where her desperate flight from Lew Quayle had landed her. What had she said? What had she betrayed? she asked herself wildly. Would Hugh's life be in jeopardy because she had been coward enough to run away?

Everything seemed to flash through her brain—the danger they were all in; the sick man in the green dressing-room; Lew Quayle's impertinence in coming to her room; the rolls of lamé and satin spilled upon her floor. All these and so much else given into the hand of the enemy by a mere moment of terrified hysteria.

Lord Chard released her and, bending down to the bottom of the bed, drew up the silk bedspread where it had been folded back, and with both surprising gentleness and accuracy placed it around her shoulders.

She held the silk firmly over her breasts and sat, tense and still, her brain racing as she tried to think of a way out of the pit into which she had fallen.

"Now tell me what is troubling you?" Lord Chard said.

"Indeed, my Lord, you must think me very s-stupid," she answered, in a voice that strove to be natural but succeeded only in being young and breathless and very afraid. "I had a . . . nightmare and ran—as I have done so often before—to Hughie for . . . consolation."

"It must have been a very potent nightmare," Lord Chard said. There was a dry, sarcastic note in his voice and though she could not see his face she guessed that the expression in it was cynical.

"Indeed, it was," Leona said. "Perhaps it was something we . . . we . . . ate for dinner. But that is not s-surprising for it was an ill-cooked meal, for which I have already apologized."

There was a moment's silence and then Lord Chard said:

"Will you not let me help you?"

The question was so unexpected, the tone of his voice so inviting, that for a moment she almost surrendered. It would be so easy, she thought, to tell him the truth; to tell him how terrified she was by Lew Quayle, to relate how she was being persecuted by a man notorious along the whole length and breadth of the south coast.

And then almost before the idea was formed in her mind she remembered how much more was at stake. Hugh, their home, the people on the estate, and the villagers she had known and loved since she was a child. All were involved, all stood to lose their lives or their freedom if she but spoke one word.

"But you have helped me already," she said lightly. "I swear, my Lord, when I first came in here I was half asleep, still encompassed around with bad demons in my dreams. Now I am clear-headed again and they have vanished, so I must thank you for that and retire back to my bed-chamber."

"I think it would be best if I accompany you," Lord Chard said. "If any demons are still lurking there then I will dispel them."

"No . . . no, there is no . . . need," Leona said quickly, conscious even as she spoke of the dismay in her voice.

She felt he was unconvinced and added desperately:

"I would not in-incommode your Lordship. You have passed a bad enough night as it is—a smoking fire in your own bed-chamber, the inconvenience of having to move into Hugh's room, and now to be awakened by m-me. Could anything be more disconcerting?"

"So you will not trust me!"

She could not misunderstand what he meant.

"It is n-not that I will n-not," she said at length in a very low voice. "It is that I c-cannot."

She would not have said so much had they not been talking in the darkness. Somehow at that moment she found it impossible to be afraid of him or even to fear what he might do. It seemed to her instead that they were alone in a world that had no substance or reality, that was just a figment of their imagination. She only knew that he was very close and that his mere presence gave her a sense of security and of safety.

It was all an illusion, she knew that. He was the danger! But while her brain told her one thing, her body told her another. She tried to remember that in fleeing from Lew she had become involved in an even more dangerous situation. Nevertheless even though she knew it to be the truth, her heart could not credit it.

It was Lew whom she feared: Lew who terrified her, with his thick, grasping fingers, his full, sensuous mouth and glinting eyes. There was something about Lord Chard which made her feel as if he were a harbour to which she had fled from a tempestuous sea outside. As long as he was there she was safe!

It was not the truth, and yet some ridiculous, inconvincible part of her body kept feeling it, while her brain told her she should think something very different.

"I understand," he said softly. "I would not force you

to do anything against your will. Will you promise me one thing, Leona?"

"What is it?"

"It is that should you be in danger again, should the demons of which you dreamed just now be pursuing you, you will come to me. I will save you, I promise you that."

His voice ceased and then, as Leona did not answer, he said:

"Will you not promise me that I may help you?"

"I want to say y-yes," Leona whispered. "But I know that while I think like this tonight, tomorrow I shall think d-differently."

"It is easy to talk at this moment, is it not?" Lord Chard asked. "I cannot see your face, but I know that you are there. I can hear your breath coming quickly between your parted lips and I can smell the perfume of your hair. You smell always of roses, Leona."

She shut her eyes for a moment. This was a dream—a dream of the darkness. She could listen to such things and wish to hear more. Always before, when she had been paid compliments, she had been frightened and tried to run away. That was because they had been Lew Quayle's compliments, Lew's mocking, taunting words accompanied by the terrifying fire in his eyes, the sensuous twist of his lips.

This was different. This was how she had dreamed, sometimes when she had sat alone in the long evenings, that a man would talk to her and she would stay and listen.

"I think that when you came here tonight," Lord Chard said, "I was dreaming of you. I fell asleep with the sound of your music in my ears. Did you know how much you told me in that music, Leona? You talked to me of your loneliness here in this big, empty castle. You told me, too, how you had peopled it in your imagination. I seemed to see you reaching out your arms to a life as full and as varied as any I had known even though I have travelled all over the world."

Leona sat very still as she listened to him. She knew now that when she had been playing to him she had, indeed, tried to express all that she felt. And he had understood! Never before had she believed that anyone, any living person, would understand what she tried to say.

Lord Chard drew a deep breath.

"And now you must go back to your room," he said and his voice was deep and full of an emotion she did not understand. "I would like to keep you here, talking to you, but I know it is one of the things I must not do, for reasons you are, perhaps, too young to comprehend."

"I can go back by myself," Leona said quickly.

She felt as if his words were like a douche of cold water. She had been drifting away into the darkness, lulled into security by the softness of his voice. Now she remembered Lew Quayle. Would he have gone? Or would he have been fool enough to wait, thinking perhaps that Hugh would have sent her back to him?

"I will go at once," she said. "And there is no reason for your Lordship to come with me. I shall be perfectly s-safe."

She rose to her feet and as she did so she heard him throw back the bedclothes and get out on the other side of the bed.

"No, please, I . . . I would rather go . . . alone," she said, her voice hesitant and at the same time tremulous.

She could not disguise her fear and she knew that he must have sensed it for he hastily slipped on his dressing-gown, which he must have flung across a chair, and by the time she reached the door he was beside her.

"I am coming with you," he said, and because she felt there was nothing more she could say or do she opened the door and stepped into the passage.

The tapers had gutted away in the sconces and instead, to light their way there was only the very faint grey of the dawn coming through an uncurtained window. As Leona moved with bare feet down the carpet, she heard the silk bedspread that she still clutched sliding behind her and making a soft rustle which reminded her of the movements of a snake.

"Have I betrayed them?" she whispered to herself, and then began to pray with an intensity which came from the very depths of her soul. "Let the room be empty! Oh, God, let the room be empty!"

She did not turn her head or look at Lord Chard as he walked behind her. Only when they reached her bedroom door did he move forward and open the door so that she could enter.

For a moment Leona was afraid to look; and then she saw that her prayers had been answered. Lew Quayle had gone, and the shimmering rolls of silver lamé and gold-sprigged satin had vanished too. She would have thought his presence had been in actual fact, a dream, if there had not been her white shawl lying on the floor in a crumpled heap as it must have fallen from his hands. And there were, too, the tapers still burning by the bedside where he had put them so that they might illuminate the presents he had brought her.

"You see, my Lord," Leona said with a note of relief in her voice. "There is no-one here. I was, as I told you, but having a bad d-dream."

"No, there is no-one here," Lord Chard said, a little grimly, she thought.

He crossed to the window, threw back the curtains and looked out. She saw him glance round the room, taking in every detail of the furniture as if he suspected that a man might be hiding in the shadows of the wardrobe or behind the dressing-table.

She looked at him for the first time and saw that with his hair slightly tousled and without his high cravat he looked much younger and less formidable. His brocade dressing-gown, with its wide cuffs and collar of blue velvet, threw into contrast the frilled collar of his white night-shirt.

For a moment she had the impression that he was little more than a boy. Then she remembered his errand and forced herself to say:

"You perceive, my Lord, how foolish I have been, running away from nothing but s-shadows."

"Then bolt your door so that they shall not disturb you again," Lord Chard replied.

He looked down at her for a moment and she fancied there was a strange expression in his face she had not seen before. And then he took her little cold fingers in his and kissed her hand very gently.

"Good night, Leona," he said. "And for the rest of the night, at least, you need not be afraid."

She did not know exactly what he meant by that; she suspected that he would keep guard so that no-one should approach her door.

He went from the room and, obediently, because he commanded it, she locked the door behind him and stood for a moment listening to his footsteps going down the passage. No-one could come to her room without passing his, and though it gave her a sense of security from Lew Quayle, it also terrified her with the thought that if he did come again Lord Chard would be waiting for him.

But Lew had gone, and she was certain that he would not run any further risks that night. Besides, she remembered with a shiver, he could always find her when he wanted to.

She crept into bed, conscious that she was cold and yet her cheeks were burning. Now that she was alone the full import of what had happened faced her accusingly and she shrank in shy embarrassment from the thought of what she had said and what Lord Chard must think of her.

How could she have known that he had changed rooms with Hugh? she asked herself. And even if she had known, would it have made much difference? Because she would have had to turn to someone to save her from Lew Quayle.

She had known when she saw his face in the mirror what he had intended. She had known when she felt his hands grasping at her breasts, his arms pulling her backwards so that her head must rest against his shoulder.

She felt herself shudder again with the terror that he always invoked in her. He was like a wild beast, she thought, and she never knew when he would strike next. She hid her face in the pillow and tried to find some avenue of escape which would seem practicable and not insane—for she knew it was insane to trust Lord Chard, insane to think for one moment that she could turn to him for safety or security. In his own way he was more dangerous than Lew Quayle, and certainly more of a danger to Hugh.

"Helplessly, because she was tired, bewildered, and despondent, she began to cry. Not as she had cried before, frantically, in a tempest of terror, but quietly and hopelessly, the slow, difficult tears which seemed to be squeezed out of her by an inexorable hand from which she could not escape.

She did not sleep but she must have dozed for a little while because when she opened her eyes, still wet with tears, it was to find the sun shining in through her window. She sat up with a start, then got out of bed and picking up her shawl wrapped it around her.

There was the sick man to be attended to. She must see to him before anyone else was awake. She unlocked her door, lifted the latch very quietly. She did not really suspect that Lord Chard might listen, but she had no desire to face a barrage of embarrassing questions.

The house was quiet and there was no sound save the tick of the grandfather clock in the hall; and her feet hardly seemed to touch the carpet as she moved hurriedly and silently along the passage to the green dressing-room. She opened the door. The curtains were drawn and the room smelt stuffy and a little airless so she crossed to the window first to let in the sunlight.

Then she turned towards the bed. It was empty! For a moment she could not believe her eyes. When could Lew have taken the man away?

There were stains of blood on the pillowcase and the blankets had been thrown back, perhaps hastily. She wished she knew what had happened. At the same time, she realized the risks that had been run were terrifying. A few seconds one way or another and she and Lord Chard might have walked straight into Lew. She felt herself pale at the thought of what might have happened then. No amount of lying, no amount of pretence would have been able to extricate them all from that situation.

She wondered if Lew would have fought for his freedom. It would have been like him, she thought, to attack a defenceless man and to leave him dying, as he had left so many others. She had a sudden vision of Lord Chard in his brocade and velvet dressing-gown lying dead in the passage, and almost cried out at the idea. Then she turned from the room, closing the door behind her, went back to her own bedroom and dressed hastily.

There was no time to think what she should wear or of arranging her hair in an attractive manner. She only knew that she must talk with Hugh, must tell him what had occurred. She wondered where he was sleeping and guessed that as he had given up his room to Lord Chard he himself would have moved into the old nursery. There was usually a bed kept made up and aired in there for the attorney who came once a month to see to the estate accounts.

Yes, she thought, that was where Hugh would be. And sure enough, when she opened the door she found him fast asleep beneath a picture of some white lambs which she had always loved as a child.

She sat down at the end of the bed and called his name:

"Hughie! Wake up! I want to talk to you."

He turned over, yawning, and stretched.

"What time is it?" he asked.

"Quite early," Leona answered. "But wake up. Things have been happening that you must know about."

"What things?" Hugh inquired, yawning again.

His fair hair was tousled on top of his head and there was a night's growth of beard on his round chin.

"Lew came here last night," Leona answered.

She saw that Lew's name had the power to arouse Hugh. He opened his eyes and raising himself on his elbow, said:

"I know that. He woke me to say he had taken Andrews away."

"He woke you!" Leona ejaculated. "How did he know where you were sleeping?"

"Rose told him, I believe," Hugh replied. "You know that she is in love with Gideon, the man who sees to the pack-ponies. She is always hanging about with the tub-carriers, and last night she was down getting them drinks when they were moving off with the cargo."

"So Rose is in it too, is she?" Leona said. "Oh, Hughie, is there anyone who is free of this hideous coil?"

"You will not think it is so hideous," Hughie said cheerfully, "when you see last night's work translated into rolls of soft. I had to put Chard in my room as the chimney was smoking fit to choke a cove. When I thought he was settled down I slipped outside to see what was happening. I learned that they had got all the cargo out and I told Rose I was going to sleep in the old nursery and to make up the bed when she got back."

"I suppose you did not think to tell her that Lord Chard was sleeping in your room?" Leona asked.

"I do not think so, why should I?" Hugh inquired.

"Because Lew tricked me into opening my door and I ran to your room for help," Leona said.

Hugh jerked himself upright.

"Good Lord! And you found Chard?"

"Yes, I found Lord Chard."

"What did you say? What did you do? He did not suspect, did he?"

The questions came out quick and fast and in answer Leona rose from the bed and walked towards the window. She opened the latticed pane wide and stood looking out. From here she could see the sea, pale and iridescent in the early sunlight, the horizon so indistinct that it was hard to tell where sea met sky.

"Hughie, we cannot go on like this," Leona said.

"Do not talk such fustian," he admonished her. "We are in it up to the neck—all of us, and there is no drawing back. What I want to know is did Chard suspect?"

"Yes, I think he did."

"Then we shall have to tread softly. Thank God he has asked us to Clantonbury today. We will get the cargo in tomorrow, as arranged, and then lie low for a bit. The sales of these two will set us on our feet."

"Do you really mean to bring cargo in tomorrow?" Leona asked.

"Yes, why not?" Hugh inquired. "We shall be at Clantonbury keeping an eye on Chard. Lew will keep his eyes open here. We may have to store some of it in the cellars for a short while as all the pack-ponies will not be back in time."

Leona turned to face him.

"Not here! Not in this house, Hughie!"

"Why not? The stuff has rested here often enough before, and if Chard searches the village he will find nothing. There is no reason why he should suspect the hidden cellars—no-one has so far."

"I do not know why but I feel he might suspect anything," Leona said a little hysterically.

"What did you say to him last night?" Hugh asked with a sudden suspicion.

"Nothing about the cargo. Nothing like that," Leona answered. "But I thought it was you. I asked you to stop Lew pestering me."

"Perhaps he will not know who Lew is," Hugh said unconvincingly.

"He is certain to know that," Leona said. "Lew Quayle is notorious and when the Dragoons came last they were looking for him. They knew him by name, the Coastguards too."

"Well, they will not catch him, at any rate," Hugh said. "There is not a man, woman or child in the whole length and breadth of Sussex who would betray him."

"You mean they would not dare," Leona flashed.

Hugh shrugged his shoulders.

"I would not care to be in anyone's shoes who betrayed Lew," he said.

Leona shivered, then she said:

"How did he get Andrews away—if that was the man's name?"

"Just took him out through the back door, I believe. There were a couple of men there ready to help him home. Lew said I was to thank you and that he was much better."

"He was not really well enough to move, not until this morning," Leona said.

"Much better to get him out of the house," Hugh said practically. "We did not want Chard bumping into him." He gave an impatient sigh and then added: "I forgot to tell you. Chard is having his own carriage sent here today to take you to Clantonbury."

"How kind!" Leona exclaimed .

"Kind!" Hugh ejaculated. " 'Twas as I suspected. The coachmen, outriders and servants have been waiting at an inn in Worthing! 'Tis damned degrading for us when a man like Chard does bring his carriage and his valet with him for fear he should uncover our poverty."

Hugh spoke with such bitterness that Leona looked at him wide eyed.

"Do you think that is the reason?" she asked.

"Of course," he answered. "And you cannot be such a muttonhead as not to see it. You do not suppose a man of Chard's address travels without a valet, do you—and a couple of outriders? But he comes here like a poverty-stricken parson."

"We could have put up his valet," Leona said.

"Of course we could," Hugh answered roughly. "And a number of other servants as well. But Chard did not think so. Oh, no! He is ready to rough it with the Ruckleys. That is the sort of insult I have to put up with, Leona. Are you surprised I want money? And I will get it any way I can lay hands on it."

"Oh, Hughie, does it matter to you so much?" Leona asked, a pathetic note in her voice.

"Yes, it does," he snapped. "I want to take my place with other men of my age. I want to be able to walk down St. James's without wondering if the duns are waiting in the shadows. I want to be able to gamble, to own some decent horseflesh, and drive a curricle of which I am not ashamed."

He gave a hoarse laugh which had no humour in it and went on:

"I want, too, to be able to entertain my friends. It is the outside of enough to come back to this ramshackle, tumbledown, old place! Look at the dinner we had last night! 'Twas not fit for the pigs! And served by old Bramwell, who ought to be in the grave."

"Oh, Hughie! Hughie! Do not speak like that," Leona begged, her voice breaking a little. "This is your home and I want you so much to be happy here."

"Happy!" he snarled. "How can I be happy? There is no money."

"But if this next cargo gets here safely, will that be enough?"

"Enough for what?" Hughie questioned. "To live in comfort for a short while? To pay off some of my debts to Lew? Oh, I suppose so. But there has got to be more cargoes; more and more, Leona, if we are going to be rich! And then we can do up the Castle, employ decent servants and I can go to London and enjoy myself. And I'll take you with me too," he added, as an afterthought.

"Thank you, Hughie," Leona said in a very small voice.

It was difficult for her to speak, with the tears rising in her eyes, choking in her throat. The whole thing was hopeless, she thought—a danger and horror to which she could see no finish. More money wanted, more cargoes, more risks. It was an endless spiral and behind it all she could see Lew Quayle waiting for her.

She felt a wave of hopelessness sweep over her and without saying anything, her eyes blinded by tears, she went from the room, knowing that as she did so Hugh buried his head once again in the pillow and pulled up the bedclothes. He could sleep with a clear conscience whatever was happening.

Leona went downstairs and started to tidy away the things which would not be wanted while she was at Clantonbury. And now she forced herself to concentrate on what she was doing, wiping away, with her tiny lace-edged handkerchief, the tears that fiercely came to her eyes and trying to tell herself that it was no use crying and bewailing. Men must be what they were. She must accept Hugh as he was and not try and make him into anything different.

She knew there would be another struggle later in the morning when she asked him for money to pay Bramwell's wages and to provide Mrs. Barnes with something to expend on food for the household.

She remembered then, almost for the first time, the problem of her clothes. It had been easy enough for Lord Chard to tell her that his sister would lend her what she wanted, and because he had said it in that quiet, comforting voice which had such a strange effect on her, she had believed him and, for the moment, was prepared to accept the situation.

Now she realized how stupid it was. Her face suddenly

burned with shame as she thought of how she would appear to the Duchess and also to the supercilious superior servants who would see her arrive and realize how little she had brought with her.

And yet there was nothing she could do about it. She knew that Hugh was set on leaving so as to get Lord Chard away from the Castle. She knew, too, that after last night she did not wish to remain behind alone. For the first time in her life she was afraid of being in her own home.

She was still thinking of this when she heard a step outside the Salon and guessed that it was Lord Chard crossing the hall in search of breakfast. She felt the blood fly to her face in sudden embarrassment. How could she face him again after last night? How could she appear calm and unconcerned when she could remember only how she had cried out to him in the darkness and how, later, they had talked as if everything else in the world was forgotten except themselves?

Yet, surprisingly, things were better than she anticipated. Resisting the reluctance which made her leaden-footed, she went out in the hall to find Lord Chard on his way to the breakfast room, and Nicholas Weston descending the stairs.

She bade them good morning and found, after all, it was easy to talk almost unconcernedly of the weather, what a nice day it was for a drive to Clantonbury and how kind it was of his Lordship to have ordered his own carriage to convey her.

Breakfast was better cooked than the dinner had been the night before and while the gentlemen ate heartily Leona toyed with a cup of chocolate and some strawberries from the garden. She did not look at Lord Chard but though her eyes were downcast she was well aware that he often glanced at her.

Hugh was in the best of spirits and Leona knew that it was because he was so relieved at the thought of Lord Chard leaving the Castle. Yet, perversely enough, Leona, who had also longed for him to go, now had a pang of regret.

She could not understand her own feelings, yet, she felt a curious reluctance as she watched his smart leather boxes being brought downstairs and saw him, resplendent in his many-caped riding coat, giving instructions to the coachman as to the best road that they were to take.

Leona had so very little packing to do. Rose had put her few things together in a small, very worn, trunk, Mrs. Mildew had pressed her batiste gown and she had set her only bonnet, which she knew was sadly outmoded, on her golden hair and tied the ribbons under her chin.

"Look after everything, Bramwell," she said as she turned, with a last glance round the hall, to ascend the steps to the coach.

"Do not worrit about us, Miss Leona," the old man replied. "You have a good time—'tis something that's been coming to you for many a year and, as I says to Mrs. Barnes only this morning, I says 'no-one deserves it more than our Miss Leona'."

"Thank you, Bramwell," Leona said bravely.

She wished she was optimistic that she would have a good time at Clantonbury. She could only think what a drab she would look and how *gauche* and foolish she would appear in her old grey gown! As she stepped into Lord Chard's carriage she had an insane desire to run back into the Castle.

Even that was more luxurious than anything she had believed possible. The silver lamps, soft cushions, sable rugs, were all incredibly luxurious and the whole vehicle was so well sprung, besides being built for speed, that she felt as if she were leaning back against a cloud of swansdown!

Nicholas Weston and Lord Chard were travelling in the coach beside her, but Hugh was riding, as Lord Chard had suggested that he should bring one of his own horses with them.

"There is plenty of horseflesh for you to choose from at Clantonbury," he said. "But if you would desire to ride one of your own then, of course, we should only be too delighted. I, personally, prefer my own mounts to anyone else's."

"So do I," Hugh replied, not to be outdone, but Leona knew that when he got there he would wish to ride the Duke's horses, being quite certain that they were superior to anything he owned himself.

"Poor Hughie?" she thought with a little throb of her heart as she watched him through the window of the coach, riding down the drive. He looked so elegant in his new riding coat. She felt, at the same time, there was an air of defiance about him. He was pitting himself against such enormous odds and she felt suddenly there was something very gallant about him as if, right or wrong in what he attempted, his courage atoned for many of his sins.

Lord Chard and Nicholas Weston were having a long discussion about the relative values of soil in this part of the country. She lay back in the corner of the coach and after a while, because it was warm, slipped her shawl from her shoulders.

She saw Lord Chard glance at her once or twice and wondered if he was thinking how shabby she looked in contrast to the rich furnishings of his carriage. And then she chided herself.

"It is Hughie who matters," she whispered beneath her breath. "It is Hughie who is being saved because we are going to Clantonbury. Whatever I suffer, however awkward I feel, it is worthwhile if it means that the cargo comes in safely."

As they passed through the village she saw in the soft mud caused by the rain of the day before, the imprint of the ponies' feet leading from the riverside towards the roads to London. She glanced under her eyelashes at Lord Chard. But he was busily talking to Nicholas Weston and she knew he had not seen them.

The village looked quiet and peaceful enough in the morning sunshine. There were several yokels in smocks sitting outside the inn, mugs in their hands. She guessed that the ale they were drinking would have been paid for by the work they had done last night. She gave a little start as she heard Lord Chard say:

"That inn, Nicholas, is notoriously supposed to be used by smugglers—'Gentlemen' they still call them in this part of the world."

"Why do you not have it searched?" Nicholas Weston asked quickly.

"Because if I did I should find nothing," Lord Chard replied. "'The Gentlemen' are not such amateurs at the game that they leave their goods lying about for anyone like myself to find."

" 'Tis a pretty profitable game, I believe," Nicholas Weston said.

"So long as it lasts," Lord Chard replied.

Leona felt that Lord Chard was conveying a warning to her in what he said. She averted her face, looking out of the window to where Hugh was riding a little ahead of them.

What could she do? she wondered desperately. How

could she impress on him that the game was not worth the candle. Like the tolling of a grave-yard bell she heard Lord Chard saying with a sudden emphatic note with which he had not spoken before:

"Sooner or later, Nicholas, even the cleverest smuggler makes a mistake—then he is either caught or he dies!"

7

CLANTONBURY was built near the sea and as the crow flies was only between eight and ten miles from Ruckley. But there was no road along the Downs and to get to it the coaches had to go many miles inland, making the drive nearer twenty miles before the passengers had their first sight of the magnificent stone mansion which had been designed by Robert Adam.

Leona was tired by this time, but this did not prevent her feeling a sudden thrill of excitement as they rolled down a steep hill and saw below them the great house encircled by its terraces and gardens and beyond, shimmering in the evening light, the English Channel.

On this part of the coast the cliffs had dipped down to a low, marshy land with a wide river, turning and twisting to the sea. There were woods to protect the house and Robert Adam had chosen his site well so that from one side of the house there was a view of the undulating country and from the other the majesty of the emerald and blue sea, beautiful in whatever mood it might be.

"It is lovely!" Leona exclaimed, and Lord Chard looked at her with a little smile, noting her parted lips and shining eyes and the way in which, in her enthusiasm, she had clasped her hands together almost as if she reached out to hold this treasure and make it her own.

"I wish my sister loved the place as much as you do," he said. "I always tell her that she has no artistic soul if she prefers the smoke and dust of London to the fresh air and the fragrance of the Clantonbury gardens."

Leona hardly heard what he was saying. She was watching the house as they drove towards it down a long avenue of oak trees and vaguely, at the back of her mind, taking in the information which came from Nicholas Weston that the trees had been planted for another house which had been the ducal residence before this one.

Then they crossed a bridge over the river and the horses swept round in front of the house. Now she could see the wide stretch of stone steps leading up to the colonnaded front door, while on either side two great wings stretched out to portray, in perfect proportions, the great arched dome which surmounted the centre of the building.

It was only as the carriage drew up and the footmen, with powdered hair and purple and silver livery, came running down the steps to roll out a red carpet for their feet, that Leona remembered her own appearance.

With a little inward grimace she thought that so far as she was concerned she should enter this magnificent edifice by the servants' entrance. "Even a chambermaid would look smarter than I do," she thought, and shrank from the prospect of leaving the carriage.

How much easier it would be, she thought, if she could return home, having seen Clantonbury but not being forced to enter it. Then she knew that there was no escape, for Lord Chard descended from the carriage and turning round held out his hand to assist her to alight.

Just for one moment her fingers touched his and she felt as if the warm grasp of his hand reassured and strengthened her. She glanced up at him and saw that he was smiling at her.

"Do not be afraid," he said softly. "My sister will welcome you and there will not be a vast party as she has only just arrived from London."

This was comforting. All the same, Leona's heart was beating quickly as she walked up the broad steps and into the huge marble hall with its Corinthian pillars, tall stone statues, and magnificent furniture displayed under massive glittering chandeliers.

Leona gave a little gasp as a major-domo, more pompous in his authority than anyone she had ever met, led them forward into what he described as "the small Salon" but which, to Leona, seemed the size of a vast ballroom. It was a pretty room overlooking the rose garden, but it was empty and Lord Chard, after a quick glance, said he would go in search of his sister.

Nicholas Weston, who had entered the house with them, had already disappeared and there was no sign of Hugh, who Leona guessed was seeing to the stabling of his horse. She would have liked the reassurance of her brother's presence but she knew that once Hugh got into the stables it might be hours before he emerged.

The major-domo closed the door behind Lord Chard

and, alone, Leona looked around the room and felt again her own insignificance. In her sheltered life at the Castle she had never imagined such luxury could exist.

It was not only the polished furniture, exquisite silk hangings, the pictures and mirrors, the gilt frames and the rugs on the floor, each one of which she realized was worth a fortune. It was also the little trifles which decorated the room and which, ignorant though she was of such things, she was convinced that each one was worth far more than she was able to spend at Ruckley in a month—or even a year.

She moved from object to object, touching with sensitive fingers the soft satin of the cushions, the velvet and brocade of the chair covers. At length she wandered to another part of the room where there was a window overlooking the rose garden. The window was open and from beneath it she heard voices. She was just about to draw back for fear she would be seen when a high, gay voice exclaimed:

"Really, Julien, you are indeed asking a great deal of me, even though I am your most adoring sister. I do not see you for weeks—nay, months—except across the room at some Assembly. And then you turn up here with some country doxy who has taken your fancy and ask me not only to extend to her my hospitality, but also to lend her my prettiest gowns. I declare, it is the outside of enough!"

A deep voice answered this accusation but Leona did not hear what he said, for she had run from the window, her cheeks burning, to the other end of the Salon, to sink down in a chair, her head bowed, her hands clasped together in a very agony of shame and humiliation.

So this was what came of trusting Lord Chard's assurances that his sister would welcome her and that she had not the right clothes to wear at Clantonbury. How could she have been such a fool as to trust him? she asked herself.

She felt her flushed cheeks burn and burn again, both with embarrassment and anger. A country doxy, indeed! How dare the Duchess say such a thing of her?

She thought of her father, with his handsome, aristocratic features, the family tree of which he was so proud and which went back to the Ruckleys who had defended Britain against the invader, William of Normandy, at the Battle of Hastings.

"How dare she?" Leona said aloud, and felt a sudden

pride sweep away her embarrassment to bring her to her feet, her chin held high, her eyes suddenly defiant.

"I will not let them say such things of me," she thought, even as the door of the Salon opened and the Duchess entered, followed by Lord Chard.

Her Grace's ideas must have been moderated by her brother's arguments on the way into the house, but even so she was not prepared to capitulate entirely in her attitude towards the newcomer and as she walked across the room it was obvious that her manner was regal and there were many reservations in the formal welcome with which she was prepared to greet Leona.

Leona had somehow expected her to be a tall woman— perhaps because Lord Chard was tall. But instead she saw someone about the same height as herself although very different in appearance.

At twenty-eight the Duchess of Clantonbury was at the height of her beauty. She was a brunette with hair that had blue lights in it, and winged eyebrows over almost purple eyes, which seemed by contrast to make the magnolia texture of her skin even whiter than nature intended.

Lovely, small and vivacious, Helen Clantonbury could, when she pleased, be awe-inspiring. This was one of those moments.

"May I present Miss Leona Ruckley?" Lord Chard asked, and frowned as the Duchess in a clear but icy cold voice said:

"How do you do, Miss Ruckley? My brother, I understand, has brought you to visit us."

Leona swept to the floor in a deep curtsy, at the same time holding her own little fair head high, her eyes meeting the Duchess's determinedly. She was shy and yet her pride surmounted all other feelings.

"I must offer you my deep apologies, Ma'am," she said softly, "that my brother and I should impose ourselves on you uninvited, but Lord Chard was most insistent we should come here—I think, perhaps, for reasons other than that we should enjoy the visit."

If the Duchess's voice had been cold, Leona's contrived to be even colder. In fact, that she was so young made the reserve and ice in her voice even more obvious than in the case of the older woman's.

The Duchess looked slightly surprised and Leona was well aware that Lord Chard was looking at her intently, and though she held her chin proudly, she was well aware that her breasts were moving agitatedly beneath the grey cotton of her gown and that her hands, which held her white shawl, were trembling, try as she would to keep them steady.

Quite suddenly the Duchess relaxed.

"Why!" she exclaimed, "You are but a child! And an outrageously pretty one at that. And Julien did not tell me. . . ." She broke off her words, bit her lip and glanced at her brother. "I'm quite certain, Julien," she added, "that Miss Ruckley is right and there is some reason behind this visit. What is it? Come, tell us the truth."

"I assure you——" Lord Chard began.

The Duchess snapped her fingers and turned again to Leona.

"Oh, la!" she exclaimed. "Pay no attention to him for he is about to prevaricate. I know my brother so well that I can tell immediately when he is able to fob me off with a falsehood. You must tell me why you are here and what this is all about. For I swear we shall get no sense out of him."

Her tone was warm and now she smiled, an entrancing smile that would have melted into forgiveness any member of the opposite sex she might have offended. But Leona was still on her dignity.

"I regret, Ma'am," she said, "that I have no secret knowledge which can enlighten you as to Lord Chard's insistence that we should visit Clantonbury. I thought perhaps it must be a habit with him to spring surprises on his hosts, for I had but half-an-hour's time in which to prepare for his visit to our own home."

"Now is not that like Julien?" the Duchess said. "Always inconsiderate and, what is more, always turning up when one least expects him. But we all have to forgive him because when he does arrive one is so ridiculously glad to see him."

She smiled at her brother over her shoulder as she seated herself on a comfortable, brocade sofa and with a little gesture of her hand invited Leona to sit beside her.

"Now you are here," she said effusively, "we must not trouble ourselves why you have come or how, but see that we make your visit an enjoyable one. Your brother is with you, I understand."

"Hugh will be in the stable seeing about the horse he has ridden," Leona explained. "He is very particular as to the treatment of his horses and I am afraid does not trust anyone—even Your Grace's grooms—to see that they are rubbed down exactly to his satisfaction."

"The Duke is just the same," the Duchess confided. "I swear that sometimes I feel quite embarrassed and rather envious of the fuss he makes about his horses, while any sort of accommodation will do for me."

It was quite obvious that the Duchess was now relaxed and ready to talk on almost equal terms to her visitor. But Leona was not entirely mollified. The words "country doxy" were still ringing in her ears and looking up at Lord Chard, who was still standing, she said:

"I hope your Lordship will permit us to return home tomorrow, for there are many things to be seen to at the Castle and which I am persuaded will be neglected if I am not there."

Lord Chard raised his eyebrows but before he could reply the Duchess said:

"Oh, but, indeed, that would be impossible! We could not let you go after one night. It would make the journey hardly seem worthwhile. And, besides, I am sure that my husband would wish you and your brother to view the many things to be seen at Clantonbury and that one certainly could not do in so short a time."

"It is, indeed, gracious of you, Ma'am," Leona said stiffly. "But I am sure my brother will support my conviction that we could not possibly leave our home for longer."

She felt almost a delight in the knowledge that this was upsetting Lord Chard's plans, whatever they might be. She saw the sudden frown between his eyes and the sudden tightening of his lips and knew that he was put out by her decision and not quite certain how to cope with it. He even glanced at his sister as if for help.

Impulsively the Duchess put out her hand and laid it on Leona's.

"I think," she said, "that you are angry with me because I was a little stiff in my greeting. You must forgive me if that was so. It was not you I was annoyed with, but Julien, because he had not troubled to send a groom ahead so that we might have been prepared for you."

"It was, indeed, inconsiderate," Leona said. "And had I been in your place, Ma'am, I should have been just as angry as you were. In fact, I spoke severely to my own brother when he arrived home two evenings ago to tell me that Lord Chard was but half-an-hour's journey away."

"These men! These men!" the Duchess exclaimed.

"All the same," Leona went on as if the Duchess had not spoken, "that does not excuse my brother's and my lack of consideration in imposing ourselves upon you. I see now that we should have refused Lord Chard's invitation until we had received a note from your Grace. I am afraid, Ma'am, I was lamentably ignorant of the etiquette which prevails in fashionable society. At the same time, I was well aware that this was the right procedure and should not have let myself be overruled by Lord Chard's insistence."

Even as she spoke Leona felt there was a slight injustice in her words, for it had not been Lord Chard who had been so insistent as Hugh. If only she could have stayed behind, she thought. And yet she knew that with Lew Quayle about she could not have faced the Castle alone tonight.

"Oh, please, Miss Ruckley, you are not to be too angry with my poor Julien!" the Duchess exclaimed. And then before she could say any more the door opened and Hugh was announced.

If the Duchess had realized that Leona was not what she had expected, as she saw Hugh she was certainly aware that, however unconventional their visit, here were two distinguished young people who were quite obviously a lady and a gentleman.

Leona felt proud as Hugh crossed the Salon with an ease and an unhurried gait which showed him to be perfectly at home at Clantonbury.

He bowed with a grace that could not have been equalled by Lord Chard, and told the Duchess, with a most obviously sincere glance of admiration, that he was her most humble servant.

"I am, indeed, Your Grace's most faithful admirer," he added. "Ever since I saw you at Almack's about a month ago looking so beautiful in your diamonds that you made the very tapers and chandeliers pale in comparison."

"Sir Hugh, you are a flatterer, that is quite obvious," the Duchess scolded, but Leona could see that she was pleased as she added. "I am so delighted to welcome you and your sister to Clantonbury. Julien informs me that you live but a short distance away and as we are neighbours we should have met before, although I understand you have not been at home."

"No, indeed, he has been with me in France," Lord Chard interposed. "One of my most trusted officers,

Harriet. In fact, I think I may have written of his exploits in some of my letters."

"If you had I should have remembered it," the Duchess retorted. "Your letters were usually monstrously dull—full of tactics, battles and endless complaints about the French, whom I have always found a most cultured race with a real appreciation of good food."

Lord Chard laughed.

"Harriet, you are impossible; I really believe you would have dined with Napoleon on the eve of Waterloo if he had promised you a good dinner."

"Why not?" the Duchess inquired. "All these masculine bickerings and fights are so exhausting. I swear I cannot keep count of them."

She spoke like an irresponsible schoolgirl but her eyes were twinkling and Leona suddenly realized that she enjoyed teasing her solemn and serious brother. It made her see Lord Chard in a different light, but before she could follow this train of thought the Duchess had turned to her with one of her quick changes of subject.

"Come, Miss Ruckley, I will take you upstairs to your room," she said. "We will have a quiet gossip together without being overheard by these tiresome men. Let them converse pompously together of the 'good old days'. I am certain that subject will be produced before the evening is far spent. But we have more important things to think of."

"It is monstrously unfair of Your Grace to deprive us of your company," Hugh said, but the Duchess only laughed at him.

"If you are good you will see us at dinner," she said. "And when my husband appears start your talk of horses right away for I will not tolerate a discourse on the subject while we eat, for then Miss Ruckley and I will wish you to concentrate on us."

" 'Twould be impossible for us to do anything else," Hugh replied gallantly and the Duchess laughed again as she drew Leona from the room.

"How handsome your brother is and what a diplomat!" she exclaimed as they walked up the stairs.

"Hughie has been in London recently and has learned these graces," Leona replied.

"And do you never go to London?" the Duchess inquired.

Leona shook her head.

"No, I stay at the Castle. I have many things to do there."

"But that is ridiculous," the Duchess told her, "for I swear you would be a great success in St. James's. I did not believe Julien when he told me that he had brought me a beauty, but he made an understatement of what is a very obvious fact."

"I thank Your Grace for such a kind remark," Leona said, "but I assure you my looks, whatever they might be like, play very little part in my everyday life."

Even as she said the words she realized they were a lie. If it were not for her looks Lew Quayle would not be pursuing her, would not be frightening her and making her terrified of returning to her own home. She knew, with a little shiver, that in future every step on the stair, every creak in the passage would make her think he was coming. She would never feel free of him, not while he held the key to the secret passage beneath the Castle.

"You are shivering!" the Duchess exclaimed. "I have always said that even in June this house is as cold as the sea itself. Let us hope your bedchamber will be warm. If we had known you were coming the fire would have been lit the day before. It is the only way to get these great rooms to the right temperature."

She opened a door as she spoke and let the way into a room which was, indeed, so vast that Leona could not for a moment credit it was the bedchamber in which she was to sleep.

Then she saw her own pitiful belongings, already unpacked and laid on the great carved, gilt and marble dressing-table, and her white batiste gown draped pathetically over the big velvet armchair near the fire, and her shabby bedroom slippers reposing at the foot of a high four-poster surmounted with ostrich fronds which nearly touched the painted ceiling.

"Ah I have just remembered," the Duchess said, looking around her, her eyes lingering for a moment on the batiste gown, "Julien tells me that you have not had time to bring many gowns with you. If you will permit me I shall be only too happy to lend you some of mine."

"I thank Your Grace for your kind thought," Leona said in a low voice, "but I am perfectly content with my own wardrobe, such as it may be."

The Duchess looked at her intently, then said unexpectedly:

"And what has happened to hurt you, to make you feel that you will not accept a favour from me?"

Then suddenly she put her fingers to her mouth.

"I know!" she exclaimed. "I know what it was! The windows in the little Salon were open and Julien and I were in the rose garden. You heard what I said."

There was no need for Leona to answer. The Duchess could read, by the sudden colour in her cheeks and the confusion in her eyes that she had hit upon the truth.

"Oh, my dear, I am sorry!" she exclaimed. "My troublesome tongue will run away with me, will say things before I think, before I consider what I am doing. I get myself into such scrapes. But you must forgive me."

Leona turned towards the fire, her head bent. The dancing flames brought out the glinting lights in her fair hair, dressed unfashionably but still like a soft halo, framing her tiny, aristocratic features."

"Your Grace must not apologize to me," she said. "It was an exceedingly irresponsible action on my part to come here without a proper invitation."

"How could I have been so thoughtless and so unkind?" the Duchess asked in sudden consternation. "I have hurt you, and I would not have done that for the world. The moment I saw you I realized how mistaken I had been in what I thought.

"In fact, to tell the truth, I did not think that Julien would, in truth, have brought a doxy to Clantonbury— for he is very meticulous about such matters and would not, I know, allow me to associate with any friend of his, be it man or woman, who was not exactly *comme il faut*. But I enjoy teasing him because he is so solemn and because he takes life so seriously. Did you hear his reply?"

"No, Ma'am."

"Then I will tell you what it was," the Duchess went on. "He replied, 'How dare you say such a thing? The girl I have brought to stay is the purest and most beautiful creature I have ever seen in my life'. There, does that mollify you?"

"He . . . he said . . . that?" Leona stammered, her eyes wide. "I cannot . . . credit it, Ma'am."

"But it is true," the Duchess assured her. "And I think to tell the truth, I was a little jealous. That was why I was so stiff and cold when we first met. You see, Julien has been wholeheartedly mine until now."

"I do not know . . . what you mean, Ma'am," Leona said. "Lord Chard is not . . . interested in me, I assure you, but in . . . a very different matter which concerns my . . . home."

Her voice trembled on the words and to her surprise the Duchess did not press her to explain herself. Instead she said:

"I can only apologize again for my ill taste in what I said. To show that you forgive me will you allow me to lend you what gowns you need while you are here?"

"There is no need for that," Leona said. "I have a gown to wear tonight and tomorrow we shall be gone."

She made a little gesture towards the batiste gown, wishing as she did so that it did not look so deplorably shabby and out of fashion.

"Then you are still angry with me," the Duchess said. "And if you are so unkind I swear I shall retire to bed and not join the gentlemen for dinner. It is a way I punish my husband when he has been tiresome. He dislikes above all things, that I should not be there to preside at meals. But you will upset me so much if you will not forgive me, that I swear I shall stay in bed and eat nothing."

Leona stood resolute and the Duchess looked so determined that she could not help but be convinced that if she did not get her own way she would do exactly as she had said.

"Oh, please, Ma'am . . ." Leona hesitated. "You cannot possibly wish to lend your lovely clothes to anyone, and I do assure you there is no reason for it."

"There is plenty of reason," the Duchess said. "I am selfish, self-centred and terribly inclined to say and do things without thinking of other people's feelings. I am ashamed of myself and have got to make reparation. Please help me or I vow I shall be in a fit of the sullens all night."

She spoke so dramatically that Leona could not help smiling.

"Oh, Ma'am, you do exaggerate," she said.

"No, I mean it," the Duchess assured her. "You do not know how foolish I am when I have a fit of remorse. The Duke gets furious with me but it does no good. I sit in a melancholy and brood over my sins until I feel everything is black and miserable and that I shall never smile again."

"Please do not be like that, Ma'am," Leona pleaded.

"Then come to my room and let us choose you something to wear," the Duchess coaxed.

Still reluctant and yet with the last remnants of her pride melting like a mist before the sun, there was nothing Leona could do but acquiesce.

"Very . . . well," she faltered, only to find the Duchess's cheek pressed against hers.

"Bless you!" that impetuous lady exclaimed. "You have forgiven me and I am happy again. Come, we will have fun. There is nothing I adore more than dressing up. We will both look our best and confound those stupid men. It is all their fault from the very beginning—it always is. Come!"

She took Leona by the hand and hurried her from the room and across the landing to an even larger and more magnificent room. Here all the hangings were of white brocade embroidered with the Ducal crest, and the bed was of silver with white ostrich fronds and a bed cover of ermine edged with Brussels lace.

"The furniture came from Italy," the Duchess explained as Leona stood spellbound at the beauty of the room. "The silver toilet set was given by Charles II to one of his mistresses. I love the little Cupids plucking a harp, don't you? And the carpet was worked by the third Duchess with her own hands. Look at those tiny stitches. What a labour! I assure you I have got something better to do with my time than sit stitching away—but then I hear the third Duke was very romantic and always in love with someone other than his own wife."

The Duchess rattled on as she crossed the room to fling open a huge wardrobe at the far end of it. Leona gave an exclamation. She had never seen so many gowns. As the door opened they fluttered in the breeze like the wings of a colourful cloud of birds—blue, green, crimson, orange, gold and pink. They moved as if they were alive, waiting eagerly for a chance to step down from their hangers and appear in the world that would appreciate them.

"I have never seen so many clothes," Leona half whispered.

"Oh, these are but a few of what I possess," the Duchess replied. "I have a big cupboard of them in my maid's room and there are many that I leave in London. 'Tis useless bringing my ball gowns here, for instance. But we will find you something lovely. Let me look at you."

She turned to inspect Leona with an experienced eye.

"The vivid colours I wear would be quite wrong," she

went on, almost as if she was speaking to herself. "You are so young and that gold hair and fair skin needs a frame that will throw it into prominence. You should wear white or pale blue, and perhaps, sometimes, the soft mauve of Parma violets. But tonight I want you to be magnificent. I want you to surprise them all."

Leona could not help but feel a little excitement creeping into her. To surprise them all meant, for the moment, to surprise Lord Chard. He had seen her among the luxury of Clantonbury in her old grey gown. Had he been ashamed of her shabbiness, she wondered. She had only to compare herself with the Duchess to know what she looked like to him.

The Duchess suddenly gave a little cry.

"I know!" she said. "The white gauze! I bought the material but a month ago in Bond Street and they swore it was the very latest thing from France."

She took down a gown from the wardrobe and Leona saw it was indeed lovely; something she could never have imagined for she had never seen one like it.

"Try it on," the Duchess commanded. "Oh, but this is fun! I swear you will not recognize yourself by the time I have finished."

It was a threat which Leona felt admirably fulfilled when two hours later she looked at herself in the long mirror and, indeed, a very different person to the rather frightened, retiring girl who had entered the Duchess's bedchamber.

Everything she had on had been changed. There was silk next to her skin. Her hair had been arranged by the Duchess's maid in the very latest mode. There was even a touch of powder on her little nose and a hint of salve on her red lips.

"Do not overdo it, Marie," the Duchess had admonished her maid. "She is young and needs little artifice."

"But, *Ma'm'selle est ravissante!*" the maid exclaimed, and Leona realized that one of the things for which the Duchess admired the French lay in the skilful fingers and good taste of her lady's maid.

"And now for the gown, Ma'm'selle," Marie had said when finally she had clasped round her neck a necklace of tiny diamonds.

The gown fitted as if it had been made for Leona. There were bands of soft blue and silver ribbons to cup her breasts and cross over her shoulders. And the white gauze, which was flecked with silver, fell straight from the high waist. With it was a stole of blue and silver.

"Now let me look at you," the Duchess commanded. "Oh, Marie, the fan, and the bracelet which matches the necklace!"

She stood back to admire her handiwork and Leona looked in the mirror and saw a very strange and very lovely young girl on whom she had never set eyes before.

"That cannot be me!" she said aloud.

The Duchess gave a cry of pleasure.

"That is exactly what the others are going to say," she laughed. "Wait until Julien sees you."

Leona felt herself flush and then she said:

"Perhaps he will not notice."

"Of course he will notice," the Duchess answered. "If he has got eyes in his head he cannot help but do so. Besides, has he not already said you are beautiful? Beautiful in that old grey gown and that white shawl! My child, where did you buy such things?"

"I am afraid I have had them a long time," Leona said apologetically. "But they are all I have."

"There I go again, saying the wrong things," the Duchess said. "And in such bad taste. Oh, dear! Oh, dear! When shall I curb my tongue? The Duke has often spoken to me about it, I assure you. I did not mean to be rude, my love. But you see as well as I do what a real gown can do for you."

"Yes, I know," Leona answered. "And please do not think I am offended by what you say about my grey gown. I know it is terrible, but when I have had any money—which is not often—there have always been so many things to buy which were really important, like food and wages, and even sheep!"

"Sheep!" the Duchess exclaimed. "Who would want to buy sheep? And you, at your age, should not be bothered with bills or wages. Make your brother do it; he is a man."

"But the war has kept him abroad for so long," Leona answered, "and there has been no-one else to look after things at home, except me."

"Oh, these men! They like getting away from us!" the Duchess exclaimed. "It is always the same. I declare, wars are a delight to them just so that they can forget all their responsibilities."

She laughed, her eyes sparkling and added:

"But we will punish them, you will see. Now, when

Julien pays court to you—which he cannot fail to do—just be very cold and distant to him. Flirt with Nicholas Weston."

She stopped as Leona made a little involuntary grimace.

"You do not like him?" she questioned. "Well, I do not blame you. I think myself that he is a dead bore. Very well, I will allow you to flirt a little with the Duke—but not too much. He belongs to me and I would not wish him to have a sudden penchant for a golden head."

"I promise you, Ma'am, I shall flirt with no-one," Leona answered.

"Oh, but you must," the Duchess insisted. "It is very important that we should prove to these men we are not in the slightest interested in them personally. They are so spoilt, all of them. You should see the way the women run after Julien just because he was a hero in France and because he is a good-looking, rich bachelor. They are all at his heels, I assure you."

"I am sure they are," Leona said in a quiet voice.

She did not know why but she felt as if the lights in the room were suddenly dimmed a little. Now as she looked in the mirror she did not feel that the stranger she beheld there looked as attractive as she had a few minutes before.

Was the white gauze gown really so becoming? Did not her hair, arranged so skilfully on each side of her face, look a little artificial? She turned from her own reflection to find the Duchess was watching her.

"Do you love him so very much?" the Duchess asked softly.

8

Leona could not sleep. It was not only the big bed which seemed overpowering, with its huge, lace-edged pillows and fine linen sheets. It was not the vastness of the room which she could vaguely discern in the still glowing light of the fire; it was not the atmosphere of luxury and the faint fragrance of the Duchess's perfume which still lingered in the room. It was not even all that had happened during the evening.

It was simply the question that the Duchess had asked when she was ready for dinner, which seemed to echo in her ears, repeating itself over and over again:

"Do you love him so very much?"

She found herself trying to give a very different answer —in fact, a number of answers—to the one she had actually made. Stammering, the colour coming quickly into her cheeks, she replied:

"No . . . no, no . . . of course not. Indeed I . . . I have not . . . thought of such . . . a thing."

The Duchess laughed softly and putting her hand under Leona's chin turned her face round to hers.

"I think you fabricate, my love," she said. Then before Leona could say any more, before she could protest even more forcibly, she led the way downstairs, her gown of oyster satin embroidered with pearls and diamonds rustling as she walked, and the great emeralds round her neck twinkling at Leona as if they were little evil eyes laughing at her discomfort.

She had been in such a confusion that she thought nothing but to follow where the Duchess led, until they reached the hall. There the Duchess put her fingers to her lips and said:

"Do not forget what we have planned. Act your part well. I swear it will be vastly amusing to see what the gentlemen's reaction will be when you appear."

She remembered with a start that the Duchess, while they were dressing had planned that she should be announced before dinner as someone else, a visitor to Clantonbury. Then they would wait to see who would be the first to penetrate her disguise and know her for no other than the little, insignificant girl in grey cotton who had arrived earlier in the evening.

" 'Twill be of the greatest assistance that the Duke has not seen you before," the Duchess smiled, "for he will act his part quite naturally. It is Julien and Nicholas Weston we must watch and, of course, your own brother —though he should recognize you at once."

It had seemed a great joke upstairs when they had talked about it. And Leona had only been too glad to acquiesce in the Duchess's idea of a masquerade. She felt that because the pretence gave her Grace so much pleasure it was, in some ways, a compensation for the loan of one of her prettiest gowns to a complete stranger.

But now that the moment had come when Leona must play-act, she was afraid. Nothing in her quiet life had prepared her for this type of entertainment or, indeed, for the Duchess's childlike excitement.

"Tomorrow we have a large party arriving," she said to Leona. "Tonight by great good fortune we are by ourselves. I expected it to be a monstrously dull evening but I assure you I have not enjoyed myself so much for a long time."

She spoke with such sincerity that Leona could not help but believe her and, inexperienced though she was, she could in a way understand how the endless rounds of balls and masques and assemblies which the Duchess enjoyed in London could begin to pall.

This was something new, something out of the ordinary, and so her Grace was intent and absorbed by it as she would never have been by a more conventional social amusement.

"You look entrancing, dearest, so do not be shy," were her last words to Leona as she swept away from her at the foot of the stairs. She passed through two big doors which the two footmen held open for her into what, Leona guessed, was yet another beautiful Salon.

She waited as she had been told to do for fully two minutes. Never had two minutes seemed to pass so slowly. The footmen stationed in the hall—a mere half-dozen of them—kept their eyes rigidly before them.

Nevertheless, Leona felt they were watching her, perhaps laughing to themselves at the change in her appearance. Even if they were, she decided, she could not help but feel elated.

In a long gilt-framed mirror, which stood on the farther side of the fireplace, she could see the whole hall reflected. Her gown was silhouetted against the ancient panelling, and she could glimpse the glitter and sparkle of the diamonds around her neck.

What would Lord Chard think of her? She knew, as the thought came to her, that it had been there all the time. It was not Nicholas Weston or Hughie with whom she was concerned but Lord Chard, who had seen her in so many guises—in the bloodstained gown which she had burned, in the shabby threadbare dress she had worn earlier today and in her nightgown last night when she cried at his bedside.

Leona blushed at the thought of how shocked the Duchess would be if she knew what had occurred at the Castle. And then she remembered his kindness to her and it brought a little flicker of warmth to her heart.

"Do you love him so much?"

What a ridiculous question and how insane she had been not to answer it squarely and with more forthright vehemence. Yet she had been taken unawares. She had, indeed, not dreamed of such a thing. Did she not hate him as an enemy who had come to spy out the land, to trap Hugh and all those who trusted and depended upon him?

"No, I hate him!" that is what she should have answered. But she knew it would not have been true. It was impossible to hate Lord Chard as she hated Lew Quayle, for instance. But love! That was a different matter.

"What is love like?" she wondered innocently. Was it a sudden excitement and almost a sense of suffocation in the throat? The feeling that one's own eyes were drawn irresistibly to someone else's? The knowledge that you could trust them and they would not harm you? Was that love? How, indeed, could she answer such a question if she had never known love?

She saw the footmen move to grasp the handles of the door into the Salon and knew that the two minutes were up. And now, suddenly, she had stage fright. She felt she could not go on with this masquerade. She must run away from it, run upstairs and hide in her bed chamber. Or, better still, change into the clothes that were worn and familiar, which seemed to her now a very part of herself.

Then, almost without her conscious volition, her feet carried her forward. Step by step they took her nearer and nearer to the doors as they swung inward; and then, strident, resonant, the flunkey's voice seemed to echo round the room.

"The Viscountess Mayfield, Your Grace!"

It was a name that they had chosen at random, a name which the Duchess declared would sound so commonplace that they would be certain of having met someone of that name.

And now Leona was walking down what seemed to her the longest room she had ever seen. The lights, the flowers and the kaleidoscope of glorious colours seemed to encroach upon her and then recede again until in bewilderment she was able to focus only on one figure—that of the Duchess moving towards her, her eyes twinkling although there was a conventional smile of welcome on her red lips.

"How kind of you to come, my dear Lady Mayfield," she said in what Leona knew was her "Society" voice. "I was just telling my husband and our guests how glad I was to learn that you were in the neighbourhood and would honour us this evening by your presence. You are, indeed, in great beauty."

Leona dropped the conventional curtsy and as she rose the Duchess took her arm and drew her forward.

"Your Grace," she said to her husband, "this is my dear friend, Lady Mayfield, of whom I have so often spoken. I was exceeding glad to find that she could honour us tonight with her presence."

"You are, indeed, welcome, Ma'am," the Duke said, bowing over Leona's hand, and she was surprised to find that he was not in the least as she had imagined him, but short, rather bald-headed, with a long face and with an indescribable air of horsiness about him which not even his elegant satin knee breeches and brocade coat could disguise.

"And now you must meet our other guests," the Duchess said, drawing Leona on. "Mr. Nicholas Weston, who is an old friend."

"Your servant, Ma'am," Mr. Weston said solemnly, and Leona felt a sudden desire to laugh for it was quite obvious that here, at least, was someone who did not recognize her.

"And Sir Hugh Ruckley, a near neighbour," the Duchess continued.

Leona saw that Hugh was not only not in the least suspicious as to who this newcomer might be, but certainly not interested in her. He was watching the Duchess. She saw the admiration in his eyes and did not blame him for it.

"But lastly," the Duchess said, "you must make the acquaintance of my most beloved brother, Lord Chard."

"My Lord," Leona murmured, and as she curtsied unable to meet his eyes, her eyelashes touched the sudden flush of colour in her cheeks.

"He does not know me either," she thought to herself, but as she rose she heard Lord Chard say in his quiet voice:

"You have made her look entrancing, Harriet."

"Oh, Julien! You have recognized her!" the Duchess cried reproachfully.

"But of course!" Lord Chard replied. "Did you really believe that you would deceive me?"

"What are you saying?" Hugh interposed. "This is not Leona."

While Nicholas Weston raised his quizzing glass to his eye and exclaimed:

"By Jove! What a transformation! I would never have credited it."

"Will somebody inform me what you are all talking about?" the Duke inquired.

"Yes, dear love, of course we will," the Duchess replied. "But I declare, it is too bad of Julien not to be taken in and after all the trouble I have taken to make sure that Leona would deceive you all. What made you guess, Julien? Nicholas and Sir Hugh had not the slightest suspicion."

"You had forgotten to alter her eyes," Lord Chard answered gravely.

The Duchess pouted and looked exceedingly beautiful as she did so.

"How ridiculous you are! As if it were possible to do such a thing. But Sir Hugh was entirely deceived, were you not?"

"I was, indeed. I have never seen Leona look like that before," Hugh replied.

"Do I understand," the Duke inquired painstakingly, like a foxhound trying to follow a very elusive scent, "that this is not Lady Mayfield but Miss Leona Ruckley?"

"Oh, how clever of Your Grace! You have guessed it in one!" the Duchess cried.

"Then why should her brother and Julien not recognize her?" the Duke inquired, turning bewildered from face to face.

It was Leona who answered him.

"Because, Your Grace, I arrived here in my own old unfashionable clothes and Her Grace has tried to magic me into a fashionable lady. And, as you see, she has succeeded very well, for even my brother did not know me."

"Well, that was certainly an achievement," the Duke smiled.

"It would have been more fun if we could have kept it up longer, but Julien always spoils our games. He always has been far too perceptive for me to fob him off with a falsehood," the Duchess said petulantly.

"It is his training," the Duke said soothingly. "A man who commands a regiment gains experience in ferreting out the truth. And now Julien has even a more difficult job; he will need all his wits about him."

"A more difficult job," the Duchess exclaimed, looking from her husband to her brother. "What is this, Julien? And why have you not told me?"

"It is not really a job," Lord Chard replied.

"An appointment then," the Duchess insisted. "It is to the Royal Household?"

Lord Chard shook his head.

"No, no, indeed! Nothing like that."

"As Julien is being so evasive," the Duke said, "I had best tell you myself. He has been appointed by His Majesty to clean up the smuggling along the coast. It is a task that would frighten most men but then, of course, Julien is frightened of nothing."

"Oh, but how dull!" the Duchess exclaimed. "I thought at least you were to be in attendance on His Majesty at the Coronation. But smugglers! What harm do they do? I swear that if you continue to make bringing the French materials across the Channel more difficult, the prices in Bond Street will soar beyond the reach of everyone's pocket."

"It is women like you who encourage the criminals," the Duke said severely. "I think Julien should enforce the law and if necessary the penalties for making it."

"Dinner is served, Your Grace!"

The butler's voice boomed from the other end of the

room and to Leona's relief the conversation turned on another subject. She was, however, acutely conscious that Lord Chard's eyes followed her as the Duke offered her his arm and led her towards the dining-room.

There they were served with a variety of dishes of a strangeness and delicacy which prevented her from recognizing more than half-a-dozen of them. There was gold plate off which to eat and the table was decorated with orchids and great candelabras made to hold twelve tapers each.

Leona found herself seated on the Duke's right with Lord Chard on her other side, and after exchanging the conventional pleasantries about the countryside with her hosts, she turned towards Lord Chard and found him smiling at her.

"What are you thinking?" she asked involuntarily as he did not speak.

"I was thinking how easy it is for any woman to change her plumage."

"So that the humble little sparrow becomes a peacock?" Leona asked sharply. "It is for but one night, my Lord."

"For much longer than that, I hope," Lord Chard said. "My sister is already making plans to introduce you to the County tomorrow night. Listen to what she is saying to your brother."

It was true enough and Leona realized that Hugh was agreeing with everything that the Duchess suggested.

"The following day," she heard her Grace say, "you must ride with the Duke over to Lord Seaford's kennels. They are magnificent, built in the very latest style. In fact, I think the hounds are better housed than their owners."

"I should like that above all things," Hugh answered, and Leona realized that her own wishes were not to be consulted.

Was she glad or was she sorry not to be returning home? She was not sure. There were so many conflicting themes in her heart and mind that she did not know the answer. Of one thing she was quite sure. She was shy of Lord Chard. There was something in his eyes tonight that made her feel it was impossible to look at him. There was something in his voice which made it hard to answer him.

When dinner was over and after the men had joined the ladies in the Salon, the Duchess proposed a game of cards.

"I suggest you ask Miss Ruckley to play to us," Lord Chard said.

"Oh, no!" Leona cried, embarrassed, but the Duchess swept imperiously over to the piano.

"It will be lovely to listen to you," she said, and then proceeded, with the rest of the party, to talk, laugh and quarrel over the cards until Leona soon realized that she had no audience.

As always she became immersed in her music and as the notes trickled from beneath her fingers like cool raindrops, she found herself improvising a little, playing of the beauty of Clantonbury, of the terraces and gardens, the green sea beyond and the majesty of the house itself.

"What dream are you describing now?" a voice asked unexpectedly.

She started to find Lord Chard standing beside her. She had not seen him approach nor realized that he had left the others. He drew up a chair and placed it so close to the stool on which she was sitting that his knee touched her gown.

"Play to me of the sea," he said, "for I know it is a part of your life."

"Why do you say that?" she asked involuntarily.

"You love it and fear it," he answered. "It is our feelings about something that matter—not the thing itself. Is that not true?"

"I do . . . not know," she said. Yet she knew that he spoke the truth. Love or fear of something or somebody. Of her it was true enough and she was not certain if she was thinking of the sea or Lord Chard. She only knew that they both seemed to arouse a tempest within her breasts and that her heart appeared to her to be at war with itself.

She played a few chords and then her hands sank into her lap.

"I cannot play with you beside . . . me, my Lord," she whispered.

"Why not?" he inquired. "You played to me last night."

"That was . . . different," she said.

"But, why?" he persisted.

She also asked herself the question and to her consternation found the answer. It was because he encroached too closely upon her, because he seemed too near, because she was afraid of him coming nearer still. At the back of her mind was the Duchess's question: "Do you love him so much?"

She rose hastily to her feet.

"My fingers are tired, my Lord. I . . . cannot play any more."

"Come on to the terrace," he said commandingly, and before she could collect her wits and refuse, he had led her through one of the long French windows on to the grey stone terrace outside.

The gardens below were discernible from the lights of the house. It was a starlit night with the pale crescent of the new moon in the sky and involuntarily Leona remembered that the day after tomorrow there would be moonlight and therefore the cargo must arrive while the night was still dark. Moonlight would reveal too much to enemy's eyes watching for the long, dark shadow of a cutter.

"What are you thinking?" Lord Chard asked, repeating the very question she had made to him at dinner.

"I was thinking of the moonlight," she answered truthfully.

"But there is no moonlight tonight?" he questioned.

"Yes, I know," she replied.

She saw in the light from the windows the look he gave her.

"May I give you some advice, Leona?" he inquired.

"If you wish," she replied lightly. "But I warn you that it will be unlikely that I shall take it, for advice invariably exhorts one to do something that one does not wish to do or to give up something which one enjoys."

He threw back his head and laughed. She realized that when he did that he seemed younger, much younger, than when his face was in repose.

"You are incorrigible," he said, "and a complete contradiction in terms and appearance—in fact, in everything."

"A contradiction?" she queried, looking puzzled.

"Yes," he answered. "You look frail and weak and very pliable; yet I believe you are strong and determined and, if the truth be told, a little obstinate."

"It sounds horrid," Leona said.

"That is a word that can never apply to you," Lord Chard replied. "Have you any idea how lovely you look tonight?"

There was a caressing note in his voice which should have caused her to take flight. Instead, perhaps because of the quietness all around them and the star-strewn sky above, she merely looked at him a little inquiringly and smiled.

"I have told you that it is only the peacock's plumage," she murmured.

"I thought you were even more beautiful in the little grey gown you wore today when I brought you here," Lord Chard answered. "It was you, if you remember, who complained about it, not I."

"Now you are teasing me," Leona faltered.

He reached out a hand and covered hers as she leaned across the balustrade with them clasped in front of her. At the touch of his fingers she expected to feel that strange sense of security and comfort which she had felt before. Instead, almost to her consternation, she felt something very different.

She felt a sudden quiver run through her, a sudden quickening within, as if something came to life, something awoke which had been asleep before. She felt her breath come a little quicker from between her parted lips. Then as she stood there trembling because he had touched her, she saw his face grow nearer and heard a sudden hoarseness in his voice as he spoke her name.

"Leona! . . ."

What he was about to say she was never to know for at that moment there came a cry from the room behind them.

"Julien! What are you doing? We are waiting for you to deal."

The Duchess's voice broke the spell and Leona, moving quickly, took her hands from beneath Lord Chard's and turning, walked blindly into the lighted room.

Of what was said and done for the rest of the evening she had no idea. She only knew that strange feeling within her breast was still there, her pulses were fluttering, there was a constriction in her throat.

Hours later, it seemed to her, they went up to bed. There were many good nights, last minute arrangements made for the morning, the soft kiss on her cheek from the Duchess, and then at last she was alone in her own room . . .

"Do you love him so much?"

It seemed to her that she could never rest until she found the answer to this question. It had to be faced. She could not run away from it any longer.

Quite suddenly Leona put her hands up over her face.

"No!" she whispered aloud. "No! No! No! It cannot be true!"

The following morning passed pleasantly enough and

without any heart searchings or emotional upsets. The gentlemen, the Duchess told Leona, had gone riding immediately after an early breakfast and were not likely to be back until late in the afternoon. The Duke, it appeared, had heard there was a sale of horses taking place about twenty miles away, a forced sale for some poor rake who had lost his whole fortune gambling and had been obliged to sell up everything he possessed, even his lands.

"Of course, when His Grace learned that some bloodstock that he had admired in Rotten Row was to be included in the sale," the Duchess explained, "nothing would suffice him but he must post off at once in the hope of getting them cheap."

"And, of course, Hughie wanted to go with him," Leona said with a smile.

"And Julien was nearly as eager," the Duchess added. "Oh, these men! Horses fill their heads and their hearts too! If they were as eager to hurry to a woman's side, we might feel better complimented!"

Leona was not upset at the thought of spending the day alone with the Duchess. There were so many things to see.

The pomp and grandeur of Clantonbury which the Duchess took for granted left her breathless. The great hordes of servants in the house and the seemingly army of them who served the estate made Clantonbury a small independent kingdom in miniature.

There were not only gardeners, stable-hands, park-keepers, kennel-men, gamekeepers and woodmen. There were so many others besides, for Clantonbury had its own brewhouses, laundries, workshops, its stone masons, painters, carpenters, blacksmiths and glaziers.

"Now we have become acquainted you must come and stay with us very often," the Duchess said generously. "Come and look at the carnation houses. They are amongst my favourite flowers."

They were indeed, breathtakingly beautiful with their thousands of blooms—crimson and white, pink and mauve —but Leona privately preferred the flowers out of doors, especially the roses which made a perfect picture framed by the soft green velvet of the lawns.

She picked several buds and was tucking them into the high blue sash of her gown late in the afternoon when she saw the men returning. She could not help the sudden leap of her heart as she watched Lord Chard walking across the lawn towards her.

The Duchess hurried forward to speak to the Duke and Nicholas Weston and Hugh joined them, so that for a moment there was no-one within earshot as Lord Chard came up to Leona and stood for a moment watching her without speaking.

Because she somehow felt a silence between them was dangerous, Leona said quickly:

"You have enjoyed your ride, my Lord?"

"Greatly, though it cost us all a lot of money," he replied.

"Not Hughie?"

The question came almost like an ejaculation from between her lips.

"Your brother only bought two animals, I think."

"Two!"

Leona said the word almost despairingly. This meant yet another debt, something else to be paid for by one of Lew's cargoes, yet another steel chain to bind them to him.

"Do not look so tragic," Lord Chard said. "I do not think the horses were expensive."

"What do you call expensive?" Leona replied.

"I think one was one hundred guineas; the other a little less."

Leona felt as if a heavy weight had dropped upon her spirits, thrusting them down into a sudden despair and despondency. How could Hugh be so mad? He knew that they could afford no more horses than they had already. Besides, apart from that, there was only old Abbey, the groom, who was nearly seventy, to look after them. It would be impossible for him to undertake any more work. She gave a little sigh of exasperation.

"Do not look so worried," Lord Chard said. "It is not for you to be your brother's keeper."

She wanted to laugh almost hysterically at the remark. No, indeed, it was not for her to be her brother's keeper, but she was forced by circumstances to be the keeper of their home, to be responsible for the staff, the paying of the wages the housing of the old retainers. If people like old Abbey, Mrs. Mildew, Mrs. Barnes, and Bramwell were turned away what would happen to them? They would merely starve, for no-one would engage them at their age.

"You do not understand," she said coldly.

She saw Lord Chard's face change and in a voice that was suddenly sympathetic and understanding he said:

"Forgive me, I did not mean to add to your worries. Indeed, I thought there was no harm in Hugh making a small purchase."

"It may seem small to you, my Lord, in surroundings such as this," Leona answered. "But one hundred guineas is a great fortune to us."

She saw his lips tighten.

"Do not let it worry you," he said. "I will see what I can do about it."

He turned from her and sauntered to where the others were talking.

"We were just hearing about Sir Hugh's purchases," Leona heard the Duchess say.

"I was just going to speak to him about them," Lord Chard replied. "I was hoping that he would be friend enough to allow me to re-purchase from him the grey. It was the one thing I wanted in the sale and, fool that I was, I had forgotten to tell him so. Then when the bidding started I thought there was no point in the four of us bidding against each other. What about it Hugh? Will you do me a great favour and let me have her? She is just what my stable needs."

"Of course, my Lord, if you want her all that much—she is yours," Hugh said.

He was not pleased, Leona could see that, but she felt her heart lighten at the thought that they were free of one liability at least.

"And what have you been doing all day, my dear?" the Duke inquired.

"Leona and I have had a quiet time preparing for our guests this evening, visiting the greenhouses and generally enjoying ourselves," the Duchess said with a smile.

"I am glad about that, my dear," the Duke replied. "I was half afraid you would miss us."

"You are too conceited!" the Duchess teased. "I shall not tell you whether we did or not, I shall just leave you guessing."

She walked towards the French windows and then turned back as if she had suddenly remembered something.

"Oh, by the way, my dearest! Your agent was in this morning just after you had gone. He said it was urgent so I saw him on your behalf. It was not of real import. The Captain of the Dragoons who camped here last night wished to offer you his sincere thanks for your hospitality and for the ale you sent for his men."

"Oh, yes, I remember," the Duke said. "I told Richardson to send a couple of barrels to the camp."

"They were very grateful," said the Duchess smilingly, "and I gathered they were quite sorry to be leaving."

"Where are they going?" the Duke asked.

"Oh, to a small village called Al . . . Alfriston, I think. They have been ordered to trap some smugglers. Let us hope they are unsuccessful! You know my sympathies are always with the hunted fox."

The Duchess gave a little light laugh and went into the house. Leona's eyes met Hugh's and then, without a word, she followed her hostess and, hurrying up the stairs, waited in her bed-chamber. She knew without being told that Hugh would join her as soon as he could get away.

Sure enough, after about five minutes there was a quick, impatient knock at her door, the handle was turned and he came into the room.

"Did you hear that?" he asked in a low angry voice. "They must have got wind of the cargo."

"Are you quite sure that the cutter is coming in tonight?" Leona inquired.

"Of course I am sure," Hugh answered. "That is why I wanted to get Chard away from the Castle. That is why Lew had to clear the other stuff out of the bay."

"But we cannot be absolutely certain the soldiers were going to Alfriston," Leona said, knowing her words carried no conviction.

"Certain! Of course we are certain!" Hugh snapped. "The whole thing is quite obvious. Chard, by going away with us, has lulled everyone's suspicions. I must say he had me puzzled. He seemed to be abandoning the whole idea of capturing a cargo at that particular spot. Now we can see exactly what he was up to!"

He strode up and down the room, talking as if to himself.

"Lew will be off his guard, the cutter will come in and the Dragoons will invade the beach at the very last moment. They may even hide in the Castle itself—it would be like his damned impertinence to use it as a hiding place for his troops."

"Oh, Hughie, you are jumping to conclusions. We cannot be sure of this," Leona cried.

"You can be sure of one thing," Hugh answered, "and that is the Dragoons, on Chard's instructions, are closing in. If they surround the place how can the pack-ponies get away even if Lew has a chance to load them?"

"W-w-what can we do?" Leona asked despairingly.

"We have got to warn Lew," Hugh said.

"How can we do that?" Leona inquired.

Hugh put his hands to his forehead.

"That is the cursed question to which I am trying to find an answer," he said. " 'Tis impossible for me to move. If I made the smallest attempt to go home now I am persuaded that Chard would stop me, by force if necessary."

"Then what can we do?"

Hugh threw out his hands.

"You must go!" he cried. "You must warn Lew not to bring the cargo in under any circumstances."

"Not to bring it in?" Leona said, puzzled. "I do not understand."

"Lew is aboard the cutter, nit-wit!" Hugh cried impatiently. "He sailed for France yesterday morning. 'Twas all arranged and the cargo was waiting at Dieppe. All they had to do was to ship it aboard and bring it back. They should be coming into the bay some time after midnight. Damn it, before they do you've got to stop them."

"But it is impossible! How could I?" Leona cried.

"You have got to do it," Hugh said. "If you do not we are ruined. And, besides, if Chard captures Lew and the men he will have enough evidence to hang me as well. Do you want that to happen, Leona?"

Hugh threw himself down on his knees beside Leona's chair.

"God! but I'm in the devil of a coil!" he said. "Save me, Leona! For Heaven's sake, save me, for there is no-one else!"

The appeal in his voice went straight to Leona's heart. Without thinking of how she could do it or what, indeed, there was she could do, she put her arms round her brother and spoke impulsively, her cheek against his.

"I will save you, Hughie darling!" she said. "I promise —that somehow I will save you!"

9

"Ma'm'selle est charmante!" Marie exclaimed, standing back to admire the effect two of her undermaids had created.

Leona heard her absent-mindedly. It was difficult to concentrate on herself and her appearance when her whole thoughts were on what lay ahead and the dangers and difficulties which must be encountered before the night was out. She smiled, however, as Marie went on:

"I told her Grace that gown might have been made for *Ma'm'selle*. 'Tis too delicate, too pale a colour for her Grace's beauty, *mais pour Ma'm'selle c'est ravissante."*

She said the last word with all the enthusiasm of an artist who faces a masterpiece. Leona could only murmur a shy "thank you" force herself to behold her reflection in the mirror and know that Marie was not exaggerating.

The gown was very pale blue with tiny dewdrops twinkling in the flowers embroidered all over it. The ribbons of cyclamen pink were embroidered with *diamante,* and on her head, instead of the conventional tiara which she learnt the Duchess was to wear tonight, she had a wreath of blue and pink flowers. They were skilfully interwoven with a necklace of diamonds, so that every time she moved, her head glittered and sparkled.

With the maids' praises ringing in her ears she went from her bedroom on to the landing, only to stand irresolute as she heard from below the sound of voices and laughter. She felt a sudden shyness, a curious reluctance to go down and join the throng of distinguished society people who had arrived that evening to stay at Clantonbury.

She had heard their names. They were all very important, all people who graced the gay, rakish, exclusive set which until last year had been known as "The Regent's Clique"! They were now to serve the new King with the laughter and frivolity which he expected almost as if it were a Royal command.

"May I escort you?" a voice asked behind her.

Leona started and turned round. She was not surprised to see who stood there. There was no mistaking that grave, quiet voice. What she had not expected was the sudden leap of her heart, the sudden quickening of her veins, the upsurging eagerness which brought a sparkle to her eyes which had not been there before, and a quickening of her breath.

"How lovely you look!" he said. "I was half afraid you were not real, but a ghost from the ruins of the old Clantonbury."

"No, I am real enough," she answered, hardly aware what she said, conscious only of Lord Chard's magnificence and of his smile above the snowy whiteness of his elegant cravat.

And then she remembered—remembered with a sudden stab as if a dagger was driven into her—that he had betrayed and tricked them. He had brought her and Hugh here, virtually his prisoners, while the troops moved towards the Castle and unless she could circumvent it, their whole future lay in ruins and Hugh's very life was in danger.

Her eyes must have clouded suddenly, her smile vanished because, as if he read her thoughts, Lord Chard said:

"I should like to ask you to trust me. You are too young to be involved in many of the things which have become part of your life."

She knew exactly what he meant. And she looked away from him, her head held high.

"I am afraid I do not comprehend you, my Lord. You speak in riddles."

"Leona, do not play with me," he pleaded.

"Why not when you are so skilful an adversary?"

She heard him draw a sudden breath and knew her thrust had gone home. Then as she moved towards the top of the stairs he cried:

"Leona, wait! There is something I want to say to you."

His voice was urgent and compelling and once again she felt that little flame flicker within her. She had a wild desire to put out her hands towards him, to ask him to save them both. She had the strangest feeling that if she appealed to him he would do so.

Then she knew that such an idea was madness, and would commit Hugh to the enemy. Could anything be more insane? And yet why did Lord Chard seem so trustworthy, strong, stalwart and, in some extraordinary manner, a haven of security?

For a moment she hesitated and then she saw, on the floor above them, peeping over the well of the stairs, the white mob caps of the chambermaids. They were watching the gentry go into dinner, admiring the fashionable gowns of the ladies, the elegance of the gentlemen.

Lord Chard followed Leona's glance and said quickly:

"Not here, but after dinner come on to the terrace with me. I must talk with you."

Leona gave him an enigmatical smile.

"I will consider it, my Lord."

"And do not be angry with me," Lord Chard added in a very low voice.

"I am not angry," Leona replied, "only af-afraid."

She moved quickly before he should say anything else, hurrying down the staircase without a backward glance, so there was nothing he could do but to follow her.

She reached the hall and in her anxiety to be free of him, entered the Salon where the guests were assembled, without even feeling nervous. It was a chaos of colour, noise, laughter, the clink of glasses and the glitter of jewels. The Duchess saw Leona approaching and moving forward took her by the hand.

"My dear, you are enchanting," she exclaimed. "I must present you to my friends."

The Duchess herself was looking so beautiful that Leona could not understand how anyone could have eyes for anyone else. With a huge tiara of rubies and diamonds in her dark hair and a gown of white and red brocade, she seemed to sparkle like some exotic firefly as she moved from group to group, laughing, talking, introducing and jesting, and making everyone more animated and gay just because she was there.

Leona was introduced to innumerable people whose names she never heard and who were in her agitation nothing but vague, blank faces and voices which mouthed conventional greetings or compliments.

At last, as the Duchess swept away to greet another guest, she found herself beside Hugh.

"It is arranged," he said almost under his breath.

"What time?" she asked.

"Half-past nine," he replied.

Leona glanced at the clock on the mantelpiece. It was a few minutes to seven. She realized, with a strange emptiness, that was almost like an ache within her, that she had two-and-a-half hours more!

She thought she knew now what men must feel who were told that a battle would begin at a certain hour. They must wait, doing their ordinary jobs, knowing, even as they moved about and talked quite naturally, that it might be the last time they would ever do them. But for her it was not a question of her own life, but of Hugh's that was at stake.

She looked up at him, her eyes very soft, a tender smile on her lips.

"I will do my best my very dearest, you know that."

"There is no-one else who can help me now," he answered. And then out of the corner of his eye he saw Lord Chard approaching and added in quite another voice: "You are, indeed, in good looks this evening, Leona. I swear those flowers become you as nothing else could possibly do."

"Just what I wanted to say myself," Lord Chard interposed as he reached them.

Leona glanced at him and felt she could bear no more. She could not fence, could not pretend any longer; she was too frightened. Besides, his presence did something to her heart that she could not bear to contemplate or try to understand.

A little wildly she glanced across the room.

"Forgive me," she said, "but I must speak with Mister Weston."

He was the last person with whom she wished to converse, but she went to his side.

"Hugh has told me of the excellent horseflesh you saw this afternoon," she said. "Did you buy anything for yourself? I am most interested to know."

Nicholas Weston looked at her in astonishment. He was not so insensitive that he had not realized Leona disliked him and until now had made every effort to avoid him.

"No, indeed," he said slowly, as if choosing his words. "There was nothing low enough for my pocket—but then I am neither a rich man nor a gambler."

Leona realized that he was being deliberately disagreeable. But she did not care. It was enough to know that for a moment Lord Chard would not pursue her, would not come to her side and have that strange effect upon her so that she longed to cling to him, longed to tell him how frightened she was of the terrors that lay ahead

Nicholas Weston said something more and she must have replied. She did not know what it was She only heard dinner stentoriously announced and found a strange man she had never seen before bowing before her and offering her his arm.

She must have chattered lightly to him during dinner because once or twice she realized he was laughing and that the man on her other side was only too anxious to claim her attention.

Oh what she said she had no idea. She was only aware that the hours were passing and that as course followed course and the crowds of flunkeys removed the golden plates only to replace them with another, the minutes were ticking by on the big marble clock on the mantelpiece.

At last dinner ended. It must have been nearly nine o'clock. The Duchess rose in her seat and signalled to the other ladies that it was time to leave the room.

"I have a deal more to impart to you, my fair charmer," the man on her right whispered. "I shall pray that the gentlemen will not linger over their port and their stories."

Leona smiled at him but made no reply. She caught Hugh's eye as she walked towards the door and realized that he was deliberately making his expression blank and inscrutable.

She felt, rather than knew, that Lord Chard was looking at her too. She could almost feel his eyes boring into her but she did not look round. Instead, with her head a little bent, she followed demurely in the Duchess's wake. The other ladies proceeded with her, their gowns billowing over the carpet like ships in full sail.

They reached the Salon. Leona drew a deep breath. She went to the Duchess's side and waited for a moment before she could attract her attention.

"What is it, my love?" the Duchess asked, as soon as she was aware that Leona wished to speak to her.

"I must beg your Grace to excuse me?" Leona answered. "I have such a dreadful headache that I swear my forehead seems about to split in two. If I slip upstairs no-one will notice my absence, but I would not wish to incommode you in any way."

"Oh my dear, I am indeed sorry!" the Duchess exclaimed, all kindness and sympathy. "Call Marie when you reach your room and ask her to bring you my hartshorn, and if you cannot sleep, take a small dose of laudanum. It is what I always take when I get one of my migraines."

She paused a moment and then added:

"You have made a number of conquests tonight. I can see when the gentlemen join us they will be desolate not to find you here."

"I wish I could stay," Leona said a little vaguely, putting her fingers to her forehead. "But my head throbs and I feel I should be boring company."

It was true enough for her head was throbbing and her heart, too, but it was with apprehension and with a sudden terror of what she had to do.

"Be sure to ring the bell for Marie," the Duchess admonished, and when Leona reached her bed-chamber feeling it was best to act this farce to the end, she did as she was told.

Marie was as full of solicitude as the Duchess had been. *"Mon Dieu, quel dommage!"* she exclaimed, "when *Ma'm'selle* is looking so attractive. *Hélas* there is always another day. I will fetch the hartshorn."

She brought it to the bed, with another bottle, set them down and helped Leona to undress.

"I will not take the laudanum," Leona said, "unless I cannot sleep. At the moment I feel so tired that all I ask is not to be disturbed. Please do not let anyone waken me."

"Non, non," Marie replied. "No-one shall disturb *Ma'm'selle*. And if you need anything, or if you feel indisposed during the night, you have but to pull the bell by the bed. It rings straight into my own bedchamber and I will come to you at once."

"Oh, thank you, Marie, you are so kind," Leona said.

She felt a little pang of conscience that she should deceive anyone so genuinely sympathetic.

Marie looked round the room.

"I think there is nothing else that you will require, *Ma'm'selle*," she said. "I go now to have my supper. If you should want anything within the next hour, be gracious enough to ring the bell by the fireplace. After that I shall be upstairs."

"Thank you," Leona replied. "But I shall want nothing, I am sure of it."

Marie went from the room. As soon as she had gone, Leona slipped out of bed, locked the door and began to dress again. By sheer good fortune she had included amongst the clothes she had brought to Clantonbury her riding habit. It was very old but it was well cut because it had belonged to her mother. She had thought that perhaps Hugh and Lord Chard might have insisted on her riding with them to see the kennels of which they had talked so enthusiastically.

She was thankful now that she had it as well as her riding boots, though it took her a little time to find the latter as they had been secreted away by the chambermaids in one of the vast cupboards in the room. She could not find her riding hat, however, and so she tied a soft linen handkerchief over her fashionably arranged hair and, picking up her gloves and riding whip, moved swiftly towards the door.

She unlocked it and listened, turned the handle very cautiously, opened the door a crack and listened again. Far away below she could hear the voices of the ladies; the gentlemen were still in the dining-room. There appeared to be nobody in the passages.

She slipped out of her room and closed the door firmly behind her. Hugh had described the way she must take, having already reconnoitred that part of the house.

"Turn right, take the first passage that leads to the left, turn right again and go straight on till you come to a flight of stairs," he had said.

It all seemed much longer than she had anticipated and she thought that perhaps she had taken the wrong turning, until as last she found the stairs—narrow, insignificant ones—which led her, as Hugh described, to the ground floor. There was a small hallway from which a door opened on to the outside of the house.

The door was unlocked; Hugh must have seen to that. Opening it, Leona felt a sharp blast of cold air on her face and found herself behind some laurel bushes. Moving cautiously round them she stepped into the drive. There was a pale light still in the sky from the setting sun to percolate the twilight and she discerned a horse standing under the shadowy branches of a great tree.

Drawing nearer she saw that holding the horse's head was a young, rather vacant-looking stable boy and guessed that Hugh had bribed him.

" 'Ere you are, m'lady," he exclaimed as he saw her. "I was a-worriting t'at I'd come t' the wrong place."

"No, this is where I expected to find you," Leona answered.

She looked at the horse and saw it was "Kingfisher", Hugh's favourite stallion, and thought that only the urgency of her mission would have forced him into lending it to her. The side-saddle had been borrowed and as the stable boy helped her to mount she hoped that Hugh had made it worthwhile for him to risk getting into trouble on their behalf.

"Thank you very much for doing this," she said quietly, not daring to raise her voice.

"That's a'right, m'lady," the boy answered. "I'll lob off now afore anyone sees I. The swell cove 'at told I t'be 'ere said no-one 'd know as long as I keep me bone-box shut."

"Then remember to tell no-one," Leona answered.

She touched Kingfisher with the whip and he responded instantly, moving eagerly forward as if he guessed he was going home and was only too glad to return to his own stable.

Hugh had described the way but Leona knew that it would require all her brains and ingenuity if she was to reach Ruckley at anything like the time he expected of her. She glanced across the park, found a way out of it which led on to the Downs, and then began to move forward at a steady trot.

She guessed by his freshness that Kingfisher had not been exercised that day. At the same time, she had to preserve his strength. They had at least eight miles before them, and if she was lucky, eight miles back.

She wondered if Hugh had been unduly optimistic in believing that she could return to Clantonbury and that no-one would notice her absence. She had a feeling that for this part of her journey he had drawn freely on his imagination, or perhaps he had only wanted to reassure himself that such a thing was possible.

"If I am not there in the morning what will you say?" she had asked.

He avoided looking at her and then said gravely:

"I shall explain that you were homesick, that you must have gone home because you were worried about your animals. I shall swear you did not take me into your confidence."

Even as he spoke Leona had known that Lord Chard would not believe him. But she had put the thought from her. It was not the return journey that mattered, but what she achieved when she reached home.

She wondered what Lord Chard would say when he came from the dining room into the Salon and found she was not there. Would he wait a little, thinking that perhaps she had gone upstairs to adjust her gown or tidy her hair? Or would he immediately ask the Duchess where she was? Perhaps he might even think she was waiting for him on the terrace.

She found her thoughts carrying her away and in imagination she waited for him. What would he say when he came towards her? What had he been about to say in the garden when they had been interrupted? She felt her heart give a little throb.

Then she knew! Knew as the breeze from the sea whipped the little tendrils of curls around her forehead and against her cheeks. Knew as she smelt the fresh sweet smell of the downs, felt the movement of Kingfisher beneath her and heard the cry of the birds swirling overhead.

She loved him! That was what the strange feeling within her meant when she saw him and when he came near to her. That was why her fingers had trembled beneath his, why it had been hard to meet his eyes, and why, at the mere sound of his voice, her breath came quicker between her lips.

It was absurd, incredible, and yet she loved him! She wanted to be near him, wanted to feel him close. She thought again of that night when she sat on his bed, when he had comforted her and, because she had shivered, pulled the bedspread around her shoulders with hands that were as gentle as any woman's.

She loved him! And tonight she was throwing away her only chance of winning his love in return.

She laughed a little bitterly and heard the sound go out into the darkness like the cry of a wounded animal. How absurd to think that he might even have loved her! Lord Chard—the rich, the fêted, the distinguished; the hero from France who could have any woman whom he desired.

No, he had only been kind to her as he might have been kind to a child. What he had to say to her could not have concerned love. She was sure of that. He might have pleaded with her to leave Ruckley and to escape from all the consequences of Hugh's ill-fated enterprise. He might have offered her a home with his relations; he might have done a dozen things to make amends for the chaos and disruption he was bringing to her family. But love! Not love!

Why should he love the "little country doxy", as the Duchess had called her before they met? She felt the tears welling into her eyes; tears because she suddenly felt lonely and lost; the only consolation was that Hugh had turned to her in his trouble and she must not fail him. That was the thought to cling to. She could help Hugh. She would save him, even though it meant that her own happiness lay in ruins.

On, on, Leona rode, Kingfisher carrying her bravely and sure-footedly. The stars were coming out. They twinkled in the heavens and it was possible to distinguish in the shadows where it was dangerous to go and where it was safe. A sudden crag or crack in the cliffside was avoidable so long as one was not going too fast. Leona realized she must have all her wits about her and she tried to prevent herself thinking about anything but the urgency of getting there and of arriving safely.

But, whether she willed it or not, she could feel her heart whispering all the time to her. She kept seeing pictures of Lord Chard's face. The moments when they talked together, snatches of their conversation kept coming back. She saw again the strange expression in his eyes as he had come up the stairs towards her and she had stood waiting for him with a basin in the crook of her arm.

"Must I think of him all my life?" she whispered to herself, and then realized, with a sense of relief, that she was drawing near to Ruckley.

This part of the Downs she knew well. She had ridden over every inch of it one time or another, and she pressed Kingfisher even more quickly. But now, he, too, knew the way and was eager to be in his own stable again.

Hugh had, however, advised caution.

"Go to Dan first," he had said, and when she reached the banks of the stream she crossed it and instead of turning towards Ruckley, rode a little farther to where Dan's small cottage stood on the outskirts of the village.

It was a poor place and Dan, who was supposed to be employed on the Ruckley estate, was a ne'er-do-well who had never been able to hold a job for long. He was also reported periodically to have bouts of drunkenness and to beat his wife.

As she reached the fence which surrounded the small garden, Leona dismounted, tied Kingfisher by his bridle to the gate, which made him snort indignantly, and then walked up the rough path to the cottage door. She rapped on it with the handle of her whip. She heard someone push back a chair on the flagged floor, then the door was opened a few inches and she saw Dan peering at her with a taper in his hand.

"God save us, 'tis th' young Mistress!" he exclaimed.

"Let me come in, Dan," Leona begged.

She entered as she spoke. The home smelt stuffy and airless and she realized that Dan's wife and children must have gone to bed for there was no-one else in the small kitchen.

"Sir Hugh sent me," she said as Dan shut the door behind her. "What is happening at the Castle? Have you seen any soldiers?"

Dan set the taper down on the table again. It was the cheapest form of rush light, spluttering and spitting because it had been moved.

"Can Oi get ye anythin', Mistress?" Dan asked. "A nip o' brandy, mebbe? A've some good spirit 'idden be'ind th' chimney."

He hiccupped as he spoke. Leona realized he was drunk and guessed he had been drinking to give himself Dutch courage.

"No, thank you, Dan. I want nothing," she answered. "Except information about what is happening."

Dan glanced over his shoulder as if the walls themselves might be listening.

"There be soldiers everywhere," he whispered. "They came in t'night when us were a-comin' back from work. There be two or three o' us trapped in th' caves, but they won't find 'em there. They caught Ted, Ben and old Coby, in th' inn, but they can prove nothin' against 'em. They were but a-drinkin', but they've got 'em boxed there 'til th' cargo arrives."

"You mean the soldiers are lying in wait for the cutter?" Leona said.

"Aye, Mistress, that's what's they be awaitin' for."

Leona realized that Dan was trembling; she had always suspected that he was a coward at heart.

"Sir Hugh said you and I were to get a boat and go out to sea to warn the cutter before it comes in," she said.

"Us canna' do that," Dan answered quickly, his eyes shifting. "There be soldiers on th' beach. Oi see'd 'em go down with me very daylights. They be around th' Castle too. They be in the inn. Us 'aven't a dog's chance of gettin' a boat, Mistress. Us'd be piked on the beach afore us reached th' road."

Leona sat down on a chair. She had thought it was unlikely that the troops would not close in on the village.

But Hugh had been convinced that they would stay out of sight until the last moment. With his memories of the skirmishes of war, he had expected that they would not show themselves until the enemy actually appeared. He had been wrong and this meant she had to adjust her plans.

"Where else along the coast can I get a boat?" she asked.

Dan looked vague.

"Nowhere, Oi be a-thinkin'!"

"Think, Dan! Think! Leona said insistently. "What about old Ben Andrews? He used to fish. I have been out with him when I was a child."

" 'E be dead these past two year or more," Dan answered.

"Well, what about his son?"

" 'E might 'ave a boat or 'e might not," Dan answered. "A' bain't actually set eyes on 'im this last twelve month."

Leona sighed impatiently. She knew only too well the people of the village rarely went outside it and were not too keen on mixing with their neighbours for fear of what they should find out. Dan was hopeless; the only thing for her to do was to go on herself and see what she could find.

It was no use asking him to accompany her. He was too drunk and far too frightened, and anyhow he would be useless in any emergency. She got to her feet.

"I will see what I can do, Dan. Do not tell anyone I have been here."

"Oi' be sure not to do that, Mistress," Dan replied, and she knew that he was intent on saving his own skin, not hers.

She slipped out of the door and heard Dan unceremoniously close it sharply behind her and push the bolt home. He did not even offer to help her mount Kingfisher. Fortunately she was used to getting on and off by herself.

She swung herself into the saddle and turned Kingfisher's head east. It was only a short ride along the cliffs to the next creek where one could descend by some rough-cast steps on to the beach.

There were one or two little fishermen's cottages near the steps and after puzzling for a moment, Leona chose the second cottage and knocked on the door. It was opened after some moments by an elderly woman wearing a shawl over her nightgown.

"And wot would ye be a-wanting at this time o' night?" she demanded truculently.

"Are you Mrs. Andrews?" Leona inquired

"Aye, and who be ye?"

"I am Mistress Ruckley from Ruckley Castle."

"Ah, so ye be," was the reply "I recognize ye now. What would ye be a-wanting, Lady, at this hour o' night?"

"I want to know if your son is here and if he has a boat," Leona replied.

The woman lowered her voice

"Ye know where 'e be—or, at least, ye should."

"You mean he is at sea?" Leona asked.

" 'E is tonight at any rate," the woman answered, her voice hardly above a whisper.

"Let me come in," Leona answered.

The woman shook her head.

"Nay, ye canna' come in, Lady. Me son-in-law is sleeping 'ere and 'e's a stranger to these parts and not to be trusted."

"Then listen," Leona whispered. "Your son is in danger. I have got to get out to sea and warn the cutter before they bring it in."

At the word "danger", the woman came out into the darkness and pulled the door closed behind her.

"Danger do ye say? Be it th' coastguards?"

"The soldiers," Leona replied.

"The Lord save 'im!"

The prayer was heartfelt and the voice broken.

"I will try to save him," Leona answered, "if you will help me. I must procure a boat. Is there no-one we can trust?"

"No-one 'ere," the woman answered. "Oh, I begged Jim not to join that cut-throat lot. But Mister Quayle, his very self, came for 'im two day ago. Begged 'im to go out with 'em, 'e did. They were short-'anded, he say, and 'twas worth th' risk. Jim wanted th' money and 'e agreed. I knew no good 'd come of it."

It sounded as if she was very near to tears and Leona said sharply:

"There is no time for regrets. Come and help me get the boat off the beach. I can manage by myself once I am out to sea. But you must lend me a lantern. I have a good candle for it."

Without a word the woman went back into the house. Leona could hear her moving very softly about the kitchen as if afraid of waking her son-in-law. When she returned she had fisherman's boots on, a skirt over her nightgown and a shawl draped over her head. In her hands she carried a stoutly-made lantern of the type that most fishermen used for night fishing. Without a word she led the way down the steps to the beach.

Kingfisher was tied to the gate, but now Leona knotted his reins on his neck.

"Go home, boy," she said softly, giving him a little slap. "We do not want questions as to why you are waiting here."

The horse looked at her for a moment, wondering what she meant, and then, as she flicked him gently with her whip, he started off the way he knew so well, back to his stable.

Leona hurried after the elderly woman to the beach. There were three boats drawn up just above the high water mark. Fortunately the tide had not long turned and it did not take a tremendous amount of strength on their part to get a small boat down the shingle and into the waves.

The older woman's skirt was sodden and clinging about her ankles, but Leona, by tucking up her riding habit, managed to keep dry as, finally, with the last push, she swung herself over the side and into the boat.

"Thank you," she said. "Thank you very much."

She did not dare to raise her voice but the woman's reply came to her quite clearly.

"God bless ye! I'll be praying ye can reach me lad in time."

The boat was bobbing on the waves and Leona got out an oar and pushed it clear of the shore. She rowed for a little while, getting away from the cliffs for fear she should suddenly be swept in on the tide and dashed against a rock. Then when she thought she was safe, she shipped the oars and brought out from her pocket a candle that she had taken from a candlestick at Clantonbury. She fitted it inside the fisherman's lantern.

"Take a good candle with you," Hugh had said. "The trash the fishermen use will not show above a few yards."

It was a little more difficult to kindle a light—in fact, she had to crouch down in the bottom of the boat and use her body as a protection from the wind. At length she managed it and now, at last, the lantern was burning brightly.

But that in itself was a danger. There might be eyes watching her, watching from the top of the cliffs. She had to take off her coat and wrap it round the lantern. She had only a soft white lawn shirt beneath her coat and she felt herself shiver as the rough wind seemed to cut through her.

"I shall be able to keep warm rowing," she thought, and started off moving her oars rhythmically with the precision which her father had taught her when she was quite a child. He had been a good oarsman, rowing for Oxford when he had been at the University, and Leona had learned to row effortlessly so as not to tire herself, moving her whole body with every stroke.

She wondered what the time was. It must be getting on towards midnight she reckoned, and Hugh had told her that any time after that the cutter might be expected. She moved well out to sea and then kept rowing until she was almost opposite Ruckley Bay. It was impossible to see anything in the darkness—just the outline of the cliffs against the sky.

She wondered how many eyes were watching, as she was watching, for a ship's bow. The cutter would carry no lights and she knew only too well it would be impossible to see it until it was almost upon her.

Now that she was no longer rowing she was very cold. But she dared not take her coat off the lantern and had to content herself with rubbing her hands and even slapping her arms round her body as she had seen the farm hands do on very cold mornings before they started to milk.

It was very lonely and very quiet here in the middle of the sea. Luckily the sea was calm with only the slightest swell which rocked the boat almost as if it were a cradle. There was no mist, and the starts were bright, twinkling above her head as if they, too, were a million eyes looking down at her and wondering what she was about.

"I love him!"

It seemed to her as if even here she could not escape from the whispering of her heart.

She was so small, so insignificant. Alone in the midst of a huge expanse of water under a vast sky, yet her whole being throbbed and yearned for one particular person.

"Do you love him so much?"

She could hear the note of interrogation in the Duchess's voice and she knew now only too well what in truth her reply should have been.

"I love him with my whole heart!"

She gave a sudden start. She was certain that she had heard a little sound ahead of her. It came again, the sound of twenty or thirty oars moving in the water. She whipped the coat off the lantern.

"Ahoy!" she called. "Danger! Danger ahead!"

She shipped the oars and stood up to wave the lantern.

"Danger!" she cried.

Her voice, thin and high, seemed to come back at her in the darkness and yet she felt it must carry its message.

"Danger!"

The cutter came nearer and now she could see it silhouetted against the sky and the men at the oars.

"Who is it? What do you want?" someone cried.

"It be th' Coastguards," a man said in a sudden panic, and she could hear the fear in his voice.

"Danger! Is Lew Quayle there?" Leona called.

"Mister Quayle! Mister Quayle!" Half a dozen voices shouted his name.

"Who is it? Who are you?"

The cutter was ever nearer to her now and she could see Lew hanging over the rail at the stern.

"Do not go into the bay," she called. "The soldiers are waiting there."

She held up her lantern as she spoke and the light was on her face.

"Good God!" she heard Lew Quayle ejaculate.

Then one of the oarsmen exclaimed:

"Bust me boots if it b'aint a woman!"

She heard Lew give some orders and now he came down the centre of the boat to the bow so that he was nearer to her.

"Row in alongside," he said. "We will take you aboard."

"No, thank you, I will row myself back," Leona replied. "I have only come to warn you that the soldiers are in the bay."

"Do as I say," he commanded.

She shook her head.

"I am going back," she replied. "As long as you do not go near the bay you are quite safe."

She saw Lew Quayle turn his head and say something over his shoulder. She did not hear what it was because now she was concerning herself with putting her lantern down in the boat and blowing out the candle. She also picked up her discarded riding jacket and began to put it on.

It was only as she heard a splash in the water beside her that she realized what had happened. One of the men had dived from the boat and was swimming towards her.

Hastily she tried to get her oars out but it was too late. He grasped the side of the boat and, tipping it precariously, swung himself into it.

"I do not want to come aboard," she said furiously, speaking to Lew.

"It is dangerous for you to go back," he replied. "They may have seen the light of the lantern and, anyway, they will realize soon enough that we are not running into the trap that they have set for us."

Helplessly Leona watched the man who had climbed into the boat pick up the oars and start to row her towards the cutter. He was grinning and she realized that to him it seemed a huge joke that Lew Quayle had got his own way.

With her anger mounting within her, she found herself carried closer still to the cutter, a dozen men shipping their oars so that the boat could draw alongside the centre of the vessel in its lowest part. And then, before she could say anything or protest even further, strong arms bent down from above and lifted her bodily from out of the rowing boat and into the cutter. She felt herself set on her feet and found Lew confronting her.

"You have no right to do this," she said to him in a low voice. "Hugh had arranged everything. When I had warned you I was to return the way I had come."

"I am but doing you a kindness," he answered. "I am taking you back to Hugh."

"What do you mean," she inquired.

"I have been thinking what to do with the cargo," Lew replied, "and I have hit on the perfect solution."

She had no wish to bandy words with him, and yet she could not help but be curious.

"What are you going to do?" she inquired.

"I am going to drop it in Clantonbury Bay," he answered. "They will not be expecting us there."

"No, do not do that," Leona pleaded. "Take it farther along the coast or back to France."

"What, and lose all we paid for?" Lew inquired with a sudden note of laughter in his voice. "You must think us mutton heads. To Clantonbury Bay, men! And someone tie that boat on behind."

"It belongs to young Andrews," Leona said, and heard a voice say:

"Oi thought Oi recognized 'un. Tie it up tight. Oi dunna want ter buy a new 'un."

"Ye'll have plenty o' meggs, lad, with which ter buy a dozen boats after this run," an older man's voice replied.

"Come with me, I will look after you," Lew Quayle said into Leona's ear.

She saw his face near to hers, felt his hand under her arm and was revolted at the nearness of him. But there was no escape. He helped her to walk between the oarsmen into the bow of the boat. There was a cabin there, piled with cargo of all sorts and descriptions, but room enough for two people to stand just inside the door.

There was no light and Leona instinctively drew back at the door of the cabin.

"I would rather sit outside," she said.

"I want to talk to you where no-one can hear," Lew answered.

"You know I do not want to talk to you," she replied.

They were so close that she could hear him draw a deep breath. Then he said:

"You saved my skin tonight. Is it not right I should thank you?"

There was that mocking note in his voice that always made her shudder.

"I came to save Hughie," she answered, "and the other poor fools you have inveigled into this mad, dangerous venture which can only end in death or worse—not you."

"You entrance me," he replied, and as she shivered at his words she knew, with a feeling of desperation, that she could not escape from him.

10

It was dark in the shadow of the cabin, and the smell of the cargo—tobacco, brandy and a fragrance which must have come from a French perfume—mingled with the stench of bilge, sea water and the sweat of men who had been engaged in moving heavy bales and barrels at an almost superhuman speed.

It was not only this combined with the close proximity of Lew Quayle which made Leona shiver and feel a sudden sense of panic sweep over her. It was a premonition of the dangers that lay ahead.

It seemed to her madness that they should turn towards Clantonbury Bay, and yet she knew that nothing she could say or do would alter Lew's decision. She had a sudden picture of the Duchess seated at the card table; of Hugh talking gaily and animatedly to the pretty women around him and Lord Chard watching them with that faintly cynical smile at the corner of his lips as if he saw their frivolity and frailties and would have nothing to do with them.

At the mere thought of Lord Chard she felt a sudden yearning and wild desire for him, which was so strong that she felt as if she called his name aloud. If only she could have trusted him. If only she could have told him of her worries and anxiety about Hugh. If only she had not been forced to prevaricate, lie and deceive him. And in that moment she knew the hopelessness of despair that she could never mean more to him than a tiresome country girl who had tried to circumvent the forces of law and order.

"Come and sit down!"

It was a command rather than a request, and she winced away from Lew Quayle because he had put his hand on her arm and touched her.

He laughed at the gesture, quietly, almost beneath his

breath, and though she could not see his face in the darkness, she knew he was amused at her weakness and her inability to defy him.

She sat down because there was nothing else she could do, finding the seat was a bale of some material, not very wide, so that when Lew Quayle seated himself next to her there was little room for her to move far away from him.

To her relief, for the moment he was occupied with planning the movements when they reached the bay.

"I will row you ashore," he said. "You must get back into the house and when you see Hugh tell him what I have decided to do and warn him that it may be some time before we can move this particular cargo."

"I think it is crazy to take it there," Leona said.

"On the contrary. Why should they anticipate that we should deliberately run into danger? It it the old story of attacking a man when he least expects it. No, the cargo will come to no harm in Clantonbury Bay. The Duke and Duchess are seldom in residence and when they have departed for the excitements of the city we will raise it at our leisure. I have many friends amongst the employees on the estate."

"You have used this particular place before?" Leona asked curiously.

"A dozen times," Lew Quayle boasted. "And who has a better right to the private beaches and the gardens of Clantonbury than I?"

He was boasting with that unpleasant brand of sarcasm and resentment that she had heard before. She remembered the stories of his birth and knew that he was hinting that his father had been none other than the Duke's father, a handsome man who everyone in the county knew had been somewhat profligate in his love affairs.

"As soon as you return to Ruckley," Lew continued, "I will come to see you and give Hugh an account of what has been obtained from the last cargo."

"Did you get a lot for it?" Leona asked.

She could not help the eagerness sounding in her voice. It meant so much to Hugh.

"Not too bad a sum considering the risks we ran to obtain it," Lew answered. "Though not enough, my dear, to free Hugh of his obligations."

"Oh!"

The monosyllable was little more than a sigh, and then suddenly Lew's arm was round Leona's shoulder and his hateful face was near to hers.

"There is a much quicker and easier way in which he can be free of everything he owes," she heard him say. "You know what that is."

Leona struggled against him.

"Let me go," she said, but her voice was little above a whisper for she would not have the men rowing just outside the cabin know she was struggling with their leader.

She heard Lew Quayle laugh above her head, the laugh of a man who knows that he is the victor and that anything he wants is there for the taking. And then his free hand was on her chin, tipping her head upwards, pressing it back against his shoulder until even as she struggled and opened her lips to scream, his mouth came down upon hers.

She tried to struggle, tried to fight him, but she was as ineffectual as a small bird that had been taken prisoner, making her feel defiled and degraded, as if he had dragged her down into the very slime.

Her hands beat against his chest but his great strength was like a clamp of steel holding her, subjecting her to his will, so that finally, breathless with horror and utterly his captive, she could only endure his kiss until she felt she must faint from the horror of it.

At length he raised his lips from hers, and now she was past speech, gasping for breath, tears rolling from her eyes and down her face.

"You shall be mine, debt or no debt!" Lew said between his teeth, and as he spoke he fumbled at the buttons of her riding coat.

She gave a little cry of terror and then deliverance came in the voice of the man at the tiller.

"We be a-nearing th' bay, Mister Quayle!"

Lew started to his feet.

"As silently as possible, boys," he said. "There may be a look-out around—tho' I doubt it."

He went from the cabin, leaving Leona to rub her lips roughly with her handkerchief as if she would scrub away the memory of his kiss. But even as she did so she knew that was impossible to erase what had happened. The touch of him, the horror of his embrace, his triumphant assumption that sooner or later she would be his, was seared deeply into her mind and soul.

Was there no escape from him? Would it be impossible for her even to be free of him? She knew then, with a sudden hopelessness, that she fought alone. It was useless to appeal to Hugh. He was too deeply in Lew's debt.

Looking out through the door of the cabin, she saw the lights of Clantonbury. It was sheltered from the sea and yet it was possible to see many of the upper windows of the great house. They were golden with light and she had a sudden yearning for the security they represented.

If only she had wings. If only she could leave this boat with its illicit cargo and crew of law-breaking yokels and be back in the great bedroom where the Duchess believed her to be sleeping off the effects of a headache. If only the evening could start again, and she could stand on the landing and know that Lord Chard was there beside her.

Lew's voice broke in on her reverie.

"Are you ready? There's no time for hanging about, we've a devil of a lot to do."

"I can row myself ashore," she answered.

"No, I will take you," he replied. "The men'll start putting the cargo overboard as soon as we reach the bay. The whole operation will not take more than a quarter-of-an-hour, and then we shall be away again."

Leona looked towards the shore.

"You are certain that it is safe?" she asked.

"Would I be doing it otherwise?" Lew inquired. "You'll have to learn to trust me, my pretty one, as many another wench has been only too eager to do."

There was an unmistakable taunt in the words and she knew that he referred to the other women who trusted him and whom he had betrayed. She felt her face flush in the darkness that he should speak to her in such a way.

There was no time for conversation. The men were shipping their oars and letting the cutter, still moving, glide silently into the bay. Lew dropped over the side and into the row-boat which was pulled into position by two men.

Then, as Leona waited hesitantly, another man picked her up in his arms and handed her to Lew. He took her and as he did so tried to kiss her on the mouth. She turned her head swiftly, striking at him with her clenched fist, and she heard him laugh as a man might laugh at the gesture of a child.

"You excite me," he whispered, and set her down in the boat.

She wanted to rage at him, to tell him what she thought of him, but knew that she must not speak for fear of endangering the lives of them all.

There was something uncanny in the silence; thirty men moving in the darkness as if they were ghosts and Lew

Quayle dipping the oars with the quietness of a tiger prowling through the jungle.

"That is what he is like," Leona thought suddenly. "A tiger waiting to strike, waiting to pull down his prey, so strong that none can gainsay him."

Her breath was still coming brokenly between her lips from the horror of his kiss. She still felt herself shivering with the revulsion which had rocked her whole body. Yet a new emotion was rising in her—the anticipation of being free, of knowing that in a few minutes she would be able to step ashore and run to the safety of Clantonbury away from this man whom she hated and feared, away from the pregnant terrifying silence.

The boat ground suddenly on the soft shingle and Lew sprang out, his high boots protecting him from getting wet. He pulled the boat a little way up the beach then bent towards Leona.

"I will get out by myself," she whispered.

"The sand is wet," he replied. "I will carry you."

"No, I will manage," she tried to say in vain, but it was no use. Lew's arms were round her and he was lifting her as easily as if she were a doll, without thought or will of her own.

"Do not be afraid," he said. "This is no time for love-making. That will come later when you return to Ruckley."

It was a statement more than a threat, but she felt the full horror of it as if he had given her a blow. Not even her home was to be safe or sacred from this man.

He carried her above high water mark and set her down on her feet. Behind them Leona could hear the faint sounds of heavy objects being lowered into the water—a little splash, a sudden muffled oath. It was amazing how quiet it all was considering how much was going on.

Then suddenly there was a shout, a cry which seemed to shatter the stillness and to echo and re-echo around in the darkness.

"Get out! Danger! Put to sea!"

It was a voice full of fear yet somehow there was courage in its very loudness.

"Danger! They are waiting, you fools! Put to sea!"

The voice came again and now someone came running down the beach, running towards Leona and Lew as they stood seemingly paralysed by the suddenness of the noise. And in that moment Leona recognized the voice and knew who it was.

"Hughie! Oh, Hughie!" she cried.

She went towards her brother and as she did so there was a sudden loud report, a flash of fire; and even as she reached him, Hughie fell, thrown to the ground with a violence which made his very fall seem as explosive as the shot itself.

"Hughie! Oh, Hughie!"

Leona reached his side and fell on her knees beside him. By now pandemonium had broken out. She could hear Lew's voice shouting orders. There were shots coming from every side of the bay. She could see vivid orange bursts of fire, hear the bullets whizzing overhead.

"God's curses on you! Get your oars out!" "Holy Mother!" "Us be betrayed!" "The devil take you for your slowness!"

The noise was indescribable and without warning there was a light on Leona's face. She looked up, her eyes agonized in their anxiety for Hugh, and saw that the lantern was held by Lord Chard.

"He is dead!" she cried wildly. "Dead! And you have killed him! I hate you! Oh, I hate you! Hughie is dead!"

"I will get help," he said quietly.

She had a brief glimpse of Hugh's face covered in blood as Lord Chard turned away taking the light with him. And then, before Leona could speak again, before she could cry out in fear, someone lifted Hugh in his arms. She knew it was Lew, but could do or say nothing as he strode away over the shingle. She guessed that he went towards the boat in which they had reached the shore.

She knelt there, stupidly, not realizing quite what had happened, only racked with her own emotion, until a few seconds later he returned and jerked her to her feet.

He carried her the few feet to the water and almost threw her down in the boat.

"Crouch down," he admonished her, shouting above the noise of firing. "Get as flat as you can."

She was too bemused to do anything but obey him. Hugh was lying in the bottom of the boat and she put her arms round him, conscious as she touched his face that her fingers were wet with blood.

There was another explosion. She heard a bullet whine over their heads. Lew was rowing like a man possessed. Already they were out of the bay and raising her head a little she saw the cutter was ahead of them. The men were rowing surprisingly well and at every stroke they drew farther and farther away from the beach.

In the distance she heard someone shout:

"Load again!"

And another voice called her name:

"Leona! Leona!"

She felt sure it was Lord Chard who called, then when she did not hear it again thought she must have imagined it.

By now they were in the open sea and Lew cupped his mouth in his hands.

"Ahoy there!" he shouted. "Stop to pick us up."

They drew alongside the cutter and Lew picked up Leona and handed her to the men aboard.

"Be careful of Hughie! Oh, be careful of him!" she begged, forgetting, in her anxiety, the rough hands that were handling her.

"We'll be careful right enough, Mistress," someone said kindly. And now Hugh was aboard and carried by two men into the cabin.

It was too dark for Leona to see anything but she knew they set him down on the floor. Then, a moment or so later, someone kindled a lantern and for a second, as the light illuminated the body lying on the straw-strewn, wooden floor, Leona was afraid to look.

Had Hugh's face been blown away? Was he so mortally wounded that there was no hope of him even being alive? The men who had carried him turned to look at her and she forced herself to go to Hugh's side.

She dropped on her knees. His face was a mass of blood and for a moment she thought that the mere sight of it must make her faint. Then she drew from her pocket a small cambric handkerchief and started to wipe the blood away.

"It is his head," she said to no-one in particular, and then Lew appeared beside her.

"Get to your oars," he said to the man with the lantern and the others who had carried Hugh. "And keep the door shut."

The men slunk away from the sharpness of his tone. Lew set the lantern down on the floor and taking Leona's handkerchief from her without apology, staunched the wound which she could now see was a gaping gash at the side of Hugh's forehead.

"Is he . . . dead?" she asked tremulously.

Lew put his hand inside Hugh's coat.

"No, his heart is beating," he answered. "He is unconscious from the impact. When we get to Dieppe we will find a physician for him."

He turned his head suddenly, for the cabin door had opened.

"What the hell are you doing?" he asked gruffly, and then saw the answer in the dangling body that the two men carried and set down on the floor.

" 'Tis Ben Robinson," one of them said.

The man had been shot in the chest and the blood was pouring down the front of his shirt. But he was conscious and as Lew held the lantern over him, he looked up at him with glazed eyes.

"Oi . . . oi've . . . copped it . . . 'aven't oi . . . Mister Quayle?" he said. "Aye . . . but it were . . . a . . . grand . . . game . . . while it . . . lasted. . . ."

There was a strange gurgling in his throat, the blood gushed from his mouth and his head fell back. One of the men who brought him in crossed himself and murmured a prayer.

"Put him overboard," Lew Quayle commanded.

"Oh, but . . . you cannot do that!" Leona cried.

Lew turned to look at her.

"Why not?" he inquired. "A cargo of corpses is not welcome in Dieppe, I can promise you."

"To be buried without . . . a service or . . . a prayer," Leona faltered, feeling her protest was unjustified yet somehow shocked at such an ending for any man, whatever his life might have been.

"There is nothing to stop you saying one," Lew replied mockingly.

The two men who had brought Ben Robinson in, picked him up again, took him out through the cabin door, and after a moment's pause there was a sudden splash. Leona closed her eyes. Was there no end to this night of horror? she wondered.

Lew Quayle went to the door.

"Anyone else injured?"

"Jake's got a splinter through his finger," someone volunteered. There was a guffaw of laughter at this, to be instantly silenced by Lew.

"Keep your voices low, you muttonheads," he snarled at them. "Do you want the Revenue cutters to hear us? They're as thick as pilchards in the Channel and well you know it. Keep rowing, you blasted landlubbers. Let's get to Dieppe and then you can start shouting, if you've anything to shout about!"

He came back into the cabin, slamming the door behind him.

"Sapskulls!" he cursed. "And may the soul of Lord Chard—or whatever that fancy friend of yours is called—rot in hell."

Leona did not answer. She was kneeling by Hugh, aware now that he was breathing but terrified by the pallor of his face and the blood which kept oozing beneath her soaked handkerchief and running down his pale cheeks.

Lew bent over Hugh, to look closely at his face. "He's alive at any rate," he said after a pause.

"He saved you!" she said. "He risked everything to save you."

"He certainly did his best to warn us," Lew acknowledged grudgingly.

"If he had not done so you would have all been killed or captured," Leona said. "Do you realize that they were firing from both sides of the bay? They were only holding their fire until you were too deeply engaged to get away."

"And who planned the devilish trap, I wonder?" Lew asked. "Oh, do not tell me, I know the answer. But Hugh said that he thought his nosy lordship had found nothing at Ruckley, that his suspicions were allayed, and re-directed elsewhere."

There was no doubt about the accusation in his words and Leona flushed.

"How could Hughie think anything else?" she retorted hotly in defence of her unconscious brother. "Lord Chard seemed so pleasant and so unsuspicious. It was only when we arrived at Clantonbury that we realized his invitation had only been a ruse to take us away from the Castle."

"He must have learned that we have used the bay at Clantonbury before," Lew mused, his eyes narrowing. "It will go ill for the man who betrayed us."

"No! No more bloodshed!" Leona cried. "Has there not been enough? One man is dead and Hughie barely b-breathing."

"Two casualties out of thirty-two men," Lew said. "One cannot really complain."

"You would complain if you were the one who was wounded," Leona retorted. "Or if you were the wife or mother of that wretched man who has died. Cannot you see that the game is not worth the candle. What do you get in exchange for lives? Only money!"

"Money is what most men—and certainly all women—want," Lew answered. "And when we get to Dieppe, my dear, you will certainly need it yourself."

His glance flickered over her as she knelt beside Hughie

and Leona felt as if he suddenly undressed her. There was something humiliating and degrading in his very glance. She looked down at her bloodstained, dusty habit and knew that with her dishevelled hair falling around her face she looked wild and unkempt with little dignity and no pride with which to combat him.

"I care not about my appearance," she said defiantly, speaking as much to herself as to him.

"But you do care whether Hugh has a good physician or not," Lew answered. "And that, too, costs money. So you have to remember, my little firebrand, who holds the purse strings."

Leona felt the tears of humiliation rise in her eyes but she turned her head so that Lew should not see them.

"Leave me al-alone," she said. In spite of her effort to sound defiant, her voice broke on the words and they were soft and unhappy, the cry of a hurt child.

He laughed and went from the cabin. Outside she could hear him spurring the men on, telling them to row quicker, to get away from the accursed shores of England.

She rose a little unsteadily to her feet, collected the straw which littered the cabin from the packing cases and bales which had already been deposited into the sea, and placed it beneath Hugh's head to make him more comfortable.

Thinking that he seemed cold she would have taken off her riding jacket to cover him had she not been afraid that Lew would come into the cabin and find her wearing only her thin cambric shirt. She knew that it clung to her body and she was afraid that the sight of it might tempt him to touch her.

Instead she found a sack thrown into the corner and she covered Hugh with that, hoping he would feel a little warmth from it. She held one of his hands in hers, caressing and stroking it, holding it against her breast to keep it warm. And all the time she was conscious of the fact that they were moving away from England, away from the only security that she had ever known—away from Lord Chard!

She could not help wondering, as she sat there, what he had thought when he returned to where he had left her on the beach to find her gone and Hugh with her. Was he distressed or merely angry that his prisoners had escaped?

Hugh had betrayed himself, there was no question of that. And though she hated to admit it, she knew she must be grateful to Lew Quayle that her brother was not at this moment in irons and being taken to the nearest prison. Would his life be forfeit if he were caught, she wondered, or would he merely be transported?

She shuddered at the thought, remembering a ship which she had once seen setting out from Southampton, the prisoners being taken aboard all chained together. They were being hit and whipped into the hold with a cruelty and a violence which even now made her sick to think of it. And it might have happened to Hugh!

She knew then that whatever she felt about Lew Quayle she had to be grateful to him that he had saved Hugh from that. Supposing she had flung herself on the mercy of Lord Chard. Might he not have been able to save Hugh, too? She did not know the answer. She could only hear again his quiet voice saying: "I will get help," and remembered that he moved away into the darkness.

What had he thought of her outburst? Had her voice rung into his ears?

"I hate you! I hate you!" she had said.

Quite suddenly Leona covered her face with her hands.

"It is not true," she whispered to herself. "I love him, whatever he has done to us. Even if he had killed Hughie, I should still have loved him."

She knew it was disloyal and was appalled at the contrariness of her own feelings; and yet she must be honest. It was because she loved Lord Chard so deeply that she had cried out her hate.

"How can I love him," she argued, "when he has done this to Hughie?" But she knew even the sight of her brother lying silent and still with the wound in his forehead, could not change the throbbing of her heart, the yearning of her soul for the man who had awakened the strange flame within her.

"I must be mad," Leona whispered. But she knew she was not mad; only in love, as she had never imagined love could be.

She had thought of it as something quiet, beautiful and wonderful that came into a woman's life. Instead it was a torture and an agony, a dividing of loyalties, the destroyer of all peace of mind and all chance of contentment.

Love was a flame, a tempest, a rough sea. And all she had believed it to be was a soft light and a harbour of refuge.

Because she was so bewildered and confused and, at the same time so desperately anxious about Hugh, she began to cry. At first softly, holding his limp, cold hand against her cheek while the tears ran down on to it. And then in a very paroxysm of grief, crying in a hopeless manner which shook her whole small body, with tears which seemed to come almost like drops of blood from her very heart.

She cried for Hugh and for herself and for the man who had died and been thrown unshriven into the sea. She cried at the thought of leaving England and her home behind. And beneath it all, colouring everything, was the thought that she was going farther and farther away from the man she loved and that she would never see him again.

He might despise her. He might be glad of the opportunity to be rid of her. But she still loved him hopelessly and desperately, with an emotion she had never before known that she possessed.

How long she sat on the floor of the cabin she had no idea. She only knew that her tears exhausted her until she could cry no more. When the cabin door opened she did not even turn her head because, in her hopelessness, even her fear had no longer power to animate her.

"How is he?"

Lew asked the question, and when she did not answer he bent down to put his hand against Hugh's cheek.

"He is cold," he said briefly. "Well, we will not be long now. The sun is rising and we shall be in Dieppe in time for breakfast."

Still Leona did not answer and Lew crossed the room to pull back the heavy curtain from a small porthole and let the light into the cabin.

"The crossing takes but three hours in a calm sea with a ship like this," he said. "Unfortunately we are an oar short so we shall take longer. But we've been quick enough to avoid the Revenue cutters and any other ships that might have been looking for us."

Still Leona did not answer and looking at her downturned head Lew said:

"Have you nothing to say? You will find France not such a bad place to hide in. You'll want money, of course. The Frenchies do not part with anything unless they are paid for it. But I am accompanying you. Do not forget that—'tis indeed fortunate for you that I am with you."

Leona raised her head wearily. There were dark lines under her eyes from sleeplessness and weeping and her face was almost as pale as Hugh's. And yet, had she known it, she looked very lovely in the pale, cold light coming in through the porthole of the dingy cabin.

"I am not concerned with what happens to me when we

get to Dieppe," she said, her voice husky with tiredness. "All I ask is that Hughie shall have the attention of a physician as speedily as possible. But I must thank you for . . . saving him last night. I have been thinking of . . . what would have happened had he been . . . captured after he had given you the warning. And because you . . . brought him away, I can only say . . . thank you, with all my heart."

It was an effort to force the words from between her lips, although in fairness she knew they must be said. For a moment she thought Lew was going to laugh, but instead he replied with a glint in his eyes:

"So you are grateful to me, are you? Well, that is one step forward. I shall remind you of your gratitude—perhaps you can count it as a debt to be added to what Hugh owes me."

"As you wish," Leona answered, and her voice sounded hopeless and despairing even in her own ears, and she knew in that moment that she was a prisoner who must undergo a life sentence as horrible, as degrading as that which had awaited Hugh had he been left in England. She was at Lew Quayle's mercy and now there was nothing she could do about it.

There was a shout from one of the men outside and Lew left the cabin. When he had gone Leona turned, dry-eyed, to Hugh and laid her head against his breast.

"Hughie, darling, if only you could save me," she whispered, and knew it was a hopeless wish even while she made it.

But now, as they neared the shore of France, her spirits began to rise again. She had touched rock bottom, had gone down to the very darkness of despair. Because she was young, because it was against her whole nature to remain miserable for long, she felt that in some miraculous way things might not be as black as they appeared.

Perhaps it was because Hugh moved his head a little and muttered deliriously. It was only a slight movement and the words that came from between his lips were unintelligible. But at least it showed he was alive; at least it was better than that he should remain so silent, still and frighteningly pale.

"He tried to speak," she told Lew when he came to the cabin to say they would be in the harbour in another ten minutes.

"I told you not to worry," he answered. "Hugh's tough; he has been through the war, has he not? I will take you to some lodgings I know of by the quay and we will send for the best physician in Dieppe."

"Thank you," Leona could only say humbly.

And she had to thank Lew again after they had carried Hugh with great care on an improvised stretcher from the ship to the quay.

The lodgings to which Lew took them were not grand but they were certainly clean. They were situated above a little *estaminet* which Leona understood the smugglers had made a special meeting place of their own.

They took Hugh up the narrow stairs and when they reached the bedroom, with its big bed and feather mattress and clean white-curtained windows overlooking the harbour, Leona was well satisfied.

"Does this suit you?" Lew asked her.

"Hughie will be all right here," she answered.

"There is a bedroom for you next door," he said, "and the landlord has promised you his own sitting-room so that you will not have to go into the bar."

"The physician! Please get the physician quickly!"

"I will do my best," Lew answered and she heard him clatter down the narrow staircase.

The innkeeper's wife, a fat, voluble Frenchwoman, came upstairs and helped Leona to undress Hugh and get him between the sheets. Leona could speak French, but only haltingly and she was unsure how to pronounce some of the words. Fortunately she could understand all that the Frenchwoman wished to convey to her.

When Hugh was in bed they washed away the congealed blood from his wound, which Leona realized now was not so deep or so frightening as she had thought at first.

He was beginning to twist and mutter now he was warmer and it was quite obvious that he was developing a fever.

"If only the physician would hurry," Leona cried, but the Frenchwoman smiled and said:

"Do not worry, *Ma'm'selle,* your brother will be all right. I have seen many sick men and we have had wounded men here before in a far worse state than this.

Still Leona did not believe her until the physician arrived—an oldish man with heavily waxed moustaches and an abrupt, rather disagreeable manner. He examined Hugh, bandaged up his wound and said:

"*Alors!* It is not bad. The bullet struck him a glancing blow and severed the artery. That is why there was so much blood. He must be kept quiet for three or four days. If he runs a high fever I will come again and bleed him, otherwise there is nothing to be done."

"But, *Monsieur*——" Leona protested.

"I have said there is nothing to be done," the Frenchman repeated. "That will be fifty francs, if you please."

He held out his hand and Leona found the blood rising in her cheeks.

"I . . . I am sorry, *Monsieur*, but . . . I . . . I have not the . . . money on me," she explained in her halting French. "If you will be . . . kind enough to ask . . . the gentleman who . . . fetched you here, Mister Quayle, he will, I am . . . sure, pay you."

The physician mumbled rather disagreeably and left the room. Leona put her hands to her burning cheeks. To have to be beholden to Lew Quayle, to have to ask him for every penny and know that he must pay the rent and purchase every mouthful of food that went into their mouths—that was bad enough. But how long was this to continue? That was a thought that she could hardly bear to face.

But what was the alternative?

"I will get work," she told herself. "There must be people in Dieppe who want some sewing done for them. Or perhaps I could work in the *estaminet* washing up the dishes."

She shrank from the very thought, yet she knew that her self-respect would never let her rest until she had found some way of earning money.

She suddenly remembered that perhaps Hughie might be carrying something with him and chided herself for not having thought of this sooner. The Frenchwoman had put his clothes tidily on a chair and now she searched in the pockets, finding a purse in the white satin breeches that he had been wearing for dinner the night before.

How handsome he had looked, she thought with a little ache in her heart: how at home amongst the glittering social throng which had gathered at Clantonbury! And now he could never return to them again. She knew then that exile for Hugh was going to be very hard.

She emptied the purse out in her hand. Five golden guineas! That at least was something, but how long would they last? There was also Hugh's fob, she thought, with its gold and emerald seal, and the watch that had been his father's which he had worn in his vest pocket.

She put the money in the pocket of her riding coat for

safe keeping and even as she did so remembered that Hugh would want new clothes when he was well again. He could not walk about Dieppe in white satin breeches and a blue brocade evening coat. His cravat and waistcoat were soaked with blood and his only shoes were evening ones with silver buckles.

What a tangle it all was! There was nothing she could do but wait until Hugh was well enough to face some of these problems for himself.

She was thankful that as the day progressed there was no sign of Lew. The Frenchwoman brought her an omelette at midday which she found delicious, even though she could only force herself to eat a few mouthfuls.

It was not until the afternoon that Hugh stirred and opened his eyes.

"Where the devil am I?" he asked petulantly. "I have got a ball of fire in my head!"

"Oh, Hughie! You are all right!" Leona cried.

She did not know until that moment how afraid she had been that the bullet might have affected his brain. The idea had been there but she had not dared to voice it even to herself. Now the tears of relief started to her eyes.

"What do you mean, all right?" he asked, and put up his hand to touch his bandages. "What is wrong?"

"A bullet hit you at the side of the head," Leona answered.

"A bullet! What bullet?"

"Oh, Hughie! Do you not remember?" Leona asked. "You ran down to the beach to warn Lew."

"Cannot recall a damned thing about it," Hugh answered. And then, as if the effort had been too much for him, shut his eyes and fell into a deep sleep.

He awoke again two hours later and now was more coherent. He could not remember exactly what had happened when he reached the beach, but he could remember learning while they were playing cards that something was afoot.

"I do not remember who said anything first," he said, his voice weak, his forehead knitted by the effort. "I think one of the ladies remarked that she had seen some soldiers on the road that morning, and it was then the Duchess —yes, it was the Duchess—said, 'Oh, they have all gone away to Alfriston'. I was just praying that you had got there in time to warn Lew when someone else—a man I think, said, 'Not all of them. I hear they are guarding the bay tonight. There have been rumours the smugglers have used it before'. 'Oh, surely not!' the Duchess exclaimed."

Hugh gave a little groan and Leona said quickly:

"Do not tell me if it hurts you. It can wait until tomorrow."

"No, no, I want to recall it," Hugh replied irritably. "That is what she said: 'Surely not! We do not have smugglers at Clantonbury'. And then Nicholas Weston laughed."

Hugh was silent for the moment, his eyes shut, his mouth twisted in pain, before he continued:

"I knew then, just as clearly as if someone had told me what was going to happen. Lew, if he got your message, would run the cargo into Clantonbury Bay—he had done it before; I had heard him boast about it—and Chard had got the whole thing tied up. How I could ever have underestimated him I do not know. He was like that in France. You would think he was doing nothing and all the time he had a strategy worked out which would defeat the French."

"If only you had said that might happen," Leona whispered.

"He got me mesmerized, I think," Hughie answered. "He seemed so friendly, so easy, I never suspected a thing. But when Weston laughed I knew."

"What did you do?" Leona inquired.

"I went on playing as if I had heard nothing. I think I won a few guineas. But I left them on the table and rose from my seat saying I wanted a drink. It was getting pretty late by then and I reckoned that if you had got in touch with Lew and he had decided to come to Clantonbury, it would be just about the right time for him to be heading for the bay."

He coughed, then went on.

"I took a drink, talking to one or two people quite casually, and slipped out through the French windows. I thought no-one had seen me and as soon as I was out of the way of the lights from the house I began to run. I ran down through the gardens and found my way—though I do not know how—towards the beach."

Hugh stopped and wiped the sweat from his forehead with the back of his hand.

"I cannot recall much after that."

"I can relate to you what happened," Leona told him. "When you reached the beach the cutter was already in the bay beginning to unload. You warned them. You shouted out at the top of your voice: 'Danger! Get out to sea! Danger!' You saved them all, Hughie. If you had been a little later they would have been too far involved with their unloading to be able to slip away."

She drew a deep breath.

"The soldiers started to fire. They shot you down and one other man on board the cutter; he was killed but everyone else got away."

"And how did I escape?" Hugh asked. "I thought you said they shot me down."

"Yes, they did," Leona answered in a low voice. "But Lew saved you. He carried you to the boat in which he brought me ashore, and then returned for . . . me."

She tried to say something more but somehow the words would not come.

"Good old Lew!" Hugh cried enthusiastically. "That was damned clever of him, was it not? He saved me. He saved you, Leona. Indeed we must thank him!"

"Yes, Hughie, we must . . . thank him," Leona whispered.

11

Hugh was better, there was no doubt about that. He sometimes got blinding headaches in the evening if he had done too much during the day but he managed to dress and sit by the window and amuse himself by watching the people in the streets below.

Leona suspected that on top of the pain which his wound obviously caused him, he was also worrying. She would hear him tossing and turning about at night and would come from her own bedroom to ask if there was anything she could do for him—often to be told curtly not to fuss over him like a hen with only one chick.

Now, as he sat in the window, the sunshine on his pale face, she pirouetted in front of him to show off her new gown.

"It cost a paltry sum!" she said. "Only about two shillings in our money. *Madame* showed me where to buy the material—it was from a stall in the market and even before I argued they reduced everything for me."

Hugh shook his head. "What woman could resist being extravagant in France?"

"Oh, it was not really extravagant," Leona replied, taking him seriously. "I could not go on wearing my riding habit. Little boys in the street used to call after me and ask where I had left my horse and, what was more, there was blood all over the coat."

"I was but roasting you," Hugh smiled. " 'Tis a pretty gown and you look exceedingly attractive in it."

Leona dropped him a little curtsy.

"Thank you kindly, sir."

The sunshine turned her to gold and the gown, of blue cotton with ribbons to match, showed up the fairness of her skin.

"Gad!" Hughie said involuntarily. "You'll be growing into a beauty if you're not careful."

"To what purpose?" Leona asked, and there was a bitterness in her tone that he had never heard before. And then, before he could question her, she said:

"Hughie, we have to talk seriously together. I know you have been feeling too ill up until now, but do you realize that we have but a few guineas between us and starvation?"

"Fustian!" Hugh ejaculated. "Lew will not let us starve."

"Lew! What has Lew got to do with it?" Leona asked, a passionate note in her voice. "We have to stand on our own feet. We cannot go on being dependent on Lew, running to him for every penny, getting ourselves deeper and deeper into his debt."

"What alternative is there?" Hugh inquired petulantly.

Leona sat down beside him and put her hand on his arm.

"Could you not get a position somewhere in France?" she asked.

"Who would employ me?" Hugh replied. "I am a good soldier, but I cannot see the French Army welcoming one of their late enemy occupiers with open arms."

"There must be something you could do," Leona insisted.

"Well, I am a connoisseur of wine and women," Hugh smiled.

Leona gave an exasperated little sigh and turned her head to look out of the window. It was always the same when she tried to make Hugh talk seriously, nevertheless she supposed that he was, in fact, speaking the truth. He had been trained for nothing except to be a soldier and a gentleman of leisure with money to burn in his pockets.

"I suppose I shall have to find work for myself," she said.

"You'll have to see what Lew says about that," Hugh replied.

"Lew! Lew! Lew!" she stormed at him suddenly. "Cannot you think for yourself? Have you not an idea in your head except what Lew puts there?"

"Now, Leona, be reasonable. Lew has been a good friend to us. If it were not for him I should be in prison or with a rope around my neck on the gallows."

"Yes, I know, I know," Leona agreed, "and I am indeed grateful for it. But one cannot live for ever on a debt of gratitude."

"That is what Lew wants you to do?" Hugh said

impishly, and with a sudden fire in her eyes Leona opened her lips to tell him what she thought of the idea, when there was a knock on the door.

The words died on her lips. She waited, expectantly, afraid of who stood outside, as Hugh said:

"Come in!"

"It must be Lew again," she thought. Every day he called and every day under the pretence that Hugh was too weak for long visits or for a discussion of any sort, she had managed to whisk him away without anything being said but a few conventional words of inquiry. But she had known in her heart it could not go on. Sooner or later he would have to face facts. She had a shrinking, horrible idea of what those facts would be.

Fortunately, Lew had been heavily engaged negotiating for another cargo. "A bargain to beat all bargains," he had told Hugh and there had been a triumphant smile on his lips when he left the room. Leona guessed he liked nothing better than the haggling, bullying and browbeating with which he had driven a very hard bargain so far as his side of the deal was concerned.

"*Entrez!*" Hugh called, changing to French as his first invitation to someone outside had not been answered.

The door opened and the landlord stood there—a stout, red-faced man who was obviously catching his breath after climbing the stairs.

"There is a lady to see you, *M'sieur*," he said in his thick *patois* which was rather difficult to understand.

"A lady!" Leona exclaimed. "There must be some mistake."

"*Non, non, Ma'm'selle. C'est vrai. Une grande dame qui demande M'sieur.*"

"*Une grande dame!*" Leona repeated. "Who on earth can she be, Hughie?"

"I have not the slightest idea," he replied. "There must be some mistake. But ask the lady to come up. At any rate it will relieve the monotony of sitting in this damned bedroom with nothing to do."

In her careful French Leona asked the landlord to request the lady to honour them by ascending the stairs. He nodded and shutting the door went heavily down the old, wooden steps which creaked ominously beneath his weight.

"Who can she be?" Leona questioned.

"She might be my fairy godmother for all I know," Hugh replied. "If you ask me she's some fancy mort of Lew's. That bird-witted old fool of a landlord would not know a lady of quality from a bit of muslin."

"I am sure you are right there," Leona said, glad to see Hugh so bright and interested.

She had been afraid at one time that his wound would inflict him with melancholy, for the pain had made him bad tempered and he seemed listless and uninterested in anything.

"Here she comes," Leona said, for her quick ears had caught the sound of light footsteps and of what she thought was a rustle of silk.

There came a light knock on the door.

"Entrez!" Leona said, crossing towards the door.

It was flung open before she could reach it, to reveal a vision such as she had never anticipated in her wildest imagination. A woman stood there dressed in the height of fashion. She was a brunette with dark, flashing eyes, very red lips and a sweet smile that was somehow at variance with the extreme fashionableness of her appearance.

She wore a gown of finest silk which clung to her figure in the most outrageously revealing fashion, showing to anyone who was interested that it was a very full but extremely shapely figure. Over it she wore a cloak of satin, trimmed with elegant embroidery, of the brighest shade of emerald, and there were emerald plumes upon her high, pointed bonnet which was tied beneath her chin with ribbons of the same colour.

As if this were not sufficient, her jewels were fabulous. She sported a diamond and emerald necklace, which sparkled and glittered in the sunshine, and long ear-rings which were quite dazzling as she turned her head with the eagerness and quickness of a brilliantly coloured bird.

She stood for a moment in the doorway looking at Leona and then, before either of them could speak, Hugh, from the window, gave an exclamation.

"Yvette!" he cried.

There was a little scream from the vision; then, impetuous and rapturous, she ran forward leaving a whiff of expensive perfume on the air as she passed Leona, to fling herself at Hugh, her arms round his neck, her cheek pressed against his.

"Mon cher! My Hugh! My very, very dear! I heard you were wounded. It is true! *Oh, mon pauvre brave!* But how did it happen?"

"Yvette! But . . . but what are you doing here?" Hugh stammered. "How did you find me? Who told you?"

For a moment both their voices merged together incoherently, both talking so quickly that it was impossible to differentiate one sentence from another. Until, finally, Yvette took her arms from around Hugh's neck and straightening her bonnet, which had become disarranged in the excitement, said in a very different voice, cold and hostile:

"And who is this?"

She pointed at Leona as she spoke and Hugh gave a guffaw of laughter.

"Still jealous! Now, is that not like you, Yvette, to start asking questions before you have answered one of mine?"

"Who is she? I ask," Yvette replied with a little stamp of her foot.

"I am Leona Ruckley, at your service, Madam," Leona said, dropping a polite curtsy.

"My sister," Hughie laughed. "Does that satisfy you?"

"*Ta soeur!* Your sister!" Yvette exclaimed in a voice which was very different from her tone of a second before. "*Mais, je suis enchantée, Mademoiselle.* Your brother and I are old friends."

"I thought you must be," Leona answered but without sarcasm.

"Old friends! That is a good description if ever there was one!" Hugh said. "But, tell me, Yvette, tell me quickly. Why are you here?"

In answer Yvette sank down in a chair beside him and clasped her hands together as if in a sudden ecstasy.

"I cannot believe that it is true; that you are here! Here!" she said. "And I was just about to leave for England to find you."

"To find me?" Hugh queried, bending forward in his chair. "Yvette, do you mean? . . ."

Yvette nodded, her black curls bobbing on each side of her big, eloquent eyes.

"*Oui, c'est vrai!* Edouard is dead. I am a widow, Hugh, and, as I promised, I have come to find you."

"By all that is wonderful!" Hugh exclaimed. "And there was I believing he would live for ever."

"He was taken ill three months ago and the physicians, even then, held out little hope of his recovery," Yvette said. "But I was afraid to write, afraid unless our hopes were raised only to be dashed again."

"And now it is true; you are free," Hugh cried.

"Yes, free," she nodded.

Leona stood looking from one to the other in amazement. Why had Hugh not mentioned this woman with whom he seemed so intimate? she wondered. And then she realized that Hugh had, in fact, never spoken to her of his friends. Always he had treated her as a child—a child old enough to run the castle, to do all the things that bored him, but a child who was not old enough for him to talk with intimately concerning his own affairs or of what had happened while he was abroad.

Now, with a little smile, he realized she was watching and he held out his hand to her.

"Come here, Leona," he said. "Congratulate me, for I am the happiest and luckiest man in the world."

"You mean that . . . you are going to be . . . married?" Leona asked in a very small voice.

"Just that," Hugh answered, "to someone I have loved for a very long time. How long is it, Yvette?"

"Tiens! Do not speak of those years," she exclaimed. "We have all the future together and the past is best forgotten. But Edouard never knew that I loved you. He died happily, believing that he was my only love."

She raised a tiny lace-edged handkerchief to the corner of her eye.

" 'You have been a good wife, Yvette,' he said to me a little before he breathed his last. 'That is why I have left you everything—all I possess'."

"Great heavens!" Hugh ejaculated. "I thought that son of his would have inherited."

"Pierre also is dead," Yvette said. "He died fighting a duel six months after you left for England. He was always wild and dissolute and I think in his heart Edouard never trusted him."

"Then you are a woman of great wealth," Hugh said with a sudden serious note in his voice.

"Too much money," Yvette said lightly. "Too much for one woman to look after. That is why I need you, Hugh, to help me with my estates near Paris and Edouard's possessions in South America. We must go and visit them."

Hugh was silent for a moment and then he said:

"I suppose you realize that I have nothing, not a penny, and I am also an exile from my own country?"

"Oui, oui," Yvette said impatiently. "Mister Quayle told me what had happened, but it is not of consequence. I

want you to live in France. I am not interested in England."

Hugh did not speak, and she went on:

"*Oo, là, là!* Do not pull such a long face. I know what you are thinking—that you do not like your wife to have all the money while you have nothing. Englishmen are so stupid. A Frenchman would be delighted. What does it signify? I have enough for two—more than enough. Forget the money. Let us only be thankful that we can be together at last."

"Do you really mean that?" Hugh asked, and lifting her hand to his lips, he kissed it.

"He loves her," Leona thought, and knew it was the truth by the look in Hugh's eyes, the sudden quiver of his mouth and by the softness in his whole expression that she had never seen there before. There was indeed no doubt that he loved this vivacious little Frenchwoman and that she loved him.

"If you are sure you do not mind having a penniless beggar for a husband," Hugh said with a humility that Leona would not have expected of him.

"*Mon Dieu!* I only know one thing," Yvette answered. "If you will not marry me, then I shall be a widow for the rest of my life."

They gazed for a moment into each other's eyes, then Hugh drew a deep breath and kissed Yvette's hand once again.

"*Mon chéri!*" she murmured with a little catch in her voice. "I never thought to be so happy again."

Leona suddenly realized that she was *de trop* but she had been almost mesmerized by the scene enacted before her. It had all taken place so swiftly, so quickly, and now, with a sudden consciousness that she was not wanted, she would have turned towards the door had not Hugh put out his hand to stop her going.

"Leona!" he said. "Leona is here with me."

There was a moment's pause and then Yvette said with a quite obvious hesitation:

"Your sister must, of course . . . er . . . be found somewhere to live."

"Suppose I have a suggestion to make there?" a voice said from the doorway.

Leona turned and saw who stood there, with a little shiver of dislike. She wondered how much he had overheard. It would be like Lew Quayle, she thought, to have followed the Frenchwoman up the stairs and to have listened so that he could be acquainted with all that was going on.

"Why, Lew!" Hugh exclaimed with a genuine smile of welcome on his lips. "Come in! You could not arrive at a more auspicious moment. You have already met Madame Dupont, I think?"

"We are, indeed, acquainted," Lew answered, bowing.

"Yes, indeed!" Madame Dupont exclaimed. "I met this so charming gentleman at the quay-side when I was making inquiries about a ship to carry me to England. He asked if he could assist me and I told him that I desired to travel to Newhaven because I understood that Sir Hugh Ruckley of Ruckley Castle lived not so many miles from there."

She smiled at Hugh.

"He then told me that there was no need for me to cross the Channel; that you were here, here in Dieppe!"

"It was a pleasure to be of service, *Madame*," Lew said. "And now perhaps I could proffer more assistance."

"And what is that?" the Frenchwoman inquired.

"It is that I should take your future sister-in-law off your hands."

He glanced at Leona as he spoke, saw her stiffen and her face whiten. And then, before she could speak, went on:

"Hugh, I have the honour to request from you the hand of your sister in marriage."

Madame Dupont clapped her hands together.

"*Splendide!*" she exclaimed. "What could be better than we should both be married? It makes everything so simple."

"I will not marry him! You know that, Hughie," Leona said, going to Hugh's side and speaking in a low voice tremulous with emotion.

He smiled up at her from his chair.

"But, Leona, what else is there you can do?"

"She is shy, *la pauvre petite*," Madame Dupont interposed. "Monsieur Quayle, you have embarrassed *Mademoiselle* by asking for her hand so openly. But, of course, she would be glad to marry a charming upstanding man like yourself—so elegant, such address."

She glanced at him from under her dark eyelashes, a little flirtatious smile at the corner of her lips. Then, turning to Leona, she went on:

"*Monsieur* is fortunate too—*ma cherie*—for you are very attractive."

"Hughie, I will not marry him," Leona said, a note of desperation in her voice.

"But what else can you do?" Madame Dupont inquired. "Hugh has said you have no money, no dowry. Do you not understand it is very hard to find a husband when you have nothing to offer but yourself—however charming you may be. And, *enfin!* All girls want to be married. To coiffer St. Catherine is, indeed, a tragedy."

"I would rather be an old maid than marry Mister Quayle," Leona said.

"Now, Leona, be sensible," Hugh begged. "You know the situation."

"Exactly!" Lew Quayle said with an unpleasant smile at the corner of his lips. "Hugh has so much common sense, that is what I have always admired about him. He knows that a debt of seven or is it eight thousands pounds?—I have not looked it up just recently—is something which cannot be dismissed with the flick of an eyebrow or, should I say, by a foolish fancy in a very pretty head."

"Hughie will pay you back in time——" Leona began to say, but was interrupted by Madame Dupont.

"Eight thousand pounds!" she exclaimed. "How much is that in francs? Why, a fortune! Is that what Hugh owes you?"

"It is, indeed, *Madame*," Lew Quayle replied, addressing himself to her. "But as I think I have really explained before, it is a debt which I am prepared to wipe away at the stroke of a pen, to sign away on the day I write my name on a marriage certificate."

"That is a generous gesture, *Monsieur*."

"One that I am willing, indeed anxious to make," Lew Quayle said.

Madame Dupont put her bejewelled fingers on his arm.

"*Hélas!* It would be a pity if your generosity was not appreciated or accepted."

"It would, indeed," he sighed. "Can I rely on your assistance, *Madame?*"

"You can, *Monsieur*," she answered. She turned to Hugh. "*Mon chéri*, make your little sister see sense. This "*homme du monde*" is charming and obviously very rich. Where would she get a better offer? Certainly not here in France."

"I have told you I wish to marry no-one," Leona said, only to realize that no-one was listening to her, and with a sense of utter despair she realized her own impotence.

What could she do? What could she say against these three people who were planning her future with an utter disregard for her own feelings in the matter?

"You could be married here in Dieppe," she heard Madame Dupont say, "either the day before or the day after Hugh and I are wed. Our wedding must take place in a Catholic church, but doubtless we could find a priest of your own religion who would marry you."

"No! No!" Leona said with such violence that they instinctively turned towards her. "If I am to be married, I shall be married at Alfriston in the church where I was christened, the church where my father and mother are buried."

"Very well." It was Lew who spoke and she knew by the odious smile of triumph on his lips that he knew he had triumphed. "We will be married at Alfriston and, if it please you, we will spend our honeymoon in the Castle."

"Oh, the Castle!" Hugh said vaguely, as if he had just remembered it. "Why, I had best give it to you, Lew, for it seems as if I shall never be able to go there again."

"I will take it as a wedding gift," Lew said. "It will be useful so long as I wish to use it for the little transactions in which you and I have been interested. And when they no longer concern me, I might become respectable—Mister Lew Quayle of Ruckley Castle! It sounds almost pompous, do you not think?"

Leona bit her lips in an effort not to scream out at him. She saw now exactly what he was planning. She had always suspected that he was a snob and a social climber. She had known that the mystery and gossip over his birth was something he could never forget and never forgive. It was true enough that married to her, as owner of Ruckley Castle, he could have a very different position in the county. Memories were short and if, as he said, he did turn respectable, people would very soon forget.

"That is settled then," Lew said. "Leona and I will sail tomorrow night."

"But how will you go?" Hugh asked.

"In the cutter, of course. I have a cargo to drop in a very safe place north of Beachy Head. It will be a little more expensive to get it to London but it is safe and that matters for the moment more than anything else. Lord Chard's troops will be looking for me, but not where I shall be landing, and Leona with me."

"Do you think she will be safe?" Hugh asked with

a sudden anxiety, as if the dangers of such a trip had unexpectedly presented themselves to him.

"She will always be safe with me," Lew said boastfully. "And you can be sure of one thing, Hugh. I shall never lose her nor let her escape me."

He was speaking to *her* now, Leona knew that. She did not look at him as he bowed to Madame Dupont and kissed her hand, and then took her own cold fingers in his.

"So it is all arranged," he said in a low voice.

She did not answer, her head was downcast, and now he put his hand under her chin and tilted her face upwards. For a moment she resisted him and then she opened her eyes and looked him straight in the face.

He must have seen the hatred and known, too, how frightened she was, for her whole body was quivering beneath his touch. He laughed gently, his lips curling mockingly, but there was a fire in his eyes which told her all too clearly that her very resistance excited him.

He was a man who must conquer, must win, whatever the odds against him. And she knew she could expect no mercy from him, nothing but violence, and his passion would never be satisfied until she had surrendered herself and her will to him completely and absolutely.

"We sail tomorrow night," he said.

"If I am not dead by then," she answered.

He laughed at that.

"And if you are," he said. "I will fetch you back from beyond the grave, just as I shall find you wherever you may hide from me."

There was a warning underlying the lightness of his words and she knew that he spoke in all seriousness. She heard him leave the room and go down the rickety stairs and then, turning blindly, sought the sanctuary of her own bedroom.

She flung herself down on the bed, hiding her face in the pillow, trying to think, trying to find some tiny way of escape, anything, anything, so long as she need not become the wife of Lew Quayle. But she knew there was nothing she could do and, try as she would, her brain going round and round in circles, she could see no loophole of escape.

It was as if Hugh sensed what she was feeling and thinking and when Madame Dupont had gone he called her from the other room. She went to him and finding him pale and exhausted after so much excitement, assisted him into bed. And when he was comfortable against the pillow he put out his hand and took hers.

"Listen, Leona," he said. "I want to talk with you. I know you think I am being hard, perhaps cruel, in forcing you to marry Lew. But there is nothing else we can do— nothing! For one thing, you must be protected. There must be a man in your life to take care of you."

"Why cannot I live at the Castle alone?" Leona interrupted.

"My dear, you know it is impossible," Hugh replied. "It was bad enough when you were a child, but now you are a woman, do you think you would have one minute's peace or security alone there with only the servants?"

Leona shut her eyes. This was something she could not argue against because she knew it was the truth. Would Lew leave her alone? Might not other men look on her as a light woman, an easy prey, if she had no protection other than old Bramwell, who was almost senile?

She swallowed and was silent and Hugh, seeing he had the advantage, went on:

"And apart from your own security, there is that debt. Eight thousand pounds, Leona! 'Tis bad enough to go to Yvette penniless, but to ask her for such a sum the moment we are married is impossible. And if you will not wed him, make sure of one thing. Lew will demand his pound of flesh. He is like that—a devil if he is crossed."

Leona shuddered.

"That is what he seems to me," she said in a low voice. "A devil! And yet you would commit me to his keeping."

"He loves you," Hugh said simply. "You will be able to alter him, to make him do as you wish. Try to like him a bit, Leona. It will not be so hard then."

She did not answer him. She could not because of the lump in her throat, and he went on:

"If you only knew what Yvette suffered. Her husband was a monster indeed. He was a miser for one thing— would never give her a penny of money she could spend if he could help it. And he was so jealous that if she so much as smiled at a beggar he would accuse her of being unfaithful to him.

"She hated him—in fact, I never met anyone who did not. And yet she managed to make it appear to the world as if they dealt together most amicably. They know a thing or two, these Frenchwomen. And, most of all, they are well aware which side their bread is buttered. Make the best of Lew. You might find a worse husband, and as he is crazed about you he will be generous enough."

Still Leona did not speak and Hugh said:

"It is no use, Leona. I know you are trying to find a way out of this, but there is not one. Do you hear me? There is not one! So I want you to promise me something."

"What is that?" Leona inquired.

"I want you to promise me, by all that you hold sacred, that you will not try to run away from Lew; that you will marry him and help both yourself and me! It is the only way for both of us, Leona, there is not another. Promise me!"

Leona shut her eyes. She knew that this was the signing of her own death warrant if she promised. Hugh knew her well enough to know that she would keep her word, whatever the cost to herself.

She knew in that moment at the back of her mind there had lingered just the suspicion of a hope that something might happen to save her, up to the very last moment. That was why, apart from anything else, she had wished to go to England. She knew deep within her heart was the memory that Lord Chard was in England.

"Promise me!" Hugh said insistently.

It was hopeless! There was nothing for it!

"I . . . promise . . . you," she said dully.

"Promise on the memory of Father and Mother and your love for them," Hugh insisted.

"I . . . promise," Leona said again.

He let go of her hands and let his head fall back on the pillow. Leona sat looking out at the sea. It was turning deep sapphire blue in the evening light, shading to emerald where the horizon joined the sky.

Over there was England! And there, too, was the man she loved, to whom her heart had gone out involuntarily but irrevocably. It was his—his forever, whether he knew it or not.

Leona closed her eyes so that she could no longer gaze at the sea, but she knew that it was there, just as she knew that her love for Lord Chard was there, however she might try to deny it.

She rose suddenly to her feet and went towards the door.

"Where are you going?" Hugh asked.

"I am going for a walk," Leona said almost fiercely. "I want to get some air. I want to get away from my own thoughts. Do not be afraid. I shall not run away. I have given you my promise."

She repeated the same words in her heart the following day as Madame Dupont made plans to take Hugh by coach to her chateau near Paris.

"We must leave soon after noon," she said, "if we are to reach Amiens where we will stay the first night. We must do the journey in easy stages for Hugh's sake."

"Yes, of course," Leona agreed.

"It will mean that you will have a few hours alone here before Mister Quayle takes you on board," Madame Dupont said. "You will be all right?"

Leona knew only too well what the question implied.

"I shall be quite all right and I shall be here when Mister Quayle comes for me," she said steadily.

Madame Dupont put an affectionate arm round her shoulders.

"You are sensible, *ma petite*," she said. "Do not worry, a clever woman can soon make a man do what she wants. It is just a question of being clever enough."

"Then I am afraid I shall not qualify for that adjective," Leona said.

"Oh, but you will," Madame Dupont protested. "Besides, it is easy for you. Mister Quayle is in love. Only a man who is in love could be so quixotic as to cancel a debt of eight thousand pounds.

"With me, it was different. My husband married me because he wanted an heir. He had only one son—a rakish, dissolute fellow—and he determined when he was quite old to start another family. He was not in love with me. He just wanted someone young and healthy to breed children which would bear his name. Unfortunately, I was not able to do as he wished."

"Poor *Madame!*" Leona said with a sudden sympathy.

"Oh, do not be sorry for me," Yvette Dupont replied. "I have your brother now. That is all I want of life. It is something I thought I would never get. When Hugh went away I thought I would die, I was so unhappy. And yet there was nothing—*qui vaille*—I could do."

She gave a deep sigh, as if the memory of her unhappiness still had the power to hurt her.

"Hugh was billeted for a little while in our chateau; did he tell you that?"

"No, he told me nothing," Leona said.

"That was how we met," Yvette explained. "He and several other officers of the occupying armies of the Duke of Wellington stayed with us. They behaved very correctly and were very polite. But as soon as I saw Hugh there was something—*comment dites-vous*—a feeling between us, something which seemed to vibrate when we were close to each other. . . ."

She clasped her hands together as if the thought was ecstatic.

"*Hélas*. We had snatched moments of happiness," she continued, "and then Hugh went back to England and I was alone . . . with my husband."

There was the echo of tragedy in Yvette's gay voice and impulsively Leona kissed her.

"It is all over now," she said, "and I am so glad that Hughie has you to look after him. You must not let him get into bad ways again. I know now that he gambled only because he was unhappy."

"I will let you into a secret," Yvette Dupont said. "I shall keep him busy. A man who is busy has no time for mischief, always remember that, *ma chérie*."

Everything that could be done to make Hugh's journey comfortable and without strain was planned by Yvette. There were special cushions in the carriage, footrests, rugs, flasks of brandy, bottles of Cologne and a case of other medicines which Yvette swore had been efficacious in such cases in the past.

And when, finally, she came to collect Hugh, she brought a leather trunk with her.

"This is for you," she said to Leona. "A wedding present, *ma petite*, so that you shall not go to your new husband empty-handed and without a trousseau."

Leona opened the trunk. Inside there were gowns, shawls and bonnets, all in the latest fashion.

"*Et voilà*, there was not time to have them made to your measurements," Yvette explained. "But I feel sure they will fit you, with but a stitch here and there."

"But how kind of you!" Leona exclaimed.

"*Ce n'est rien*. Just a little present from your future sister-in-law, who is going to be very happy, as she hopes you will be."

"Thank you," Leona answered dully, her first pleasure at seeing the pretty things being damped in contemplation of who would see her wearing them and for whose delectation they had been given.

"What will be the most useful," Yvette went on practically, "is the cape in which you must travel. I am afraid this is not new, but one of my own. But I could not let you cross the sea without it."

She drew it from the trunk and Leona saw it was,

indeed, a magnificent present. Of dark blue velvet, it was edged with a soft grey fur down both sides of the front, and fur also framed the hood which could be drawn over the hair.

"It will be cold at sea," Yvette said with a shiver, "and this cloak is what I bought to wear myself when crossing the Channel. *Dieu merci*, now that Hugh is here in Dieppe, I shall not need it."

"Thank you! Thank you, indeed!" Leona cried. "You are quite certain that you can spare it?"

"Quite certain," Yvette replied.

She bent and kissed Leona, then called to the men to come upstairs and carry Hugh from his own room down to the carriage.

"I can walk," Hugh protested.

"*Quelle idée!*" Yvette exclaimed. "My footmen will carry you. The sudden exertion, the steepness of the stairs, might prove too much for you after you have been in bed so long. Do as I say. When you get home you can try your legs as much as you please."

Protestingly, Hugh agreed, and as the men mounted the stair, Leona came from her own room into his and put her arms around him.

"Good-bye, Hughie!" she said. "I pray that you will be very happy—I shall . . . miss you so . . . much!"

Her voice broke on the words.

"You will write to me, will you not?" Hugh said. "Tell me about your marriage and see that Lew does not get captured bringing in one of those cargoes. They have not been able to pin anything on him yet, but remember he is a marked man."

"I shall not forget," Leona said tonelessly.

"Good-bye, then," Hugh said, kissing her on the cheek, but his eyes turned towards Yvette who was waiting by the door.

As the carriage drove away Leona stood in the roadway waving forlornly. He had gone. Her only relative—going out of her life for ever. It was doubtful whether she would ever see him again.

She went upstairs and started packing a few small things that she possessed in the trunk which Yvette had given her. She had not the heart or the interest to change into one of her new gowns but kept on the dress she had made herself for a few shillings. And because it was her own, her very own, it meant more than the grand, expensive gowns that her future sister-in-law had so kindly contributed towards her trousseau.

But the cloak was useful. It was warm and though the day had been hot she knew the sea only too well to realize that there would be a night breeze which would penetrate through the thickest of clothing.

Time drew on. Still she waited. The sun was sinking slowly, throwing a golden gleam over the sea. The landlord brought her something to eat but though she tried to swallow a morsel or two, she found it almost impossible.

She was waiting! Waiting as a prisoner must have waited since time immemorial, for the sound of the gaoler turning a key in the prison door.

Still Lew did not come and Leona began to wonder if he had forgotten her, and a wild hope arose in her heart that perhaps, after all, he had regretted his contract and would sail to England, leaving her behind.

And then, when it was nearly dark, she heard him! Heard his arrogant voice speaking below to the landlord, heard his footsteps coming up the stairs. At the very first sound of him she felt every nerve in her body quiver and tremble and her heart begin to beat in a frightened manner, her lips suddenly become dry.

He was coming for her! The man she was to marry. The man who had sworn she would never escape him. Up, up the stairs came his footsteps, and now he flung open the door with an arrogant gesture as if he heralded his own arrival.

He was well dressed, as always, with a high cravat and a cape hanging from his shoulders, held by a gold chain, and his high, beaver hat was set at an angle on his head. And she had forgotten—it seemed to her—how tall and broad he was and how frightening in his very strength and arrogance.

"Are you ready?" he inquired, and try as she would she could not answer him.

"Obviously my bride-to-be is overjoyed to see me," he said. "But we must not expect too much enthusiasm too quickly. That will come when I have taught you, my dear Leona, how to love—something which apparently has been most regrettably omitted from your education so far."

He had been drinking, she thought; celebrating, perhaps, his approaching marriage. And now, as he crossed the room towards her, the light of the candle showed her that his face was a little flushed, his eyes glittering dangerously.

"Your servant, Madam."

He bowed in an exaggerated manner and she knew he was taunting her.

"Is it time to leave?" she asked, striving to make her voice cool and calm, but succeeding only in sounding hesitant and afraid.

"Yes, it is time to leave," he echoed. "Are you not excited at the thought of seeing England again? Of being at Ruckley? Once your own home—now the Castle you are to share with me, its new owner!"

Leona drew a deep breath and clenched her fingers together. She guessed that he was trying to make her lose her temper, but she was determined to say or do nothing which might excite him further.

"My trunk is ready," she said with a little gesture towards where it lay on the floor. "Shall we not . . . go?"

"All in good time," he answered. "You have not greeted me very warmly so far."

"I was but thinking of the time," Leona said. "We must catch the . . . tide, must we . . . not?"

He laughed softly and she knew that he understood how she was trying to pacify him, and was playing with her as a cat plays with a mouse.

"So practical! So sensible!" he said. "What a useful wife I shall have. I really believe that you will be worth it—worth the eight thousand pounds I have paid for you."

Leona felt, as he spoke, as if he had slapped her across her face. The insult was almost more than she could bear. Yet still she forced herself to ignore it.

"We must go," she said. "Perhaps you can send a man for my trunk."

She would have moved past him but even as she took the step forward she knew it had been a mistake. His arms went out and he caught her to him, pulling her close into his embrace, laughing above her head as he did so, as a man might laugh at the flutterings of a caged bird struggling to be free.

"A kiss before we go," he said. "Not that there will not be time for many more kisses when we reach England. Are you not excited at the thought of tomorrow night, when you will bear my name, when we will lie together in the bridal chamber at Ruckley and henceforth have no secrets from each other?"

She tried to be still and acquiescent but it was impossible. Now she was fighting him, beating her hands against his chest, striving to be free from the great arms which seemed to crush her breathless with their strength.

"Let me . . . go!"

It was the cry of a child who is frightened of the dark. "Please . . . let me go!"

And then her voice was lost beneath the pressure of his lips—hot, devouring, possessive lips, which held her utterly captive, sapping her strength as they silenced her protests.

She thought then she was drowning, drowning in a dark sea from which no-one could save her. But when she thought she must reach unconsciousness, when she had reached such depths of despair and horror that she believed she could suffer no more, he released her.

"There is no time now," he said in a voice thickened with passion. "And, as you have said, the tide will not wait."

His lips were against hers for one more horrifying moment, before he pushed her roughly from him as if she had deliberately enticed his desire.

She staggered at suddenly being free, steadied herself with a hand against the wall until one glance at his face, distorted by lust and passion, sent her hurrying ahead of him down the stairs.

From behind he called for someone to carry down her trunk. She reached the pavement and felt the cool evening air on her cheeks. For one moment she thought of running straight ahead of her, of plunging into the sea which lapped against the harbour side; of dying rather than suffering any more.

And then she remembered her promise, her solemn promise, by all that was sacred, to Hugh. She must marry Lew! There was nothing else she could do about it.

12

The men were already at their oars when Leona and Lew Quayle reached the cutter, guided there by a ragged urchin carrying a flaming torch. A man with a lantern hurried forward at their approach.

"Dinna want to miss th' tide, Mister Quayle," he said to Lew.

"We shall not miss it," Lew replied airily.

The man with the lantern looked at Leona curiously and then, when they reached the ship and he saw she was going aboard, he muttered something indistinct beneath his breath. One of the oarsmen was, however, not so discreet.

"Womin in a ship n'er brought aught but bad fortune," he growled.

"Your bad fortune will be that you will be left ashore if I have another word out of you," Lew snapped at him angrily, and taking Leona's hand to help her step down from the quayside into the cutter, he added:

"My future wife will bring us all good fortune. Let me present you, gentlemen, to Miss Leona Ruckley of Ruckley Castle, where, in future, I shall be living."

In the swinging light of the lantern Leona saw their faces—the expression of astonishment in some, the glint of admiration in others, and in one or two she suspected there was a look of pity, but she could not be sure.

Without saying anything, she turned and made her way towards the cabin. Lew took the lantern from the man standing above him on the quay and followed behind her so that when she entered through the narrow door she could see the cabin piled once again with merchandise of every description. But she realized something else had been added to it—a couch placed against the wall near to the door and covered with satin cushions.

It was a gaudy, rather flamboyant object which would

have been more at home—and doubtless had been—in one of the many disreputable houses along the quayside which catered for sailors with money to spend, rather than ornamenting the cabin of a ship.

Lew held the lantern high above it.

"You see, I thought of your comfort," he said.

"Thank you," Leona said simply.

They were the first words she had spoken to him since they left the lodgings.

"If I have time during the crossing to share it with you, I will," he said tauntingly. "You would like that, would you not, my loving bride?"

She did not answer and he laughed again softly but, it seemed to her, menacingly. Then, hanging the lantern on a hook on one of the rafters, he went from the cabin and she heard him outside on the deck giving orders to cast off.

"Double your pace, boys, and I'll double your pay," he said. "There'll be something worth having for all of us at the end of this trip."

The creak and splash of the oars and the sudden swinging of the lantern told Leona that they were moving away from the shore. Already the ship was beginning to rock a little and because there was nothing else she could do, she sat down on the couch, feeling the gaudy cushions give beneath her body and hating them for what they signified.

She loosened her cloak which she had held clutched around her tightly against the chill of the evening winds, and thrust back the hood from off her hair, instinctively pushing her curls into position but listening all the time to what was happening outside.

Lew was guiding them out of the harbour.

"Starboard five points!" she heard him say to the man at the tiller. "Ten points! You fool! There's a sandbank here!"

The oarsmen had begun to talk amongst themselves. It was hard to distinguish what they were saying, but she had a feeling that they were talking about herself and about Lew's intended marriage.

Wearily she thought of the gossip it would cause in the neighbourhood. Lew was both feared and hated. Her father had been loved. The people at Alfriston and on the estate would be loath to see a man they considered an upstart and an evil influence living at Ruckley.

She wondered, too, what it would be like to see Lew

sitting in her father's chair, handling precious possessions that had been her mother's, giving the orders to old Bramwell and perhaps cursing him for being slow and inefficient.

These were just some of the minor pinpricks she would have to endure, and endure them without complaint. She wondered how long it took for one to become numb, utterly indifferent to anything that happened to one's body. She wondered, too, if her heart and mind could ever be subdued and the last vestige of rebellion crushed ruthlessly and utterly.

She was sitting with a blind look in her eyes and her hands folded as if in prayer, when Lew came back into the cabin. The door had been slightly ajar. Now he closed it and she glanced at him, trying to seem indifferent but knowing that every nerve in her body was tense, that her eyes widened with fear.

"We are out to sea," he said briefly.

He crossed the cabin and sat down beside her, sprawling back against the cushions, watching her as she moved as far away from him as she was able to do.

"Comfortable?" he asked at last, a smile on his lips.

"Yes . . . thank you," she replied. "It was . . . kind of you to think of finding me . . . something to . . . sit on."

It was an effort to say the words but she felt that courtesy demanded them.

"Kind, indeed!" Lew said. " 'Tis the first time you have accused me of that. Well, we are on our way home. That was what you wanted, was it not?"

"How long will it take us?" Leona asked, knowing he was watching her, feeling that silence between them was dangerous.

"Not more than three hours," he answered. "Everything is in our favour. When we have landed the cargo we shall get a carriage and drive home, you and I. We might stop at the Vicarage and tell the old fool to be ready to marry us later in the day."

Leona winced at his description of the Vicar. He was an old man, it was true, but she was fond of him for he had been a friend of both father and mother.

"Is there . . . any need . . . for hurry?" she asked a little tremulously.

"That is for you to say," he replied. "For I intend to sleep at Ruckley tomorrow night."

His eyes were on her lips and she turned her head

away, understanding all too well the innuendo behind his words.

"Come here," he said suddenly.

She glanced at him wonderingly and saw his hand outstretched.

"Come nearer," he commanded. "I am tired of you sitting there looking like a suffering saint, behaving as if I was so much pitch with which you were afraid to soil your fingers. You're going to be my wife, my girl. The sooner you get used to me, the better. Come here, I say!"

Leona would have started to her feet but he reached forward and taking her hand, dragged her towards him.

She tried to resist him, pulling against his great strength. Slowly, irresistibly, he drew her nearer and nearer to him.

"You have to be taught to obey," he said, his lips still smiling. "That is what you will promise in the marriage service and I shall keep you to it, make no mistake about that. Come nearer, I say! Nearer!"

She was obeying him because she could do nothing else about it. He was pulling her across the couch, until now he had only to release her wrist, slip his arm around her waist and her head was against his shoulder.

"There, that is more comfortable," he said. And now his other hand shot up to clasp the warm, rounded column of her throat, with its little pulse beating madly in fear beneath the whiteness of her skin.

"Surely . . . surely you should be . . . outside seeing where . . . we are going?" Leona panted, the words coming with difficulty between her frightened lips.

"The men know the way," he answered. "They know, too, that I'm more pleasantly engaged. Are you really so anxious to be rid of me?"

The question mocked her and now his hand was turning her face up to his.

"Please . . . please, Lew . . ." she pleaded.

She had meant to say nothing, to suffer in silence, but somehow his proximity was too horrible to be borne.

"Please, Lew," he mocked. "Please, Lew, what? Will you plead with me tonight and every night to let you off your just payment? Oh, no! You must be a sport! You must pay up, and willingly. Eight thousand pounds! 'Tis a lot of money, my pretty."

His fingers were caressing her and she felt mesmerized by the pressure of them. Her eyes were on his face, wide open with terror, like the eyes of an animal that has been caught in a trap and from which it already knows there is no escape.

"There must be no cheating," he said. "You will pay, my dear, as long as I want you to do so. No cries of 'please, Lew', will prevent me from taking my just dues."

He bent forward suddenly and kissed her. His breath smelt of spirits but his hands held her like a vice and she could not move away from the greediness of his mouth. She could only suffer until he threw himself back again on the cushions without releasing his grip of her.

"Damn you!" he said. "You would freeze the very veins of a man to ice. But I will teach you to love me, as I have taught better women than you. In time you will cry out for my kisses and then, perhaps, I shall have found somebody warmer and more accommodating."

He paused for a moment and then shook her as a dog might shake a rat.

"But until I tire of you," he said, "you will give me what I want and give it me willingly—do you hear? Answer me! Do you hear?"

He waited for her reply and it came between lips that were dry and pale.

"I . . . I hear," Leona whispered.

"Then do not forget it," Lew said. "Do not forget that you will be Mrs. Quayle of Ruckley Castle! Mrs. Quayle! My wife! The woman who belongs to me!"

He shook her again and then, as if her very helplessness excited him, he started to fumble beneath her cloak at the bodice of her gown. She gave a little cry and tried to fight him off, but knew that in her weakness it was only a question of seconds before he obtained what he desired.

Then, as he was flinging her back against the cushions and she heard her gown tear beneath the roughness of his fingers, there came a cry from outside:

"Mister Quayle! Mister Quayle!"

It was a sound which brought Lew instantly to his feet. Without a word he released his hold on Leona and turned hurriedly towards the door, pulling it to let in, for a moment, a blast of fresh air. Then he closed it behind him.

"There's a gunboat! O'er there!"

Leona heard the words clearly, and Lew's command:

"Steer to port! Put the helm hard over! They may not have seen us."

Leona felt the ship swing on another tack. Then Lew's voice came again.

"Row, blast ye! Row for your lives! They've seen us!"

She could feel the ship move forward at a pace that she had never believed possible. The men were rowing and swearing softly at the same time.

"We're getting away from them!"

She heard the excitement in Lew's voice as he added:

"Keep it up, boys, we're gaining. We'll slip away in the darkness and they won't be able to follow us."

There was silence broken only by the grunts of the oarsmen, the rattle of the rowlocks, the splash in the water as the oars dipped and rose and dipped again.

"We're winning!"

There was relief in Lew's voice now, and then there was another cry:

"Look ye, Mister, t'port, t'port!"

"Another God-damned ship!"

She heard the fury in Lew's voice.

"Mebbe a merchantman," someone suggested.

"Nay, 'tis a man-o'-war!"

"Starboard! Starboard!" Lew commanded.

Then suddenly there was a world-shattering report, a great splash in the water and then somebody, who could have been little more than a boy, said quaveringly:

"They be a-firing at us."

"Keep rowing!" Lew shouted. "We'll be free of them yet. Keep rowing!"

There was another report, another splash, and the same young voice cried out:

"God in Heaven, save us! They've got th' range o' us right enough."

"Are your pistols primed?" Lew asked.

"Aye, aye, sir."

"Then as they come nearer be ready to shoot our way out of this."

There was another report. This time it seemed to Leona to be deafeningly near. Then faintly she heard a voice shouting:

"Heave to! In the name of His Majesty King George the Fourth, I command ye to heave to!"

"Keep rowing!" Lew said. "Keep on hard at it!"

He swung the boat again this time to startboard.

"We'll give them the slip yet," he said.

"There be another un, Mister. A gunboat. 'Tis a comin' up on us."

"Keep rowing!" Lew commanded, and Leona knew that now he was speaking between gritted teeth.

"Heave to, or we'll sink your ship!"

There was no mistaking the command this time. It was clear enough for everyone to hear.

"They're going to board us," Leona heard Lew say. "Be ready to fight for your lives. Remember what happens if you're caught—seven years or the gallows. If we've got to die we'll take the majority of them with us."

There was another explosion. This time Leona knew it had hit the stern of the cutter. She heard a man shriek in agony and then there was a fusilade of shot—some, she guessed, from the ship approaching them, some from the men in the cutter who had stopped rowing.

Amid all this pandemonium she heard Lew shouting orders. She rose unsteadily to her feet only to be flung violently to the floor as the boat must have collided with another vessel. She lay where she had fallen, too frightened to move. The noise outside was indescribable. The oaths and shrieks and the crying of someone in intolerable pain, rose above the noise of shot and the sudden clank of steel as if men were using the cutlasses which she had seen many of them wore at their waists.

Then suddenly the turmoil seemed to die away. The ship was rocking to and fro, bumping at it did so. Leona raised herself on one arm and as she did so the door of the cabin was flung open. She saw some strange faces staring at her in surprise and realized that they wore Naval uniform.

"Th' Lord save us!" one of them exclaimed. "If there bain't a female aboard!"

"Let's take 'er to the Cap'n," another man said.

He advanced towards Leona, put a hand under her arm to help her to her feet.

" 'Tis all over, Ma'am," he said. "You'll please accompany us aboard His Majesty's vessel *The Seahawk*."

"What . . . has happened?" Leona managed to ask.

"The Cap'n will explain that to you, Ma'am."

The man who had spoken to her and who appeared to be a Petty Officer, lifted the lantern down from its hook to hold it low on the ground to guide Leona through the cabin door. Outside she saw a scene of destruction which brought a cry of horror to her lips.

Men's bodies, sprawling in the grotesque position of death, were lying on the deck of the cutter. The water was seeping in at the stern and towering above them was a man o' war, a big ship with guns bristling out below the upper deck.

"Look sharp with that cargo," a voice shouted from above their heads.

"There's a lady 'ere, Sir," the Petty Officer replied.

"A lady! Good Lord! Whatever next?" was the ejaculation. "Send her up, Stevens!"

"Aye, aye, Sir! 'Tis a bit of a climb, Ma'am, but I daresay you can manage it," the Petty Officer said, and with his help Leona climbed up the rope ladder and over the gunwale into the man-o'-war.

It seemed to her there were scores of men moving about and then she saw that they were engaged in taking the wounded away from the cutter and laying them down on the other side of the deck. There was a little knot of officers at the far end of the ship, standing over one man; as she came aboard, they turned and she saw that amongst them was a man not in uniform but wearing a high-brimmed beaver hat and a long dark cloak.

She felt her heart give a sudden leap and she knew, even as he turned towards her, that somehow she had expected to find him here. She saw his face quicken and felt that she, too, in imagination had run towards him even though she had not moved.

"Leona! I had not dreamed that you would be aboard."

She tried to answer him but somehow the words would not come. Instead, she found her hands in his and stood there clinging to him as a drowning man might cling to his one hope of delivery.

"We fired on you! You might have been killed!" Lord Chard said, and she heard the note in his voice that she had longed for in her dreams.

She could only look up at him, her eyes shining with the unbelievable comfort of knowing that he was holding her hand, that she was safe. But still she could not speak; she could only look at him, her little face, framed in the fur of her hood, her eyes shining in the light which came from the ship's lantern in the mast above them.

A sudden cry from one of the wounded men recalled Lord Chard's attention to where they stood and to what was happening and he said quickly to Leona:

"Come, let me take you to the Captain's cabin."

He drew her down the deck to where, in the stern, a seaman opened the door of the deck cabin to let them enter. It was furnished simply but it seemed to Leona to be very warm and comforting, with its lanterns hanging from the rafters, comfortable chairs by an oak table and a bunk at the far end curtained with red hangings.

She crossed the cabin and sat down in the straight-backed armchair which Lord Chard held for her. And now at last she could see him; see how strong and safe and handsome he looked.

He laid his hat and cloak on a chair and turned towards her with an eagerness which was unmistakable.

"I cannot believe it is true," he said. "That you are here and safe. Tell me, where have you been? What has happened to you?"

Leona drew a deep breath. She realized that now she could find her voice there was so much to tell him. But at that moment there was a knock on the cabin door.

"Come in!" Lord Chard said automatically. His eyes were on Leona, watching her face and the movements of her lips.

"The Cap'n's compliments, Sir," the seaman said, "but they've found the man your Lordship was seeking. He's in a bad way, the surgeon says, and is asking for the lady."

"Asking for the lady?" Lord Chard said, as if he could hardly credit what he heard.

"Yes, indeed," another voice said, and the Captain came through the doorway and, seeing Leona, removed his cap and bowed a little awkwardly. "Forgive me, Ma'am, but I think it only right that you should know that Lew Quayle—for that, I believe, is the smuggler's name—wishes to see you. The surgeon says that there is not much time. He has been badly wounded."

"Then I must go to him," Leona said.

She rose to her feet and not looking at Lord Chard, but well aware that he followed her, allowed the Captain to lead the way across the deck and down the steep companionway to where, between decks, the wounded men were now being carried.

Lew was not with the others—he was in a cabin. It was an austere place with only a bunk on which the wounded man lay, but at least, Leona thought with a sudden compassion, he could die alone.

The surgeon was bending over him as the Captain held open the door for Leona to enter. Lew lay there with closed eyes and for a moment she thought he was already dead.

"He has been shot through the chest, Ma'am," the surgeon said. "His whole side is shattered. There is nothing I can do about it."

"Is he conscious?" Leona asked.

"He was," the surgeon replied, "and asking for you."

At the sound of Leona's voice Lew opened his eyes.

"Are you there, Leona?" he asked.

"Yes," Leona said. "I am here."

"And the Captain? Where's the damned Captain?" Lew said, and now his voice was stronger as if he forced it through his lips by a superhuman effort of will.

"I am here," the Captain said, moving towards the bunk. Then he added over his shoulder to Lord Chard: "Is there anything you wish to ask the man?"

"Not now," Lord Chard replied. "It is unnecessary."

"Are you the Captain?—the Captain of this ship?" Lew asked from the bunk, and Leona could see he was trying to focus his eyes.

"I am, indeed! Captain Dalgeish if you wish to know my name."

"Then, Captain Dalgeish," Lew said, "I demand that you marry me here and now to this lady, as you are entitled to do, being a commander of one of His Majesty's ships."

"Marry you!" the Captain exclaimed, obviously startled.

"Yes, marry me. It is the last request of a dying man —you cannot refuse that."

"No, but . . ." The Captain was obviously surprised and astonished at such a request and he looked first at Lew and then at Leona, and said finally:

"It must, of course, be as this lady wishes."

"It is as I wish," Lew said. "Do you hear me?"

He was obviously in pain, the lines around his mouth were deep and his face was pale beneath his tan although the beads of sweat stood out on his forehead.

The surgeon had covered his chest with bandages. But Leona could see the blood was beginning to seep through them staining them crimson. He was obviously unable to move one hand but with the other he groped around and, in pity, realizing what he was seeking, she put her hand into his and felt his fingers close over hers.

"Marry us," Lew said. "Marry us now while there is still time."

"Do you really wish this, Ma'am?"

The Captain spoke to Leona only in a low voice but Lew heard.

"Tell him," he said, squeezing her hand so that weak though he was he could still cause her pain. "Tell him."

"I . . . I wish it. I will . . . marry him."

Her voice sounded strange to her own ears and yet it was clear. She did not look at Lord Chard. She dared not look at him. But she was vividly conscious of him standing there in the background as if he was turned to stone.

"Very well!"

The Captain looked round the room and saw a Bible and a prayer book standing on the table by the bed. He took up the prayer book and began to turn the pages to find the marriage service. Even to Leona his actions seemed maddeningly slow.

"Hurry! Hurry!"

Lew could hardly breathe the words but his grip on Leona's fingers did not relax. She felt as if he not only held her to him but held her on her feet. The cabin was swimming around her yet she knew she would not faint.

Clearly she could hear the Captain's voice reading the first words of the marriage service, reading them clearly, in the unhurried, grave tones of a man who has conducted many services and who is familiar with the Holy Writ.

"What is your name?"

He stopped reading to ask the words, and now Leona could see that Lew was having difficulty in answering him.

"Llewellyn . . . Alexander."

The words came haltingly between his lips and she saw the surgeon move forward as if to help him and then realized there was nothing he could do.

The Captain turned to Leona.

"And your name?"

"Leona Mary."

"Very well, repeat after me. I, Llewellyn Alexander."

"I, Llew . . . ellyn . . . Alexander."

"Take thee, Leona Mary."

"T . . . take thee, . . . Le . . . ona Mary."

She felt Lew's fingers tighten on hers, heard him accent the word "take," and then, as he began to say her name, there came a sudden death rattle in his throat, his whole body heaved as if in a convulsion.

Even as she gave a little cry of terror and consternation, he collapsed.

"Take thee, Leona Mary. . . ."

The words seemed still to hang in the air. She could still hear them, still hear the note of triumph in his voice on which he had died.

The surgeon drew the sheet over Lew's face.

"I am sorry, Ma'am, there is nothing more we can do," he said gently.

Leona turned from the bunk, almost unconsciously her eyes sought Lord Chard for reassurance, for understanding. But he was no longer there. The door of the cabin was open and he had gone.

"May I escort you back on deck, Ma'am?"

The Captain was assisting her and now they were moving past the rows of wounded who were awaiting the attention of the surgeon, and up the companionway on to the deck. Already the sails were billowing out and sailors were running to and fro. There was nothing to show that anything unusual had happened except that in one corner of the deck was piled the cargo which had been taken from the cutter.

The bales of silks and laces, barrels of brandy and crates of tea—all the valuable things which Lew had intended to sell—would now be impounded by His Majesty's Customs.

The Captain opened the door of his cabin.

"I trust you will be comfortable here, Ma'am. I will send you a glass of wine. I feel you must need it after the ordeal you have just passed through."

Leona sat down, her fingers clasped tightly together. When the wine came, brought by one of the seamen, she did not touch it, but left the glass and the decanter standing on the table. She was waiting! Waiting for the door to open and Lord Chard to come to her.

As the time passed and as the rock and roll of the ship told her they were in mid-Channel, she knew he would not come. And she felt, then, a helplessness that was almost as frightening as had been her despair earlier in the evening.

How could she make him understand? Tell him that she could not, in honour, have refused to marry Lew?

She sat stiffly in her chair—waiting! waiting! waiting! But without hope and with the certainty that he would not come, until just before dawn the Captain came in to say they were in sight of land.

"Lord Chard has asked me to inform you, Ma'am, that we have arranged to send you ashore at Ruckley Castle. We will anchor just outside the bay and the ship's boat shall take you in."

"Thank you, that is extremely kind," Leona said.

"It was his Lordship's idea," the Captain explained. "We are taking the prisoners to Newhaven, but he felt you would wish to be spared the ordeal of giving evidence against them until you have had time to rest after your journey."

"Give evidence against them!" Leona repeated.

"But of course, Ma'am," the Captain replied. "I am afraid that will be necessary."

"But I hate to do that," Leona said. "Most of the men were inveigled or bullied into taking part in these expeditions."

The Captain smiled.

"I am afraid you will find it hard to make any Judge believe that," he said. "There have been too many murders, too many crimes committed by these men, especially Mister Quayle's gang."

He realized his reference to Lew Quayle had been tactless and coughing to cover up his error, he said briskly:

"If you will be so good as to come on deck, we have discovered a trunk which we think must be yours, Ma'am, and my men have lowered it into the boat."

"I am ready," Leona said.

The Captain held open the door for her and she walked outside. Already it was dawn—pale grey and faintly translucent with the first suspicions of gold coming up in the east, while the stars had not yet completely disappeared. It was cold and she drew her cloak round her, pulling her hood over her hair and round her face.

Lord Chard was waiting for her. She looked towards him and realized that he was avoiding her eyes.

"My thanks, Captain Dagleish," he said holding out his hand to the Captain. "I shall inform His Majesty of the excellent work that has been done this night by yourself and the men under your command. You may be sure that His Majesty will reward those on *The Seahawk* who took part in this operation.

"We are extremely proud, my Lord, to have had the opportunity of performing any service that was required of us," the Captain replied.

Leona dropped a curtsy to the Captain.

"Thank you, sir," she said in a low voice, and then, assisted by several willing hands, managed to negotiate the rope ladder into the rowboat.

Lord Chard climbed down alone and seated himself at the other end of the boat. There were four seamen to row them and they reached the shore in a few minutes. In the morning mist Leona could see the cliffs rising from the beach and because she knew where to look for it, she could see the entrance to the cave where the tubcarriers had sat watching for the first sign of the cutter so that they could let down a rope ladder and climb down on to the beach.

Never again, she thought, would they wait there. Never again would they use the tunnel of escape through the Castle itself.

She heard the boat grind on the shingle. The men sprang out to drag it in so that Lord Chard could step out without getting his feet wet, and one of them lifted Leona in his arms and set her down safely above the turn of the tide.

She heard the clink of money and saw Lord Chard reward the men. Then he turned to her and said:

"Can you manage to walk up the beach?"

"I have managed it often enough before," she answered.

She tried to smile at him but realized he was not looking at her. She felt by the coldness of his voice, by the very intonation with which he addressed her, that it was a stranger who stood beside her, a stranger whom she had never met before.

Behind them two of the seamen were carrying her trunk. She glanced back and Lord Chard said:

"Your luggage is quite safe, I assure you, and as it is a cold morning it is fortunate that you are wearing so substantial a cloak."

She felt her face burn with a sudden understanding at what appeared to be a note of sarcasm in what he said. She guessed, suddenly, that he thought Lew Quayle had paid for the cloak she wore and for the trunk that was following behind them.

She remembered the poor shawl she had worn when she went to Clantonbury. How else could the expensive velvet and fur of her cloak be accounted for? Or a trunk full of clothes, when no-one knew better than Lord Chard that when she had escaped from his sister's house she had taken nothing with her except what she wore.

Vainly she sought for words in which to tell him the truth but somehow could not bring herself to speak. They walked in silence up from the beach on to the patch which led beside the twisting river to where it branched off into the gardens of the Castle.

The irises were in bloom; the kingcups were golden— as golden as the sun which was rising now to flood over the low meadowland and move the rushes as if they whispered a song of happiness. And yet Leona could see nothing but the averted face of the man who moved beside her, and hear the sound of his footsteps.

At last the Castle door was in sight and the building itself, crumbling and dilapidated and yet beautiful in the morning sunshine, was just ahead of them.

"I am home," Leona thought. "Home! And I never need be frightened any more." And yet she could feel no sense of elation in the thought.

It was but half-past five but Mrs. Mildew would already be up and Leona could see the front door was open and a brush and some other cleaning materials standing on the step.

"You will be glad of some breakfast, my Lord," she managed to say with a curious little appeal in her voice which he appeared not to hear.

In answer he drew a watch from his fob pocket.

"As soon as your grooms are stirring," he said, "I should be grateful if one of them would go to the village and order a carriage to take me to Clantonbury."

"Perhaps you would prefer a horse, my Lord," Leona said. "There will be one in the stable."

"That would be better still, if it could be arranged," he said.

He did not look at her and she knew, with a feeling bordering on utter despair, that he despised her. His face was grave, his lips, when he was not speaking, were pressed together, and she imagined again that he was a stranger, someone she had never met before, someone who had never held her hands and looked down at her with tenderness and understanding.

She wondered what he would do if she put out her hands towards him and begged him to smile at her again. Such a thing was impossible!

"Will you wait in the Salon, my Lord?" she said conventionally, and as he crossed the hall slowly and sedately, she ran down the passage to the kitchen to find Mrs. Barnes already at her baking and Mrs. Mildew sitting at the table talking to her.

They both gave a start as she entered.

"Praise be to God!" Mrs. Mildew ejaculated. " 'Tis yourself, m' dear, and us 'alf out of our minds as to what 'ad 'appened to you."

"I am back," Leona said breathlessly, "and Lord Chard is in the Salon. Please prepare the best breakfast you can, Mrs. Barnes, and tell him as soon as it is ready."

"And what about yourself, Miss?" Mrs. Barnes inquired.

"I have to change first," Leona answered.

She returned from the kitchen and ran up the back stairs to her bedroom. There she stood for a moment looking at her reflection in the mirror, seeing her face, pale and a little frightened, peeping from between the luxurious frame of expensive fur, the velvet falling in graceful folds from her shoulders to the floor.

Of course she understood what he thought. How could it be otherwise?

She pulled the cloak from her and flung it on the floor, and then she saw, standing by the bed, open and empty, the worn leather trunk she had taken with her to Clantonbury. Someone must have returned it, perhaps by Lord Chard's orders.

She went to the wardrobe, pulled it open and, as she expected, saw her gowns hanging there. Mrs. Mildew would have unpacked them. And now she pulled off the pretty, inexpensive but new gown she had made for herself in Dieppe. Quickly she put on the old grey cotton one in which he had first seen her—the demure grey gown with its little white fichu which was worn and faded and yet which was as familiar to her as the very room in which she stood.

A few moments later she gave a sigh and looked at herself in the mirror. Now she would tell him. Now she would explain what had happened.

She ran downstairs, remembering how once he had walked up them towards her, his eyes on hers, holding her spellbound as she had stood there with the basin in the crook of her arm.

She opened the door of the Salon only to find it empty, and then ran eagerly down the passage to the dining-room. She entered the room and Lord Chard rose from the table where he had been sitting, pushing back his chair.

"Oh! You have finished!"

Leona's voice was breathless.

"I am not hungry," he replied, "though I am grateful to you for providing a meal at such short notice. Your butler informs me that a horse is here."

"Already!" Leona exclaimed. "But I had not ordered it."

"I took the liberty of requesting your butler to do so," Lord Chard said. "The horse shall be returned tomorrow. In the meantime it will be well looked after."

"But . . . must you go now?" Leona asked in a very small voice.

For the first time, it seemed, he looked at her. She

saw him glance at her gown, saw, for a moment, a sudden softening of his expression, and then his face hardened again.

"I am afraid I have many things to see to," he said. "The Justices at Newhaven will be expecting me."

He waited for her to precede him from the room. There was nothing for her to do but to walk the passage slowly.

"I think I can arrange that you will not have to give evidence in open court," he said. "A statement will be all that is required and I will send my attorney to wait upon you tomorrow or the next day."

They had reached the hall and Leona saw that Bramwell was waiting there, holding his Lordship's cloak and hat.

"There is something I would ask of you," she said.

"But of course," he replied, punctiliously correct but still withdrawn from her, with a reserve she felt she could never penetrate.

"It was just something I would beg of you," she said, leading the way into the Salon.

He stood for a moment in the doorway as if he had no wish to be alone with her. And then, almost wearily it seemed, he closed the door but would not advance as far as the hearthrug but only stood waiting as if her request was of extreme inconvenience.

"It is just . . . this," Leona said breathlessly. "There is one of the smugglers, Ben Andrews by name, of whom I would beg your Lordship to speak . . . kindly. It was his first voyage and he was forced into it by . . . Mister . . . Quayle because he was short of men."

She stammered over Lew Quayle's name, finding it hard to speak.

"I will remember the name," Lord Chard said. "Perhaps you would be kind enough to speak of him in your statement and to say how you obtained this information."

"It was his boat I borrowed when I went to warn them on the cutter that you had a trap set for them here at the Castle," Leona said.

"So that is how you managed it," Lord Chard remarked. "Well, as I say, I will do my best for the boy, but I think really all of them will have very stiff sentences. My attorney will also make a plea that you should receive what monies Mister Quayle has left behind, seeing that you were so very nearly his wife."

"The monies!" Leona said. "Do you really think I

would touch a . . . a penny of his m-money—or a-anything else that b-belongs to him?"

"Perhaps not all of it was earned in such a nefarious trade as smuggling," Lord Chard suggested.

"I care not how it was earned or how he came by it," Leona cried. "I only know that I want nothing of his. What I want is to . . . to forget."

She turned her head away to hide the tears which sprang to her eyes, and yet she heard Lord Chard say, in a somewhat different tone:

"You were prepared to marry him."

"How could I do otherwise?" Leona asked. "I had given my promise, my sacred word of honour, to Hughie."

"To Hugh!"

She heard the astonishment in his tone, and then, suddenly, in two quick strides he was beside her, staring down at her, the coldness and reserve gone from his face. In their place there was a look of searching inquiry.

"Hugh!" he said. "Hugh is dead!"

"No," she answered. "Hughie is alive. He is going to be married to someone he loves and who loves him. They will live in France. He will be quite all right."

"Then you were not in Dieppe—alone with Lew Quayle?"

She heard his voice almost break on the words, and looked up at him, her eyes wide.

"No, indeed," she said. "Hughie was there until yesterday afternoon. What did y-you think? . . . How c-could you think. . . .?"

"What else could I think?" he asked fiercely. "I thought Hugh was dead. Then you appeared in those clothes and were ready to marry Quayle."

"I had to . . . marry him. It was a . . . debt of honour," Leona said. "But how could you think . . . those other things of me?"

"Leona!" His voice reached out to her and held her, and suddenly she was still. "You told me you hated me. I believed you, and yet I had to find you to be sure. When I saw you on board tonight, I knew there was no hatred between us and there never could be. And then you promised to marry that man—the man I thought you had been staying with, alone."

"He had . . . *bought* me!" Leona said. "*Bought* me for eight thousand pounds—the money that Hughie owed him. It was the only way he could be repaid."

"My God! I have been blind!"

Lord Chard spoke the words almost beneath his breath, and now his face seemed transfigured and he was looking down at Leona as if he had never seen her before, as if he could not gaze too long.

Her little face was turned to his.

"Do you know what you have done to me?" he said in a voice so low that it was almost as if he spoke to himself rather than to her. "Do you know what you have made me suffer? Do you know what I have been through this past week?"

She drew in her breath quickly. Something was happening in the room; something which made the whole world seem suddenly golden, glorious and wonderful. And yet she could only stammer:

"S-suffer, my L-lord? I have . . . made you s-suffer?"

"When I found you had gone," he said, "when I knew what had happened; when I saw you on the beach and you told me that you hated me, I thought then that I had drunk the very dregs of suffering. But when I came back to find that man had taken you away—then I thought I should go mad."

He drew a deep breath. "I discovered from one of Quayle's men who betrayed him that you had gone to Dieppe, but I had to wait until he was out of French territory before I could attempt to catch him. I have had the ships patrolling up and down outside the harbour day after day, night after night, and I have been waiting there myself, ready to get my hands on his throat and throttle the murderous beast into telling me what he had done with you. I never dreamed for a moment you would be on board. And then when I saw you. . . ."

The voice ceased suddenly and he looked down at her, still not touching her, his eyes meeting hers.

"Then when I saw you, Leona," he went on, "I thought for a moment that you were as glad to see me as I was to see you."

Her eyes were like stars and her lips were trembling.

"I . . . I was," she said. "I was, but. . . ."

"But what?" he asked.

"But I had promised to . . . marry him and I knew there was no . . . hope."

"And now he is dead!" Lord Chard said. "What, now he is dead?"

They just stood looking at each other, his voice dying away into the silence. The whole room, the whole world seemed to wait for her answer.

And then, suddenly, with a little inarticulate cry she was in his arms, the tears were running down her cheeks as she raised her face to his and he held her tightly to him, as if he would never let her go. At last, almost as if he could not help himself, he bent his head to find her lips.

"God! How frightened I have been!" he said, after a long interval. "Frightened of losing you and never finding you again. I love you, Leona! I will teach you to love me. I will wait for you. But only say that eventually you will let me look after you, you will let me take you away to peace and security, away from all that has frightened you."

"Take . . . me! Oh, take . . . me!"

He heard the words even though they were hardly above a whisper. And now, once again, his eyes were on hers and it was as if the love shining through their faces made them both unrecognisable even to each other.

"I love you, Leona!" he said, and his words seemed to encircle their whole world and sweep away everything else. "I love you, Leona! Tell me you love me a little."

"I love you with . . . all of me," she answered. "With my whole . . . heart. There is nothing else left but . . . love."

ON SALE WHEREVER PAPERBACKS ARE SOLD
— or use this coupon to order directly from the publisher.

BARBARA CARTLAND

V3587	THE KISS OF THE DEVIL (#32)	$1.25
V4154	KISS OF PARIS (#38)	$1.25
V3474	A KISS OF SILK (#30)	$1.25
V3450	THE LEAPING FLAME (#70)	$1.25
V3174	LIGHT TO THE HEART (#56)	$1.25
V4274	LIGHTS OF LOVE (#46)	$1.25
V3909	THE LITTLE PRETENDER (#19)	$1.25
V4162	LOST ENCHANTMENT (#52)	$1.25
V3196	LOVE FORBIDDEN (#51)	$1.25
V3519	LOVE HOLDS THE CARDS (#12)	$1.25
V4111	LOVE IN HIDING (#4)	$1.25
V3910	LOVE IS AN EAGLE (#49)	$1.25
V3429	LOVE IS CONTRABAND (#13)	$1.25
V4132	LOVE IS DANGEROUS (#31)	$1.25
V4273	LOVE IS THE ENEMY (#9)	$1.25
V4148	LOVE IS MINE (#43)	$1.25
V3451	LOVE ME FOREVER (#14)	$1.25
V3079	LOVE ON THE RUN (#50)	$1.25
V2864	LOVE TO THE RESCUE (#11)	$1.25
V2768	LOVE UNDER FIRE (#39)	$1.25
V2997	MESSENGER OF LOVE (#22)	$1.25
V3372	METTERNICH: THE PASSIONATE DIPLOMAT	$1.25

Send To: JOVE PUBLICATIONS, INC.
Harcourt Brace Jovanovich, Inc.
Dept. M.O., 757 Third Avenue, New York, N.Y. 10017

NAME

ADDRESS

CITY

STATE   ZIP

I enclose $_____, which includes the total price of all books ordered plus 50¢ per book postage and handling for the first book and 25¢ for each additional. If my total order is $10.00 or more, I understand that Jove Publications, Inc. will pay all postage and handling.
No COD's or stamps. Please allow three to four weeks for delivery. Prices subject to change.

ON SALE WHEREVER PAPERBACKS ARE SOLD
— or use this coupon to order directly from the publisher.

BARBARA CARTLAND

	V3921	**WHERE IS LOVE** (#71) $1.25
	V3922	**TOWARDS THE STARS** (#72) $1.25
	V3996	**DESPERATE DEFIANCE** (#73) $1.25
	V3985	**AN INNOCENT IN MAYFAIR** (#74) $1.25
	V3988	**RAINBOW TO HEAVEN** (#75) $1.25
	V3991	**THE BITTER WINDS OF LOVE** (#76) $1.25
	V3989	**LOVE AND LINDA** (#77) $1.25
	V3992	**BROKEN BARRIERS** (#78) $1.25
	V3993	**LOVE IN PITY** (#79) $1.25
	V3986	**DANCE ON MY HEART** (#80) $1.25
	V3990	**LOVE AT FORTY** (#81) $1.25
	V3994	**THIS TIME IT'S LOVE** (#82) $1.25

Send To: JOVE PUBLICATIONS, INC.
Harcourt Brace Jovanovich, Inc.
Dept. M.O., 757 Third Avenue, New York, N.Y. 10017

NAME

ADDRESS

CITY

STATE   ZIP

I enclose $_____, which includes the total price of all books ordered plus 50¢ per book postage and handling for the first book and 25¢ for each additional. If my total order is $10.00 or more, I understand that Jove Publications, Inc. will pay all postage and handling.
No COD's or stamps. Please allow three to four weeks for delivery.
Prices subject to change.

NT-19

Are you missing out on some great Jove/HBJ books?

"You can have any title in print at Jove/HBJ delivered right to your door! To receive your Jove/HBJ Shop-At-Home Catalog, send us 25¢ together with the label below showing your name and address.

JOVE PUBLICATIONS, INC.
Harcourt Brace Jovanovich, Inc.
Dept. M.O., 757 Third Avenue, New York, N.Y. 10017

NAME_____

ADDRESS_____

CITY_____STATE_____

NT-1   ZIP_____